LONDON LIES BENEATH

STELLA DUFFY

virago

VIRAGO

First published in Great Britain in 2016 by Virago Press
This paperback edition published in 2017

1 3 5 7 9 10 8 6 4 2

A CIP catalogue record for this book
is available from the British Library.

ISBN 978-0-349-00783-0

Typeset in Bembo by M Rules
Printed and bound in Great Britain by
Clays Ltd, St Ives plc

Papers used by Virago are from well-managed forests
and other responsible sources.

Virago Press
An imprint of
Little, Brown Book Group
Carmelite House
50 Victoria Embankment
London EC4Y 0DZ

An Hachette UK Company
www.hachette.co.uk

www.virago.co.uk

A koha for the taniwha that lives
in the Thames, whistling us home.

Acknowledgements

Thank you both to Antonia Hodgson and all at Virago, and to Stephanie Cabot and all at The Gernert Company, for their continued support and faith in my work. Thanks to the Cuming Museum for giving me access to *Magic in Modern London* and to the pieces of magic themselves, to Chris Roberts for introducing me to Edward Lovett's work, Kraindel Singer, Gregor Truter, Kate Lane for Mary Chamberlain's vitally useful *Growing up in Lambeth* which led me to Maud Pember Reeves' brilliant *Round About a Pound a Week*, and to the Shaky Isles *TaniwhaThames* company – story-callers all. Special thanks to Gladstone's Library where I finally found one quiet week to begin this book and to the Friends of Nunhead Cemetery for their work in keeping this story alive.

One

A stretch of land, seven hills to the south, a sandy ridge to the north running east to west and another that heads north to south. The land, marshy in many places, downright boggy in others, with thick, claggy clay running beneath, folds itself into a shallow basin around a twisting tangle of river. It is a village and on the north shore there is an encampment with a ferry crossing, it is a site of hope and of loss.

Now it is a town with a bridge, just one.

Now a city, two big churches by the water, one rising right in the centre and another to the west.

It is market gardens and trade, and still there is just the one bridge, ferrymen risk sinking their little boats from the weight of the coin they charge to row men from the chaste north to visit Southwark geese in the south.

It is ships and shipping this city, docks that smell of trade and tobacco, sugar and spice and many things that are not nice, will never be nice, no matter how often the slave blood is sluiced away.

Sailors and shipped-out soldiers journey on, the river taking them first east and then south to battle and to blood. The ships return with Empire spoils, while the men bring back stories they will tell only when whiskey or rum loosen the locked door of memory. Women wait out the night sweats of their men with horrors of their own, tales they won't tell either, the miscarriages, the stillbirths, the abortions and the hungry mouths of little ones who lived, despite it all. The children who survive, yet never seem to profit from the ships or the trade or the wars or the churches or this new bridge or that bigger ferry or the widened roads or the train stations or the tram tracks or the factories that line the docks that line the river.

A boy looks down from Nunhead to the city. He sees Highgate Hill in the distance. He knows the houses over there that edge the heath, they are comfortable and easy, with wide doors and wider halls, sunlit rooms. Beneath the hill and the heath he sees Camden and meaner houses, though not for long, for here are the great villas of Regent's Park, white porticos and tall windows. Then it is town proper, elegant squares slowly edged out by streets of shops, the new department stores where behind every counter is a shop girl who wipes sweaty hands on a tired frock before she sells goods she could never afford. Here are the tight alleys and dangerous dead ends of the St Giles rookery, there the broad stretch of Oxford Street, Regent Street, and where it meets Piccadilly here is Mr Gilbert's statue of Anteros. True, everyone calls the statue Eros, but our boy in Nunhead knows better, knows that this is Anteros, brother of Eros, the god of love returned, given back, love requited, with arrows that not only find their mark, but are welcome.

Coming closer, the boy would walk, if he could, down the slope of Haymarket, stopping just before he turns into Trafalgar Square, looking above the tall theatres for Admiral Nelson's hat. There it is, the peak of the tricorn, and the boy dreams himself around the corner and into the square. Careful of the carriages, the trams, he crosses to the four lions guarding the base of the column. He and his two best mates stood here once and listened to an old sailor, half a leg gone, cut away right above the knee, who whispered the secret of the lions' paws, a secret every soldier and sailor knew, those that were Londoners. If you want to come home to the city, then the night before you head out, you must round the column, from north to east to south to west, touching each of the lions' forepaws as you go. The three boys clubbed together to give the old man tuppence ha'penny for his story and round the lions they went, our boy reached for the back paws too, for good measure. Lads excited to grow up, to go to the world, lads with fathers who had sailed down to South Africa, grandfathers who went all the way to Kandahar and came back different men. These lads want to go out, yes, see the world, but they want to come home as well. London is home.

London, but not this London, up town London. Home is the other side of the river. That's Big Ben ringing out the hour and so the three boys have their task – ready, set, go. Running now, along the Strand, dodging trams and carriages, swiftly round the copper who doesn't want dirty lads from the wrong side of the river running along his

3

patch, doesn't trust them far as he could throw them. A quick stop at St Mary le Strand, once round the church as they have promised they always will, it would be cheating just to turn the corner to the river, then fast over Waterloo Bridge to the south, to home. Real London, the London that is beneath. Beneath the fancy shops of the north side, beneath the big white houses with their bells and whistles and servants upstairs and downstairs and in my lady's chamber, beneath the lower lip of the river that swells full and rich with the tide, shrinking back to mud flats and dirty docks twice a day. Proper London, that's where our boy lives. Lived. Where he and his friends and their families lived, happily enough, hard enough, scraping a living but only just, crammed in tight one against the other, spreading out only on high days and holidays and then just for a day trip on the tram, back to the hearth come night, and the hearth cold unless they could scrape up coin for the coal.

Haring down Waterloo Road, building works for the old-made-new station on the right, Old Vic on the left where the smart lads go to penny lectures and their mates stay behind in the pub laughing at them, bettering themselves indeed, what good is bettering yourself for the working man when there's no one will give you a job once you tell them where you're from? Home to where they're from. Now the clock tower at the junction with Blackfriars Road. Used to be an obelisk here, for years, like Cleopatra's Needle it was, come all the way from Egypt. All three of these lads would swear blind they remembered seeing it when they were very tiny, and well they might have, though it's been gone a while now. Behind them now anyway, and here's the real boundary of what is and what is not home, the Elephant itself, and Lord, how puffed they are, here's the Underground station. The start, or end, of the Bakerloo Line is a fine shove for a boy who might be flagging, as is Spurgeon's Tabernacle. Nearly there lads, nearly home. A swift sprint along Newington Butts, well and truly breathless by Draper Street, under the train lines, finally, finally, here's Heygate with the big synagogue standing at a diagonal on the corner, then the Cuming and the library, now the dog-leg that is Larcom Street. And here they are, home. Home. Red faces, chests pumping, bare legs stinging in the wind. Not quite three miles and they've done it in under half an hour if the Town Hall clock is right. Course it is, this is the Walworth clock, course it's right. Slap on the back, punch to the arm. Good mate, good lad.

A boy, high up in Nunhead, a little further to the south, sees all this. Sees his friends and his family and his home. Sees London in the clay, and the sand, the paving, and the buildings, sees London in the river, all laid out beneath a flat summer sky.

Two

Ida Shaw stood on her stall six days a week, and sometimes part of the seventh. She was twenty-eight, going on twenty-nine. She was married to Bill who wasn't her first love, but was the love that lasted, the one that mattered in the end, the father of her three. Bill was the bloke she'd made her choice for, which made him hers.

Ida knew all about choice. The goods on her stall were to do with fate and luck and chance and happenstance – to those that bought them. For Ida, any magic those amulets held was nothing but the power the buyers chose to give them. She wasn't one for charms herself, had kept only a few in her time, had no great faith in the carved angel she kept under her pillow, but she liked that her mother had passed it on, from her own father who'd had it from his grandfather.

Ida made part of her living from the ivory, brass and wooden trinkets, because the people of the lane and round-about chose to put their faith in them, but for herself she trusted the medicines she made up, recipes for distillations, mixes and tinctures passed on from her mother like the carved angel. Ida's faith, and her income, came from the medicines, and also from helping young women, some not so young, through their births. She fell for her first baby with Bill within a month of their wedding, and everything about that baby was quick, it came early, far too early to survive. She fell with Tom not long after, and he stayed with her, stayed in her, though he gave her a hard time birthing, that was for sure. Once she'd had her two little girls after Tom, Ida knew more than she needed to about giving birth. More, certainly, than some of the doctors that grudgingly came down to these streets, hands out for their payment before they'd even glance at a birthing woman, get their hands dirty. Ida didn't mind getting her hands dirty, it was only blood and humanity after all. She knew that birth was about chance and luck and fate – and she had a living to make. So yes, there was the ginger and slippery elm bark mix she'd offer to a pale-looking young woman, no ring on her finger, or a harassed mother with too many brats hanging on to her skirt, women who would quietly sidle up to the stall and ask for it under their breath. Ida sold it with strict instructions only to take this much and no more, and to make sure they had a good friend close by for the next few hours or days. Ida sold medicines and charms, but she knew she was really selling hope, and she wished there was choice on offer.

Ida's Bill worked on the railway, he'd been there since he'd left school at eleven. Worked his way up from yard boy at everyone's beck and call, to sharing a shift with the strongest, most respected fellows in the yard. Bill's work meant there was often a big lump of coal or half a ham come home with him, fallen off the back of a wagon and stuffed into a spare sack or under his jacket. It meant they were better off than plenty around here. Luck Bill called it, choice Ida said, choice to pick that ham off a pallet destined for some elegant street on the other side of the river and a butcher's counter where they were all yes please and thank you and don't mind if I do milady, choice to risk the guardsman seeing him, and choice to bring it home. But even with this help, luck or choice, Ida was at her stall most days of the week, not least because they gave away so much of what they had. They gave to Aunty Sarah who lived over the way and wasn't actually an aunty at all, not proper family, but she'd been so kind when the first baby was born dead, even though she'd had none of her own, held Ida's hand when Ida thought the sun might never rise again. Aunty Sarah didn't say a word as she pulled the curtains and folded the untouched baby clothes, and she was far more use in saying nothing than some that suggested it was for the best, or that God had his mysterious ways.

Not that anyone said so when the poor little mite was wrapped into a tiny coffin made of an orange crate, and popped into the front of the hearse alongside Ida's great uncle, dropped into the ground alongside him too. A funeral too pricey and not the done thing for stillborns anyway. Ida had heard that when a woman had a stillbirth in the hospital, half the time the wee thing was thrown into the hospital incinerator. Ida was never one for hospitals, too many sick turned dead in the hospital.

They shared what they had with Ida's dad too. He lived on the eastern corner of their dog-leg street, unable to work now, no matter that he'd like to, only in his late fifties, though his wife was gone ten years already, the growth had got her and they'd found it too late. His own trouble came of years working the docks. Since he was just a lad he'd been unloading spices and wool and tobacco, and so much of the dust gone into his lungs he could barely stand for more than half an hour at a time, and that on a good day. Then there was Bill's sister Ena who lived upstairs with fist-happy Fred, swore blind she'd never leave him, no matter how many black eyes he doled out. Bill'd had a word, threatened to do more than that when the sound of Ena or the little one's fear was too hard to hear, but it never did any good. Fred was one of those soppy bastards who were all, I'm so sorry and Lord, but I love you, and it won't happen again, my honour, when he was on the ale at home, and a big old brute if anyone was stupid enough to buy him a whiskey down the pub. And Ena herself, fool enough to stay with him, because it was the soppy bastard side of him she'd married and she loved.

So Ida worked her stall because she cared to do it, and because it made it easier to help out a bit, and because she liked the people she met on the stall. The chaps who came to her, red-faced and stammering, so that she knew exactly what they needed before they asked for it. She'd reach for a paper, measure out a few pennies' worth of powdered celery into a twist, fold it over and over so that the smell, all peppery and tart, wouldn't get into his clothes, and wishing him a good night no matter that it was just gone nine in the morning. Ida had no idea if it worked, she and Bill gave it a go one time, but Bill couldn't stand the stink of the celery, and the drink she made it up in tasted no better, so the cup of dark liquid was thrown out into the yard and it was off to bed, just the same, good as it always had been between them, celery powder or no.

Then there were the love-sick boys wanting to cure their bad skin to get a girl's notice, and old ladies who stopped by the stall to tell Ida what she'd got wrong and what she ought to be selling now, it being harvest and time for making up hot apple poultices, or winter and why hadn't she had her onions and brown sugar steeping a week by now? Ida listened, learned. She knew the country ways were long gone round here, but the country remedies might still work.

Ida liked it when other women called her in as a wise one. It was something she'd never thought could happen after she'd lost the first baby, but then her Tom came, and the two girls, one after the other, ever so quick, and now she was one of the mothers. She'd been through the mill to get there, so she was welcome alongside to push against a sweating back, push through the strain to bring in the new life. In their turn, they appreciated the way Ida kept her tongue just as Aunty Sarah had when Ida herself needed silence. Ida was good at remembering what worked.

On top of that, and Ida didn't mind admitting, having the stall, having people come to the stall, them thinking she knew a bit, made people look up to her a little. It meant that sometimes, when she was selling a powder to cover a bruise, a charm to bring back love, she'd also whisper that perhaps there might be a choice to be made too, they might make their own luck. Often Ida felt she was fighting a losing battle with the people down the lane, all lucky horseshoes and four-leafed clovers and wishbones into the

10

bargain, but it was a battle she'd not give up. Ida was all for choice and the difference it made, she'd be a suffragette if she had the time, and the money, which she didn't. So she stayed on the stall dispensing hope and maybe, wrapped in a twist of paper.

At packing up time each piece went back in the box it had come from, remedies in one, tinctures in another, a couple more to hold each of the charms, wrapped carefully and kindly. Ida said it didn't matter if she believed in the magic or not, the stories that the charms held needed taking care of, not slammed in on top of each other, but kept separate, thin tissue between, wrapped up gently, just like the day she turned eleven and knew it was time to put away her dolls. Peg dolls they'd been, and on the morning of her eleventh birthday Ida decided to put away her dolls, she'd be off to work soon enough, it was time.

Ida laid a sheet of old white tissue over a seahorse made of pink glass, all the way from Venice she'd told a customer this afternoon. It might be Venice for all she knew or Manchester, they had canals there too, didn't they? Then she tucked away a few more of the blue glass beads for the babies, to keep them from coughs and colds, and if that didn't work they looked pretty enough around a little one's chubby neck. Lastly she lay down the most delicate of the pieces, sandwiched between two more sheets of tissue paper, a charm she'd held on to for years and would be happy never to sell, though she put it out on the stall every day. It was the Lord's Prayer, all fine and copied out, words going round and round, on a circle of paper, no wider than the nail on Bill's fat thumb. He was a big man, her Bill.

Ida closed up the boxes, made sure they were tightly

jammed, one against the other, and then yoked herself to the barrow. She enjoyed working the stall, truly she did, but some days, the sky grey and no one out for buying, Ida herself up half the night with a young girl in a slow labour and the baby another day off yet, some days she'd wish on all the charms in all their boxes that someone else might pull the barrow for her.

Three

Edward Lovett walked along the street, and the people round about, shoppers, stallholders and barrow boys knew him. Not as a friend, he was different to them, a gent for a start, but they knew him. It wasn't just the way he spoke that marked him a gent, there was plenty that told his story, before he even opened his mouth.

When he stopped by Tilly Hunt's stall, her pots and pans piled up in an old bath, the measuring cups and enamel plates neatly arrayed, she checked the careful turn on his sleeve cuff, the lovely lining as he reached out a hand to pick up this or that piece of old china. Tilly knew the coat was cut from a good piece of cloth, just as she knew that most of what she had to sell was tat, but she also knew the collector was not here for her usual stuff. Every now and then Tilly would find and keep aside a nice little piece of interest for the gent. If she timed it right, reeling him in, often as not holding back the piece until he'd looked all over her stall for the second time and was about to head off, she could make her day's money in a moment and be off home early for her tea. Samson, the tinker she had an arrangement with – two arrangements, one business, one personal – picked up all sorts of rubbish on his rounds, bits and pieces he'd repair good enough for the market. Samson was not her husband, young Bert had gone in the Boer War, and the pair of them not even made a baby of their own before she lost him. Tilly still felt too wed to Bert to take on another man's name, but she and Samson rubbed along well enough, were kind to each other, and he helped her out with a few nice pieces most weeks, neatly mended and good for another few years.

Before Samson went to work on the goods though, Tilly would have a good turn-out of whatever he'd loaded on to his cart in a job lot, emptying cups and old jugs, taking the lids off teapots with broken handles, counting through buttons, scraps of cotton. When she found something she thought the collector might fancy, Tilly put it aside until he came back down the lane. Then she'd pass the time of day with Mister Lovett, whisper that if he didn't find anything he fancied along the lane, then he should pop back to her on his way home. She might have something, perhaps. The collector would smile, and nod, and tip his hat. He knew he must wait for Tilly to produce her gifts, it was part of the game they played, a game he enjoyed.

The hat he doffed was a good hat and Tilly noted that his nails were clean. The girls on the stalls all the way down the market liked that about him. The men were not so sure.

Doesn't look like he's done a day's work in his life, Samson would say, if he happened to be by the stall, bringing Tilly a warm pint on a cold day, emptying his cart before going back out into the streets, down the road to

14

Camberwell and Brixton where the bigger houses threw out any amount of good wares far more often than anyone around here.

Lovett carried a bag too, dark leather, his initials burnished in gold, the brass clasp nicely polished, no smears. He needed the bag, not just for the papers he carried to and from his work, but also for things he bought in the market. Tilly thought he might be a lawyer, that's what all the papers must be. Her friend Ida said don't be so daft, no lawyer would risk walking down the lane, what if someone he'd had sent down was coming the other way? Ida who had the remedies and charms stall thought the man had a look of one who worked with money, she'd seen the lines on his hand once, counting out his change. Charlie, Ida's cousin, reckoned the collector was having them all for a laugh, no matter that he paid them for any old rubbish they could find a story for, and well enough too.

Charlie Hatch whose butcher's barrow was the best stall in the market, wasn't one for trusting those he didn't know. And what Charlie meant by 'know' was grow up alongside, be related to, married to. Everyone else was an outsider until time proved them otherwise. Charlie Hatch liked the sound of his own voice, all the costermongers did, of course, no point having a barrow if you couldn't do the patter, but Charlie more than most.

He had a pace to his walk, did Mister Lovett, a lick, but it wasn't like he'd found himself in the wrong street, wanting to get away from there, not as many of his sort might. Not that many of his sort came down here anyway, or those that did only to pry and poke, to note down numbers in one of their big black books, mark Ida and Charlie and

15

Tilly and Samson and all their families on the map as dirty and disreputable. Always the same questions – how many people sleep in this house? On this landing? In this room? And shaking their heads as if they couldn't quite believe it, couldn't imagine how dark it must be indoors, inside the room inside the house inside the courtyard. Mind you, most people round here knew not to tell the whole story. Who'd risk the landlord putting up the rent when he heard you'd turned the upstairs into two and what had been let to one family was now shared between two families or more, and both of them extending to grandparents and aunts and uncles?

There were other people come too, down the Walworth Road, down East Lane, into the streets and the flats, their questions even more prying, the church types. Sometimes it could feel like the whole bloody lane was hemmed in by that lot. Church of Englanders of course, St John's round the corner with its school right next door. Every now and then the high church lot would come by too, with their smells and bells from St Agnes up by the park, Kennington Common as was. There were the Wesleyans, the Baptists at the Tabernacle, Jews on Heygate Street and all. At least the Jews kept to themselves, not like the flaming Christians, all asking the same question, like it was any of their business.

Have you been to church this week, month, year?

Are you sending the children to Sunday school?

Don't you want them to get the Sunday school treat?

And then the little ones would be grabbing at mother's skirts and father's knees, asking to be let go, wanting the saint's card or the pressed flower for the missal. Wanting the sweet the Sunday school lady gave each of them as they left the lesson, more like. And the time it took in washing the kids and getting them tidied up for a lesson that would only be ignored, wasn't that just time taken from looking after the babies, time lost from cooking or a moment to clear out the yard, scrub down the barrow? That lot thought they were bringing the babes to Jesus and that was all they cared about. Ida and Tilly and Charlie and everyone else with a stall down here wished their own cares were so small.

Lovett walked with purpose, picking his way carefully over rotting fruit or fish heads, dodging the little hooligan from the passage across the way, the one who seemed always to be trying to steal a piece of meat or an old apple. He took his usual route, from one end of the lane to the other, they were used to him now, had heard the questions before. Some of those he stopped to speak with came prepared.

Here it is sir, have a look at this my love, tucked away in my pocket, hidden beneath the shawl. Have a look here, you'll like this little charm, I promise.

Once the collector was spotted at the top of the lane, the word quickly ran along the street, the locals both ready and not quite willing to part with the keepsake, the talisman, the charm, not quite willing unless – well, if you're offering a shilling, sir, then perhaps yes, perhaps, just this one time.

And with each charm, each amulet, there was a story, a history, a promise.

My mother had this from her grandmother, sir.

This piece came from when we lived way out in Kent and worked the hops and the apples.

This is real London, this is, proper London, proper London story behind it and all.

It was worth more if he had to haggle.

Lovett enjoyed the effort of the trade. His job description named him a bank clerk, and most of his work day was spent shuffling one file of papers into another. Here, in the lane, he welcomed the business of negotiating over a charm. Finally a deal was made and he would part with a few coppers for the amber beads, maybe even a shiny sixpence for the feather sewn into an arc of felt, each stitch embroidering health, wealth, long life, embroidering hope.

Edward Lovett left his home every morning and journeyed to work crammed into a compartment with the same men, sitting together and still too close despite their elevated tickets, hats, coats, scarves, each item a piece of armour, shielding one man from his fellow. He worked in the bank, a respectable job, a situation that paid for the house in Croydon, had paid for two staff to help his wife run the home and a good education for his two boys. Other men would be satisfied, his wife – when she had still lived with him – had said this often, other men would be happy enough. Home, hearth, family, a garden, a good job. But he was not satisfied, he was hungry for something more. And it was this hunger to catalogue a magic that he didn't believe for a moment, that sent him into the streets, had him walking Shoreditch, Shadwell, Bow and Poplar, up to Camden and from Greenwich to Bermondsey, New Cross and Brixton. It was what brought him here, to Walworth, to the market the locals called East Lane.

This side of the river, this end of town, no matter what time of year, the air was thick with the stink of the vinegar factory, acrid smoke from the burned leavings in the glue yard, and the warm yeast of the brewery. Lovett knew that up in Hampstead or Gypsy Hill, certainly at home in Croydon, there were rose-scented gardens, sweeter still after an evening shower, windows open to a fresh and healthy evening air. And still he walked through East Lane, Bow Road, Bermondsey High Street, because sweet-scented night was not enough, and every charm was a story to collect.

Four

I'll take that for you love, he'd said.

April 1898, the warm spring sun high in the sky, oddly warm it'd been, and Wimbledon Common covered in early daisies and cowslip and half a dozen other flowers with names and uses Ida was starting to learn from her country-bred grandmother. Only those that grew in London fields though, London commons. Ida was a city girl, a Walworth cockney and proud of it, so the wildflowers she learned were those that had cures along with prettiness, and she didn't talk to strange lads, and she most certainly didn't hand over her basket to be carried when she was already half an hour later than usual, off home on her Sunday afternoon. Yet here she was, one train missed already because them upstairs had decided they wanted a different tablecloth that evening and she'd had to iron and starch the linen all over again. There'd be hell to pay if she was late getting home for her Sunday tea, her father wouldn't hear excuses, an afternoon was an afternoon, no matter who paid the wages. Trouble with that lot was they'd no idea how to run a house. Ida's dad had

20

threatened to bring her back to the market when she came home last month, all shadows under her eyes and burns on her hands from the old-fashioned iron they made her use, too heavy by half for a girl her age. Not that Ida was that happy there herself, she'd half a mind to go home and all, but she was proud, had told her dad she'd do the job, and here she was, doing it. And she'd learn to like it, maybe.

Well, and anyway, the smiling lad was still standing there, his hand held out for her basket, and it was warm, far too warm for the time of year, and he did have nice eyes, and his hands were clean, Ida'd checked. So, against her better judgement, she handed over her basket with a fresh loaf and a few eggs, half a dozen rashers the cook had said the family wouldn't miss. Handed over a cheeky little smile as well.

That was the start of it. From then on, all through the rest of April, the windy May and into the proper summer of June, Ida met Victor at the station as she headed home for her fortnightly afternoon off. Victor would get on the train with her, change alongside at Clapham Junction where they picked up a tram, all the way up to the Elephant. Later on in the evening he'd go back with her. Not from the Elephant, Ida's dad would've taken the strop to her if he ever thought she was talking to a lad on the way back to work. Victor would get the tram a few stops along, and they'd sit together again, talking about everything, about anything, in a way that Ida had never talked before. She couldn't tell her family what was wrong with the job, all they'd do was call her daft and tell her to get on the fish stall. She couldn't tell them about the dreams she had, dreams that went beyond service or stalls, dreams that weren't for girls like her, she knew, but she had them anyway, dreams of trams and trains and ships going to the whole world. But Victor listened.

It's not bad, Ida said, it's just not what I'd wanted to do. I never pictured myself cleaning up after other people. Not like some of the girls I was at school with, daft lasses who thought they'd swan into a big house and the son of the family would sweep them off and they'd be set up, princesses for life. I knew it'd be work, but there's all the bowing and scraping that goes with it too, and none of us Hatches are very good at that lark. I've always known I'll be on a barrow eventually, but the only one with a place when I was leaving school was the fish cart, and no one really wants to work on the fish cart, no matter that people will always want fish. There's all the gutting, filleting, preparing, and keeping it cold too, damn near impossible in summer. No, I told my dad I'd go into service, I wasn't going to stink of fish for the rest of my days.

Victor nodded, listening, and here, when Ida paused, worried she'd been talking too much, was failing in being ladylike again, he smiled,

You smell of lily of the valley, Ida. Lovely it is.

Ida blushed, and Victor smiled again, which made her blush all the more, and they sat back in the tram and Ida went on, telling Victor how, because she didn't want to prove them right, and because she did like earning her own money, never mind that most of it was handed over indoors on a Sunday afternoon, she hadn't told her mother that she cried herself to sleep most nights, she never spoke to her dad of the old man, had to be fifty if he was a day, the bloke who did all the heavy work and gardening, who'd hands he couldn't manage to keep to himself. She didn't even say that she thought the young lady at the house, a cousin from the country just in town for the season, was no better than she should be, coming home at all hours with young gentlemen seeing her to the door, and only a few years older than Ida herself. She kept her counsel and kept the job.

Ida found herself falling in love because someone listened to her. A boy listened to her and he didn't think it daft that a girl from Walworth wanted to do more than black a grate or work a stall all her life.

Come June, Victor invited Ida to a ship launching. It was the Albion, down at Leamouth, his brother had been working on it for two years and he'd make sure they got a good view. The launch was to be on Midsummer's Day with the Duchess of York letting go the champagne bottle and a brass band and all sorts of jollity. Midsummer's Day though, was a Tuesday, and Ida did something she'd never done in three years of service. She took a whole day off. She had to trade three half-day Sundays with Jane, who was no end of pleased that she, a lowly kitchenmaid, had something to trade with Ida, the more esteemed parlour-maid. Mrs Cooper wasn't impressed, but it wasn't as if they were a large household and Jane had agreed the trade, so Sally Cooper went back to her baking, muttering about the way the world was going, and how this had never happened when she was pastry cook to the editor of the *Manchester Guardian*. Ida had to get her mistress's permission as well, and that was a little more tricky, finally resorting to an actual lie to get the time away. Ida had never had a grand-father to remember, both of hers were dead before she was born, so she felt only a little guilt telling the story of the

23

awful tram accident and a dear old chap dead before his time. Ida was fifteen and Victor was lovely.

Afterwards, when they were coming back to Wimbledon on the tram, when Ida had finally stopped shaking, when the sound of the screams was replaced by the quieter whispers of people soothing each other, of mothers grabbing up their children and thanking God they had found them, when Victor kissed her for the first time, Ida couldn't but blame herself. If she hadn't lied, if she hadn't told the story of a dead-again grandfather. She liked the kiss, was grateful for it, but nothing could kiss away the image of that huge wave sweeping back from the just-launched Albion, slamming into the jetty, knocking all those people into the cold, churning water. She'd liked the kiss, and it was kind of Victor to try to kiss it better, but it didn't work, she didn't feel better, and she cried herself to sleep.

The next morning, when the bruises began to come out, all along her arms, from the force with which Victor had dragged her back, lifted her up and out of the crowd, pulled her away from the mass of bodies sliding down into the Thames, when she read in the paper that thirty thousand people had been at the dockside and she'd been lucky not to be in the hundreds that went in, the thirty-odd who'd died, she was a little more grateful, and a little more guilty. How had she, the liar, escaped with her life? That Sunday fortnight Victor met her again for the journey home. He'd called in at the big house a couple of times, to check on her, leaving a note and a twist of barley sugars at the servants' door. Ida believed him when he said he cared, and so she told him the lot of it. All the way home, and again, all the way back to

Wimbledon, and Victor listened. How it was to be Ida, to have a sort of knowing, the kind of knowing that made you feel responsible for not fixing things, fixing everything, and yet how that knowing was so unsure, so vague, she could never be sure if it was real, what she imagined before it happened, or was she just thinking herself too grand.

It wasn't that Victor hadn't listened before, but this time he had seen her face, ten minutes before it happened. Had been holding her hand when he'd felt it go cold, the blood all drained. Felt himself pulled back from the jetty by Ida's fear, and that fear almost as strong as he'd been himself when he pulled her up and out of the slamming body of the crowd, a mass of people surging forward on the tipping jetty. Victor believed her, believed Ida when she said she didn't know how she knew, and that she hadn't known before they got there, and that she'd certainly never have gone if she had – but she had known a bad thing was about to happen, not ten minutes before it did.

I never know what it means, but I do feel it, and only the bad things. I'm still surprised by the good things and that's something, isn't it, Victor? That I can be surprised by good things?

When Victor kissed her then, Ida felt all sorts of things she'd never felt before, all along her body, and she smiled when Victor finally pulled away, looked her in the eye and asked,

Like that do you mean? Surprised by a good thing like that?

For the rest of that year they carried on the same way, journeying together to and from the Elephant. Ida did not tell her family about Victor, she didn't need a special knowing to guess what they'd think. Yes, she was in service, and yes, they hadn't much, but everyone on her mother's side of the family had a trade, and on her father's they were barrow people, pearlies. Victor's people were different, his mother, brother and two little sisters shared two rooms in a house where four other families also had a couple of rooms each. They lived on Giffin Street, off Deptford High Street and when Victor first left school – at ten, hiding from the School Board inspector, on the same day his mother sneaked the younger children away from the rooms where they were too far behind in the rent to pretend any longer – he'd understood he'd not be going back for any more learning. From then on, Victor spent his days with his brother Arthur, collecting driftwood and scrap from the river at low tide to sell as firewood. Now he had a proper job, grocer's boy for a real grocer's shop, but there was no father to speak of, and Ida didn't press him on the subject. She didn't need to, not speaking of it said plenty, but her father would want to meet Victor, and her mother would need to know all the ins and outs of his people and Ida knew that Victor just wouldn't cut it for the Hatches.

So she said nothing and they shared kisses in back streets and alleys in half days stolen from her constant round of cleaning and clearing for the rich people in the house on the common, the one widowed woman and her four adult children who didn't need to work. Stolen too, from the half days she might have spent back at home.

Stolen hours, stolen kisses. And eventually, time to pay.

In early December, Victor told Ida he had a plan. He was going to join up, his cousin in the army said it looked like there might be another fuss with the Boers. There was a regular wage and a chance to go further than the lop-sided triangle that was Deptford, Elephant, Wimbledon. If there was a war there'd be the chance to come back in glory and change their lives for ever.

After that, the world's ours, we'll go away, to America, Australia, somewhere no one judges us on how we speak or the street we were born in.

Ida knew Victor was ready to go, hungry to go, knew he'd leave her anyway if she didn't agree to wave him off to the war. He asked her to marry him, before he left, said they could marry now or when he came back, said he wanted her for his wife as well as for his girl. And Ida believed him, but she also knew about the bad things that happen.

Bad things like a baby made the first time, the last time, the only time.

Bad things like drinking down as much slippery elm as she could and then a night, a day, another night, and the blood constantly coming from her, coming from her in drips and gobbets and finally flow and then drips again, bloody clumps.

Bad things like a card, sent just three months later, in ragged handwriting, with an uncertain slant to the letters, telling her that they were very sorry, Victor had died, no explanation as to how or what had happened, and that he had left word for his mother to let Ida know if ever he was hurt.

He was my boy, my first boy, and I shan't be getting him back, nor you neither, so you'd best pray for his soul as I do.

The envelope also held a prayer, the Lord's Prayer, written carefully on a scrap of paper the size of a penny. It was not from Victor, but from his mother, Victor's mother said she'd no need of prayer now, and so she was sending the handwritten prayer to Ida, much good might it do her. She hoped it might do her much good.

It took Ida a long time to agree to step out with Bill, longer still to accept his kisses. And when they made love that first time, Ida's second time, she was scared he would know, scared he'd be able to tell, but Bill was the virgin that Ida was not, and he didn't know there was a difference to note. Bill was as sweet and quiet and inexperienced as Victor had been ambitious and determined. Which meant that while it was not easy to accept his proposal when it came, it was a relief. Ida would not go to America or Australia with Victor, she would not be by his side as he changed the world, but Bill was like her family, like her people, she would go home to Walworth, and it would do. And, in time, through passion and also through sorrow, the loss of their first baby, when Ida blamed herself, believed she might never keep a baby inside her having got rid of the one she'd been carrying by Victor, through all that time of dry-eyed hurt, too dark for tears, Bill was there, big, solid, waiting. It became love, and it gave her Tom and the girls, and Ida was glad of it, and still she kept the prayer that reminded her of Victor, and she hoped never to sell it.

Five

Once upon a time, a long time before you were born, when we all still lived in Russia, before the Cossacks came, in the days when we were settled, when we had a home—

This was how Itzhak's grandfather Shimon began every story, and every time he did so, his daughter-in-law Mimi, Itzhak's mother, interrupted him to say,

We have a home, we have a home here.

She said this in Yiddish – *Mir hobben à hime, mir hobben à hime du* – even though Itzhak's grandfather told his stories in English, even though Mimi used English when she shopped in the market, English when she took in sewing and delivered it back again, English when she talked to Ida, the mother of Itzhak's friend Tom, Ida who had the stall in the market. She said it in Yiddish anyway, to remind her father-in-law that no, she hadn't forgotten where they came from, and why, but also that this was home now. London, Walworth, a spit, as her neighbours said, from the river. This was where Itzhak had friends, went to school, this was where she and Lev were making a home for the children.

29

Here they had a large synagogue covering a whole corner and here was a school for the children, Jewish school for Jewish children, just round from the Gentile children's school, and it was all out in the open, no one was hiding. She also said this because she hadn't lived in Russia, she had lived in Latvia, and even if the Russians insisted it was Russia, she and her family had never agreed with them, and it was important that Itzhak knew both sides of his family, followed both lines.

Itzhak's grandfather nodded yes to Mimi, the patriarch bowing to the woman of the house, adding a wink for Itzhak and a whispered 'twas ever thus, which caused Mimi to huff and slam a pot lid noisily on the stove, handing Itzhak's grandfather a wooden spoon as she did so and telling him not to get so carried away with his stories that he let the soup overcook. She went upstairs and Itzhak could hear her footfalls overhead, the sound of his mother plumping the pillows in the lodgers' room, shaking out and folding up the eiderdowns of the two faithful men who shared a partitioned room, and then the same but muffled as she went on to the room Itzhak shared with his two brothers. Mimi told Itzhak to go out into the street and run it off whenever he was angry. She, being a lady – even if she did have to be a landlady and a seamstress and a mother, a daughter-in-law and a specialist cook for the whims of her big boys Nathan and David – could not run off her frustrations outside. She, being a lady, found other ways to express her frustrations. The pillows and the eiderdowns in their house, goose feather, the lot of them, all the way from Latvia, must have been the softest and plumpest in Walworth, Itzhak thought.

And then, the story went on.

When we had a home, when we had a village, there was a doctor. He was our mohel too of course, a proper doctor, not like the sometime-barbers, sometime-butchers you get these days. We had a doctor and a butcher and a barber and yes, they were all farmers or they had smallholdings, but they had their professions, their trade. A man needs a trade Itzhak, a daily task, it holds him up when the world would knock him down. I had my profession, I was a carpenter, a wood turner, you know this.

Itzhak's grandfather held out his hands, the shaking hands he could not control, the hands that could no longer hold a knife or a saw, and he looked at the hands and puffed out a big sigh that was as much curse as it was sorrow, and he continued,

But what our village did not have was a dentist. Every town needs a butcher, a baker, a doctor, we know this, but a dentist? Anyone can pull their own tooth when it rots, any farmer knows to check his goats' teeth once a year, and, while he does that, he might remember to check his own too. What you learn from a goat you can apply to your own mouth. There was no need to pay a man for a job we could do for ourselves, one man for his neighbour.

Then, one day, a traveller came to this village, this place where we had a home, and he said he was a dentist. We did not even know what he meant. We had not heard of the profession, we were suspicious, but when he smiled, Itzhak, you have never seen such teeth, so white, so gleaming. They shone in the spring sunlight. Spring took a long time coming in our village, winters were long and hard and

31

dark, so as soon as it was Passover, even an early Passover, everyone would work outside, play outside if they could. The old men would drink their tea leaning against the open door frame, wives pulled out a table so that they could chop vegetables in front of those little houses, children playing on the still-frozen ground.

He looked around the room they sat in now, the grandfather, nodding approvingly at the glass lamps lined up all along the mantelpiece. It was always so dark indoors when I was a boy, such tiny rooms, and dark windows, if there was glass at all. Of course, we children played in any tiny space, anywhere we could, just as you and your friends from the Christian school do now. Even, he whispered, on Shabbat, when you think your mother is not watching.

Shimon took a moment to remember his boyhood friends, Mikhail and Yaakov, boys he also ran about with, boys he fought and played with, boys he too broke the Sabbath for. Boys he lost in the terrors, whose faces were still clear to him, even now, though he had never known them as men.

And the dentist? Itzhak asked, seeing the faraway look settle on his grandfather's face. He knew that if he did not bring him back quickly, the old man would be lost for the evening, somewhere in a small Russian village, running through fields with boys who did not become men.

Yes, yes, the dentist. And so, because it was spring, because Pesach had been and gone and the women were kneading bread again, because we were outdoors that evening, we all saw him when he arrived, when he presented himself at the rabbi's house. He was sent there first, of course, it was only polite. And we all saw, when he spoke to ask directions, and then when he smiled, and then – in answer to a welcoming phrase the rabbi uttered – when he laughed, we saw a mouth full of teeth, not a single gap, and each tooth like a new piano key, made to sing out a smile.

The traveller sang that night too. The rabbi invited him to stay for supper and our mothers all sent food and the men went to the rabbi's home, his was the only one with a room big enough to hold the table that would seat them all. That night he sat around the big table, where I learned what it means to be a man, where I learned my portion of the Torah for my bar mitzvah, and he told the tales of his travels, told them to the men of the village. We boys did not sit at the table, of course, but we sat on the floor and we listened, quiet for once.

Such tales. He told us he was from Persia. A Jew, Itzhak, all the way from Persia, think of it. A Persian Jew who had been travelling the great lands of Russia for twenty years, more, always planning to go home, and never getting there, ever called away by this road or that. He had been north to the place where spring and summer arrive together at Shavuot and then leave again before Rosh Hashanah. He had been west, all the way to St Petersburg, where he saw the great buildings, glorious roads paved and cleaned by street sweepers every night and every morning, enormous houses that reached right into the sky, towering above courtyards, with windows, real glass windows that look both into the courtyard on one side and out to the light on the other, houses where it is all light, only light.

Eventually, when he had told of all his travels, and the vodka was very low in the bottle that the rabbi kept for such special gatherings, he finally told of the time he met the man who had cared for the teeth of Catherine the Great. The traveller said he learned everything he knew from that man. He said that was why he had such fine teeth, now in his sixty-fifth year. No one could believe this, the man looked forty, fifty in a harsh light, but from the stories he told, the way he spoke of himself as a bystander, a witness, the elders at the table understood that he must be speaking truth. He said that the reason he did not look as old as the other men at the table – the rabbi himself, Oded the baker, Saul the tailor – was because he had a full mouth of perfect teeth, he could still eat everything he had eaten as a boy, crisp carrots and chewy date cakes and the heaviest of our own dark rye bread, and that kept him young. His teeth kept him young.

He told the men that they too could have perfect teeth.

And the men leaned closer towards the end of the table, where the traveller sat at the right hand of the rabbi, because here was a man of sixty-five who looked forty, here was a traveller and an experienced man from Persia, here was a Jew who had learned his trade from a man who had touched the mouth of the Tzarina herself.

Itzhak's grandfather leaned back, he did not want the boy to think he approved of the Tzarina, she who had persecuted the Jews, moving them on and on from one limited parcel of land to another, ever inward, ever into the towns and the cities, away from the land they loved, away from sowing and growing in open fields to hand tools and sweatshops, but even so, she was the Tzarina. For a man such as this to have been so close to one who knew Catherine, it was not nothing.

In the morning it began. Despite wives shaking their heads and old mothers accusing their adult sons of vanity, every man in the village left home with a coin in his pocket and a little fear in his stomach, coming back later with a swollen cheek, an aching jaw, and a wide, bloody gap in his mouth. Each one of them were promised just one day to wait until the Tzarina's dentist's apprentice took the tooth and the coin and turned it into his good health and long life.

Every man, that is, except Itzhak's grandfather's father, because Itzhak's great-grandfather was a carpenter, and had told his wife he would be away three days, the length of time it would take him to fell the giant maple he was so happy to have found just before winter and had waited until the weather was good enough to bring down. It was a tree that might make several tables and chairs, a sideboard and a wardrobe, a tree that might keep him busy all the winter to come, and there would also be handfuls of early leaves for his wife to use for dye. That day, Shimon's mother, the woman whose hands would be stained with maple dye thanks to her husband's good industry, watched the men of her village walking eagerly along the dirt track outside her house, shook her head at their pride, and smiled knowing that her husband was a hard worker, a good man, and no friend of the mirror. Even if he had been at home to hear all the stranger's stories, a man as ugly as her Lev would never be persuaded that new teeth could make any difference to his face.

But the men of the village were not granted their promised good health or long lives. The men of Itzhak's grandfather's village were instead treated to the bitterness of disappointment, the shame of the gullible, and the anger of their wives. Most of their wives. The rabbi's wife Rachel contented herself with quoting Ecclesiastes, and even then under her breath, allowing herself only the first words, 'Vanity of vanities . . .' Her husband smiled a gap-toothed smile and gave thanks for his good fortune. Precious above rubies indeed, and kinder than he had expected when he'd walked into the back room they kept for guests and the needy, and had seen the bedcover neatly folded back, the pillow smoothed, and no sign of the traveller other than a note in a scrawling hand:

Thank you for your generosity. The bed is fine, the pillow a little lumpy. Your teeth will be put to good use. The Tzarina was a Jew-hating whore and you should all have known better than to give money to any man who had ever had anything to do with a person who'd lowered himself enough to touch her. Let the gaps in your mouths remind you of your foolishness.

And the rabbi thought the traveller was probably right, though he didn't share the note with anyone else, not even his wise and compassionate wife.

Beside the note was a small silver hand, flat, with intricate working on the palm, five closed fingers, straight-pointed. The rest of the note read:

I leave you a gift for the woman whose husband did not come for teeth. She does not need a gift I think, as she has so wise a man, but I leave this anyway. It is a hand of Miriam, our sisters and mothers wear it where I come from, it is to protect them from harm. Such good fortune in her husband, may she have good fortune wherever she goes.

The rabbi did not show this gift to his wife either, she

36

was a superstitious woman already and he did not want to encourage her in these ways. Faith asks of us to pray and obey, that should be enough. He passed the gift on though to Lev's wife, and washed his hands afterwards, just in case.

Days later the carpenter came home, pulling a cart heavy with carefully cut chunks of good maplewood, pulling it by hand as he had done for half of the day before, blisters on his hands, his shoulders, his feet. Shimon ran to meet his father, ran to stand on the top of the cart and help his father by shouting encouragement, even as he made it heavier to pull. When his mother came out of their tiny home and scolded him for making his father's burden harder, Lev the carpenter, the ugliest man in the village, turned instead to smile at his son, showing his mouth over-full of crooked teeth, and winked. Their Shimon could never be a burden.

Late that night Lev, who had spent all day stacking the wood carefully, so that in the coming months it would dry just enough to be worked, but not so dry that it became brittle, lay alongside his wife, silent in the cool night.

When she had told the story of the traveller, and of the teeth, and of the hand of Miriam she now wore around her neck on a thin ribbon, the wife waited and then prompted her husband, hearing his listening, waiting silence.

There is something you haven't told me.

And Lev said that he too, had met the traveller.

Oh?

Another sigh in the dark, Lev shifting a tiny sidle away from his wife, his voice softer still.

I did not meet the traveller. I felled him.

The man, the stranger, had been running fast through the forest, at the very point that Lev was forcing his bound and blistered hands to push the saw through the most dense part of the maple trunk, the very last log to cut up and load on the cart. And as the saw's teeth juddered through that last chunk of trunk, he heard the sound of a man, running, and he took his attention from his saw and the final piece of the felled trunk, just for a heartbeat. His bleeding hands though, intent on their work, kept on push-pushing, and pull-pulling. In that moment, a long and thin shard of maple, a splinter as sharp and brutal as the icicles even a small child knows to avoid in the winter forest, sheared off from the trunk. The maple shard spun through the air, and caught the man, the running man, caught in his throat and felled him.

Lev was telling his wife he had killed a man.

And Lev's wife knew what he was telling her, that he had not only killed a man, but he had also buried him, hidden him, planted a maple sapling above the body. In his silence he told her they could not inform the authorities. With no words he reminded her that a murdering Jew with blood on his blistered hands, even one who had killed in accident, with an absence of malice, even one who killed only another Jew, was not something their village could survive. Any excuse for the laws first enacted by the Tzarina to be brought down on their heads.

Even though Lev believed his wife when she told him that the man was a liar and a cheat and a thief, Lev did not forgive himself, not through a lifetime of Yom Kippur fasts.

That winter, when the cold again began to bite, and the men of the village bit less than before, Lev was in his workshop at the back of their house, the cold workshop where his teeth, all of them, chattered incessantly, no matter how warm his body became as he cut and lathed and sanded and oiled. From the old maple he made a good table, eight chairs, and a wardrobe, a sideboard. He made too, a sign, a marker, that only he would ever recognise, to leave at the traveller's grave when spring allowed. And, for the first time, he gave his son Shimon tasks of his own. Until now, the boy had been allowed to sand a little, to use the lathe with his father's hands holding his own, now he was given a job. A copying job.

Itzhak's grandfather leaned down now, and took Itzhak's hands in his own shaking hands, the hands that could no longer work. That was how I learned I was not just a carpenter, a joiner, but that like my father, I was a wood turner, someone who knew the grain. I discovered that dead wood could become something living in my hands.

Lev called his son into the workshop and closed the door behind him. He pulled out a parcel from beneath the work bench, hidden behind glass jars of oils and wood stain. He unwrapped the parcel and there was a felt hat, round, box-shaped, and on it was sewn every one of the eighty-eight teeth the man had taken from the village. And because Shimon was just a boy, he did not recoil or turn up his nose in disgust, instead he held the hat and tried it on, too big for him of course, and asked if he could keep it. Lev said yes, he could keep the hat, but on two conditions: one that he never let his mother see it, and two, that he used the teeth as models to make a new tooth that would replace each one on the hat. Eighty-eight model teeth from the offcuts of the finest maple tree Lev Ayalon had ever felled.

It was a long winter, and hard, but Lev and Shimon worked happily, mostly silently, alongside each other, the boy learning all that the father could teach him and more, showing a deeper understanding of wood with every day that passed. That winter, Itzhak's grandfather began to become the wood turner he was destined to be.

When spring finally returned with Passover and promises of next year in Jerusalem, the men of the village were able to bite down on their bitter herbs because Shimon presented each man with a denture made to match the tooth he had lost. A Pesach gift like no other.

The teeth took some swapping and trying out, of course, the traveller had not stolen them and made a note of which man they came from, but eventually each model tooth was reunited with his man, and the blacksmith smelted down whatever each man could afford, or his wife could spare, gold or silver or copper, and made a band to hold each tooth in place. Each man except the rabbi, who kept his model tooth in a small piece of cloth in his pocket, there to remind him of the danger of vanity, if not the danger of inviting a stranger to his house, for after all, every table should keep a place in case a passing stranger might be Elijah, in need of a seat at the table, a warm bed.

When he finished his story, Itzhak's grandfather reached behind him to the chest where he kept his private things, now that he lived in his own son's house, the son named for Lev, the ugly carpenter. He opened the chest and took out the hat for Itzhak to hold, to look at. And even though Itzhak had seen the hat many times before, and even though he had worn it on his own head, too big of course, he looked at it differently now, making sure to count each one of the eighty-eight teeth.

One for every key on the piano, Itzhak, so when you rattle this hat you too, are tinkling the ivories.

Shimon laughed at his own joke and took the hat back for safe-keeping.

Later that night, when Itzhak was rubbing baking soda around his own teeth and gums in the way his grandfather had taught him, the way that everyone in this family took care of their teeth, he asked his mother if she had heard the story of the hat, the true story. And Mimi laughed, holding her son close, telling him that he would need to grow less gullible if he was to have a good life in this hard world.

Of course I've heard the story. And you know what I think? I think your grandfather's mother, whose sewing box I have upstairs under my bed, was also the village seamstress with a sideline in hat-making. And I think that a carpenter as skilled as your grandfather was very good with tools. You think pliers are only for pulling nails, drills only for making holes in wood?

Itzhak wasn't sure what she meant, and Mimi wouldn't say more, but he had a feeling she didn't believe his grandfather's story.

Itzhak went to bed looking at his own hands, wondering

41

what they might be able to do. Tomorrow he was meant to go to Hebrew lessons at the synagogue, and his friend Tom to the Christians' Sunday school at St John's, but often the boys met in the street, often they found their other mate Jimmy and the three of them ran away to play instead of going along to learn the stories the Sunday teachers had to tell. Now Itzhak had a story for Tom and Jimmy, his friends would like this one. And, like Itzhak, they would believe it too.

Six

Tom waited for Itzhak and Jimmy over by the coal depot. Even though Tom and Jimmy lived just doors apart on Larcom Street and from his back bedroom in their Wansey Street house Itzhak could look right into the yard at the back of Tom's place, the boys knew that meeting in their own streets would just be asking for trouble.

Tom and Jimmy, mates since they were babies by virtue of Tom's mum Ida and Jimmy's dad Charlie being cousins, knew far too many people round this way to be able to sneak off easily. Granddad Bob, Tom's mum's father, lived at the one corner of the dog-leg, they lived at the other, and Jimmy's place was bang in between. Over the road there was Aunty Sarah, no one's real aunty as far as Tom and Jimmy knew, an old lady with one eye gone to a cataract and hairs in her chin that scratched when she kissed you, worth the itch though, for the couple of bob she always gave them. Down the back of Ethel Street, cutting through to behind the Town Hall, was where Itzhak's big brothers stood to smoke and tried to chat up girls. As if any girls round here would walk down that way, knowing those lads were waiting. As if Tom and Jimmy and Itzhak would walk that way either, when they were trying to sneak away.

Nathan and David were only fifteen and thirteen, Itzhak's brothers, but they were both working, bringing in a wage, thinking it made them the big I am. Nathan at Sarson's in Bermondsey, his hair and clothes with the smell of pickling spices and vinegar on them, no matter how hard Mimi scrubbed at them, and David with his labouring job for the ironmongers', hoping for an apprenticeship when his first full year was done. Both boys were up and out of school as soon as they had jobs to go to, no matter that Mimi had wanted an education for them, happy to work all hours extra to pay for it, or that their father had begged them to stay on, learn a little more, make their way up at school before they had to get out and struggle in the world. David and Nathan had both wanted money in their pockets and their parents understood that feeling only too well, could not but consent when the time came.

Nathan and David didn't just pick on their little brother, many was the time Nathan had teased Jimmy for his bright red hair, and Jimmy had been tempted to have a go back, tell Nathan he was just a bloody Jew anyway, no need to come all that with him, but then Jimmy thought that would mean Itzhak was just a bloody Jew too, and he didn't feel that way about Itzhak. They'd been mates for years, along with Tom, even though Itzhak went to the Jews' school. Itzhak was a yid, yes, just as Jimmy had the red hair of a mick, and Tom had those great big eyes with lashes that were long as a girl's and got him called all sorts of names,

44

but none of those names were called to have a go, not the way Nathan meant it. So Jimmy kept his mouth shut and his eyes open, and he and Tom and Itzhak took their different routes, up to Newington Causeway, where they'd watched the navvies digging the foundations for the new hospital, or up past the mortuary and then the garage, or over the backs of half a dozen tumbledown walls and through the boarded-up house, the ghost house, all three boys finally meeting up at the depot.

Tom and Itzhak had to be careful, they could only skive off every few weeks or so, turning up like good lads to Sunday school and Hebrew school the rest of the time. Rose wasn't fussed about Jimmy going to the Sunday school, and Charlie wasn't impressed by it at all, always had a mouthful for the do-gooders when they came knocking, so neither of them minded if the lad was off with his mates of an afternoon. It gave Rose some time to catch up on the week before it was Monday morning and she was to start all over again. She knew it wouldn't be long before Charlie was giving Jimmy more to do on the barrow, he should have his fun while he was young. Tom swiped extra saints' cards for Jimmy, when he could, both boys loved the Sunday school treat, so it was important they got the stamps that proved they'd been there, enough stamps and you were all right to go to the treat, the long table with tea and currant buns, and the games and the prizes, when summer came. But neither of the boys loved the treat more than they loved running about, all three of them together, especially in the long lazy afternoons, so it was Sunday school they dodged when they could, and it was as mates that they ran together.

In the Jewish kids' Sunday school, Itzhak worked extra hard on his portion of the Torah, a while yet till his bar mitzvah and already he knew it well. Worked so hard that the rabbi praised him to his grandfather Shimon when they met to talk about the old days and then, the following week, the old men expressed no surprise that the boy didn't turn up to study, poor lad was exhausted he was working so hard.

Working so damn hard my foot, Jimmy said and Tom laughed and Itzhak repeated, more quietly, working so damn hard, swear words harder for him to say, his family home more faithful, if no less superstitious, Mimi pulling at her blouse and whispering p-p-p under her breath easily as often as Rose touched wood and Ida bowed to solitary magpies. All three mothers calling on luck to pick them up when the day-to-day was too full of keeping on, husbands and families and children to worry about, always their babies to worry about.

Tom, Jimmy and Itzhak left it all behind them as they hared up towards Blackfriars Bridge from the Elephant. They ran away from stories of how the Jews killed Jesus, or how the Christians persecuted the Jews, from Charlie demanding Jimmy help him sort stock, and Itzhak's merciless big brothers and Tom's annoying little sisters. They ran off mudlarking down the river, best at low tide when there was a chance of picking up a copper or two on the shore. If there were no coppers, there were always half a dozen old clay pipes to pick up and rinse in the filthy water, then pretend they were sailors, smoking their pipes and drinking a tot of rum, watching the sun go down over the sea while a dusky Pacific maiden sang to them from beyond the waves.

When the tide was high and there was no shore to play on, they might go along to St Saviour's Dock, the one Aunty Sarah still called Savory Dock, for a look at the pulleys and the chains hanging off the sides of the huge warehouses. They imagined themselves dockers and stevedores, or men of the sea, on the water and away. The big old cranes would be still for the day, some of them, like Ida, catching their breath for Monday morning and another long week's work.

It was a sunny Sunday, with a real touch of spring in the air even though it was only the front end of March, and Tom decided they should steal a ride on the back of a tram down to Clapham. They were almost there before they were thrown off, and they ran and chased the rest of the way, then across the common and it was a prairie for cowboys and Indians, through the trees and they were crossing the Rubicon, now Scott and his men, pushing on, pushing on, to the South Pole and glory that was Clapham Common south side. They were all the explorers they knew, Livingstone, then Lewis and two Clarks, one either side of Jimmy's Lewis, blazing a new trail across the whole of America. Geography was the only lesson Jimmy really cared about, he'd come top of the class for his maps two years in a row.

Shame it wasn't top of the class for his arithmetic Charlie had said, laying into the lad one day when he'd given a customer the wrong change on the barrow, change of a pound instead of a ten-shilling note. Adding up and taking away would've been a damn sight more useful than your flamin' maps.

Jimmy wasn't bothered about his sums now, running

with his mates, wanting only to push forward. He led his men and finally, finally they came to the promised land of the ponds and settled themselves down in a patch of long grass to stalk for their quarry. It had been waiting for them.

On the other side of the pond, still dressed like little boys even though they must have been Itzhak's age if they were a day, and he the youngest of the three mates, were a couple of toff lads. Instead of running free like the Walworth boys, they were watched by a nurse or a nanny or whatever they called her, not their mother for sure, all kitted up in dark blue, ever so starchy, telling them this, that and the other about how to launch their wooden sailing ships in the pond. She'd a foghorn of a voice and a suggestion for which way the wind was coming and another about which sail to raise – Tom and Jimmy exchanged hungry looks, real sails – which stick to push them in, which hook to fetch them out, where they could lean and where not. Oh, she knew it all, and told them again and again in a pretend milady voice ringing out across half the common.

At first, for a long quarter hour, between one chime of the church clock and another, the boys simply watched, imagining those boats were theirs. Once they were in the water the boats might have been anyone's, might have been theirs. Itzhak the daring captain of the smaller red boat, Tom the fierce leader of the larger blue, Jimmy, more of a landlubber anyway, played First Lord of the Admiralty, sending his men out to the farthest reaches of the Empire, speaking his orders in an accent borrowed from the hoity-toity lads on the other side of the pond. Tom and Itzhak laughed so much at Jimmy's impersonations that Itzhak fell over and landed, splat, on the muddy edge of the pond, and then all three laughed harder still.

After a time, when a spring wind took the boats further from their owners, the Walworth lads became pirates, one seaman attacking another old tar's ship, this salty dog abusing that cur's men. And then there were arrows, flying through the sea air, from the two dozen bowmen on Itzhak's port side, dead set for their targets on Tom's blue boat. In retaliation and escalation, Tom's men fought back the only way they could, hanging over the starboard rail, blunderbusses in bloodstained hands, fighting for their lives and for the honour of their captain.

When the clock chimed and woke the nanny up to the time, the need to get her charges off home for tea and there was bound to be cherry cake, but oh dear, look at that, the boats were so far into the centre of the pond, how would they ever get them back now and there were dark clouds rushing in from the north, maybe they'd just have to go on home anyway, leave the boats behind, well she had told the boys to keep them on a string, but would they listen, no they would not, and there was an end to it.

Tom stood up. He pulled muddy Itzhak and laughing Jimmy with him. They took off their old shoes and darned socks, and strode into the pond, braving the Clapham rapids and the famed eels, squelching their toes in centuries' worth of layered mud to save the boats and the other lads their cherry cake getting stale.

It was a valiant gesture, worthy of a medal, a round of applause at least. The smartly dressed lads watched, wishing they might be allowed to do the same, and the nanny, who smelled of rose-water and carbolic soap, thanked them for their trouble and handed them a whole sixpence in payment for their good deed. She said if they were anywhere near as good explorers as they were shouters, they ought to become Scouts and put all that knowledge to good use.

As it turned out, going down to Clapham hadn't been such a bright idea in the end, it took them the best part of an hour to get home and all three lads were for it when they came in damp and muddy and later than expected. Nathan gave Itzhak a hiding for worrying their mother, no matter that Mimi herself was more worried about Nathan turning into a bully and that Shimon shouted at both of his grandsons for disturbing his nap. Jimmy was lucky to get in just before Charlie came home from the costermonger's pub on the corner, Rose whisked him into the yard with a chunk of bread and dripping for his tea and Charlie was none the wiser. Tom thought he'd never hear the end of it from Ida, though there was no hiding to worry about, Ida was never much of one for belting the kids, but didn't she go on about what might be lying on the bottom of that awful, filthy pond, and forced him to scrub his feet in the yard, scrub them for ages, and threatened to tell Uncle Charlie on them and all. She never had yet, no matter how often she threatened it, never would either, no point Ida telling her cousin when he'd only find a way to use it against her in the end, make her out to be the bad mother, the soft one, letting her Tom run wild and take his Jimmy down with him.

Ida went to bed that night, a nagging ache in her chest, a worry for Tom whistled out of nowhere, out of a pair of muddy feet, a worry she whispered into a bone carving that lay beneath her pillow, a carving she'd whispered her prayers to since the day she fell for her lad. A carving made to pass on and to protect.

They'd always had cows. The family had been milkers, herders, for generations. Ever since they'd had that little bit of land up at Brixton Causeway, alongside the Effra. Not that anyone had called it the Causeway since Samuel's grandfather's time, and even then it was only the old men and women who used the name, but that's where the farm had been, marked on the old map. The family weren't farmers as such, not by the time Samuel came along. If Samuel's father was to be believed the old farm had stretched all the way up the hill from Stockwell. When they opened the Vauxhall Bridge though, the Causeway was too busy, no good for wandering stock. Then with the railway carving up the land, well, once he started selling off a plot here and there, it wasn't long before Samuel's father could no longer call himself a farmer. A farmer wanted land, without land he might have a bit more in his purse, but the money would soon go, and coin could not be ploughed. By the time he was an old man, Samuel's father was all regret at his youthful folly in selling off the farm, and not only because the family no longer had much to their name. Where once it had all been open, now it was tied up, walled and fenced into plots and parcels, wide villas for the rich, meaner cottages for the workers, and the paths trodden by generations of family feet had become roads for a constant stream of carts and carriages. Samuel's father missed the cows too, the smell of them, the stink of them even, missed their warm breath on a cold morning, their hot piss, grass-greened shit, missed the chance to sink freezing feet into a warm cow pat. He missed, and the family mourned, the money from the dirt carts, taking the manure to the market gardens that fed the city below, bringing back a pretty penny in exchange. Nothing about farming that couldn't be used, and Samuel's father had sold it almost all.

The old man wasn't entirely to blame though, it wasn't as if he'd drunk it away like some. Samuel gained from the income in a way no one from their family ever had done before. The lad was clearly a scholar, right from the start, so they sent him to the school in Honor Oak where he mixed with the sons of gentlemen, if not gentry. Samuel raised himself in the world. He was not a gentleman, the son of a farmer could not become that, but in time, with hard work and rather more good luck, he became one of those very developers that had caused his grandfather to spit on the ground whenever he spoke of them. Once the Herne Hill and City Branch of the London, Chatham and Dover Railway started bringing City men into and out of town, there was a good trade from parcelling up ever smaller tracts of land and turning them into houses. Perfectly nice houses too, the kind of place a young couple could raise a small family in comfort and keep a maid as well. In the early days Samuel had worked with the builders himself, had no fear of getting his hands dirty, but it was the planning he most enjoyed. Had there been enough money he'd have wanted to study engineering, but even the better part of a fine old farm could not buy that sort of start in life.

As he grew older, Samuel often found himself thinking of his grandfather, a man happiest outside, no matter the weather. The old man would spend half the evening sitting out on the front step of the farmhouse, looking down to London. He'd stare out across Southwark to the silver thread river, the dome of St Paul's clear on a summer night. Then, the moment the kitchen clock chimed nine he was off to his bed. Summer or winter he was up at half four to milk his cows, and he had young Samuel up with him. They didn't talk while milking, Samuel's grandfather said it put the cows off, if they were jittery he'd hum to soothe them, but otherwise the only sound was of milk swooshing, one-two, one-two, into tin buckets, double-stomachs gurgling, and the occasional splat of shit or piss when one of the girls took it into her big daft head to welcome the morning with letting go. They'd load the milk into the pails for the dairy over at Dulwich, and then Samuel and his grandfather would head back to the house, knowing there would be fresh bread and eggs or cheese or bacon waiting for them, mushrooms quickly thrown into the pan if they'd found any on their way out to the shed.

It was on these walks that Samuel's grandfather told him the stories he said didn't belong indoors, stories he'd had from his own grandfather, and him further back. He told Samuel about how they used to dress the well, covered in patterns woven from flowers and leaves, to protect the spring and keep it flowing. When he talked of Jack-in-the-Green he'd lower his voice, no point calling Jack in when he wasn't needed, and no need either, to risk his wrath if he wasn't given the right welcome. He said how Jack might be a trickster, but we need him to keep spring returning and also to keep it at bay, no point in spring coming too soon, new lambs killed in a snowfall, early crops burned in their beds from a frost. Samuel's grandfather explained that Jack needed just the right amount of appeasement and not too much encouraging. He told Samuel about the old river, how it pulled at a dozen or more tributaries even once it was all city and docks, he taught his grandson about the stars and the land and the water and the sky, teaching him with a greater urgency as the months became years. And when he was dying he gave Samuel a task.

As a little lad, Samuel had liked to sit on the front step in the evenings, leaning against his grandfather's knees. His grand-father would drink a pint of beer, warmed by the poker, and he'd let Samuel have a little sip. When he'd finished his beer, the grandfather would take his knife from his pocket and go back to his carving. The old man had been carving that cow's backbone since the day Samuel was born, that's what he said. They'd had a cow give birth to twins and the poddy calf that would usually have been sold off was kept for fattening up, because Samuel's mother – as good a girl as any man could hope for his son – had been halfway with her first child when those calf twins came and the best way to wel-come a new baby was with a real feast. His grandfather didn't make a feast for the other grandchildren, just Samuel, the first grandson. Samuel's grandmother had been sure the baby was a girl, the way her daughter-in-law carried it, the way her hair grew different on her head since the day she'd fallen for the child, but Samuel's grandfather had been certain of a lad, and so he fattened the calf accordingly.

When the baby came they were both right, and wrong. There had been a girl, a twin girl, delivered second, hours after Samuel came from his mother in a rush and a scream, hours more labouring to bring out the cold baby girl with the cord wrapped tight around her neck. Samuel's mother was poorly for weeks after, not just with grief for her daughter, but the pain of bringing forth the dead baby had taken it out of her. Samuel was born during Lent and it was past Whitsun before his mother was strong enough to leave her bed and be churched. Baby Samuel in her arms, her mother and her mother-in-law on either side, she walked slowly and carefully down to the church at Brixton Causeway. At the church they met with her married sister, half-gone with a third child herself, along from Camberwell to join them in bringing the new mother to the church. No matter that the proverbs they placed their faith in were those about the fall of dew or that the revelations they best understood were the secrets told in the weft of a spider's web – churching was what was done, and more, it was a time just for the women, and so they went along. The boy's christening was agreed for the following Sunday, after the service, and Samuel's mother was welcomed back from her confinement, that place so close to death.

Heading home, the women took their time of it, important for the new mother and the already-mothers to speak of things they could not say in front of their men. Valuable tears were shed on the way back up the hill to the farm, baby-loss poured into the Effra in the same breath as baby-love.

By the time the cottage came into view, just over the

rise, it was gone dinner time, and Samuel's mother was surprised her mother-in-law wasn't hurrying ahead to get indoors, shouting out cooking commands and ordering the men out of the house. A good mother-in-law and a wise cook, she was generous about everything but the hearth, her hearth. Samuel's mother knew she'd never have a kitchen of her own until her mother-in-law was gone. She was even more surprised when they came close enough to smell the roasting meat, see the table set outside in the sun, wild flowers picked and strewn all along the path to the low front door. She had not left the house until that morning. She had not seen spring arrive and settle, did not realise that her baby's grandfather had killed the calf, far enough from the house that she did not hear its cries, she had cries enough of her own to listen to, respond to, to hear in her sleep when the other baby, her tiny dead girl, mewled an impossible distress.

And now the animal – bled, eviscerated, organs and brain and sweetmeats and tongue put aside for other meals, skin already cleaned for curing – now that animal had been killed to honour her Samuel. It was time. And so she smiled her gratitude and went upstairs and dressed her little boy in a new-made smock and combed out her hair, tying it up again neatly. She put on a clean apron and went back downstairs, out into the front yard where the family welcomed her with cheers.

The family fed from that calf and his preserved and potted meat well into summer. And every time Samuel's mother declared her gratitude and every time she ate up, ate well and they patted her on the back for the good mother she was, for putting away her grief, saving them having to

56

suffer it any longer. They praised the bonny lad she was raising, calf's foot jelly and brawn feeding her feeding him, and with every mouthful she stifled the scream of her loss.

When that poddy calf was done, its bones stripped of meat, sucked dry of marrow, boiled for soup, the hide was tanned and ready for belts and shoes and sacks, Samuel's grandfather made use of the bones. Ground down for the ground, to enrich the soil. He put the largest backbone aside, the knobbly chunk of vertebra that had been the base of the calf's spine, and when the bone was ready, dry but not too dry, he began to carve it. Samuel's grandfather was a skilled whittler of wood and bone, had carved the over mantel in the little cottage, made his wife a pair of bone earrings that looked very like pearls, but when he set to carve the calf's bone for Samuel, he went to the bone with no plan, just a feeling in his hands that he would make something to protect his first grandchild, a charm for all his life. Samuel's grandfather sat in the evening light at the front of the cottage, looking down to the big old city growing bigger and older every day, and he let his hands get to work while his mind dreamed futures for the boy. A week later there was the beginning of a face in the centre of the vertebra, flanges of bone either side making arms, or angel's wings, perhaps.

When he was small, Samuel had been allowed to play with the bone carving only on special occasions. When he came to being a young man himself, he set it on a high shelf, not believing it had any power of its own, but not wanting to turn away from the offering his grandfather had made him. When Samuel's mother lay dying she whispered that she had never stopped mourning his birth-and-death sister, that she hoped the bone charm would protect him as a sister might pray for her brother's soul. Samuel himself came to his death middle-aged and not at all the great man his family had hoped education would make of him. He became far too fond of a high life he couldn't afford, and when that began to fail him, even fonder of the drink. Samuel was brought low long before his own child was able to benefit from any of it, his daughter came into a poorer world, without even a spit of land on which to grow her own supper. He died too young, leaving what little he had to his wife, and just one bequest to his child:

To my daughter, the bone angel, that it may protect her better than I have been able.

She gave it to her daughter and, in time, it was passed on to her granddaughter Ida.

A bone angel, all that was left of a farm and a view and a hope of prosperity. An angel that Ida prayed to, not believing it was magic, not believing that it wasn't. Beautifully carved it was though, lovingly made, meant to pass on and to protect.

Seven

Once that lady by the Clapham pond had said about the Scouts, Tom got it in his head that he and his mates had to be Scouts, and he couldn't get it out. He spent his share of the sixpence on a third-hand *Scouting for Boys*, read it once, stumbling through some passages, skipping from one chapter to the next to find something that attracted his attention, first the tips on compass work, then Morse and semaphore, a whole page on stalking games, and then he was well away, read it cover to ripped cover three times more. And what he read told him that scouting wasn't just flag-waving and bird-calling and singing songs, the things his dad said were a waste of time anyway, weren't going to look after you in a real fight, nor was it just how to be a good son of the Empire as Uncle Charlie had scoffed when he caught the boys poring over the book together,

Son of the Empire my arse, they mean bloody cannon-fodder, that's all that lot think we're good for, Baden-Powell's no different to the rest of them, hero or no.

Uncle Charlie would always have a go if he could, but Tom knew better now. Scouting wasn't just the games and the exercises and all that outdoors stuff. It wasn't even that Baden-Powell was the hero of Mafeking that'd made his book sell so fast. There were boats.

Scouts go on boat trips, he told Jimmy. The real thing, not just going up the river to look at them, or getting the ferry to the other side, it's honest-to-god proper sailing.

It was all very well to dream of being a sailor, but Tom knew he'd never go to sea. His people were neither dockers nor watermen, he was a market kid and he'd be a barrow boy first and eventually he'd have his own stall, as tied to the market as any of them. But Tom loved his *Scouting for Boys*, and Itzhak and Jimmy loved it because Tom loved it, and then Tom found out that there was to be a Scout troop, right where they were. Based at St John's school, church and Scout troop all joined up, and a young fellow from the Dulwich Mission was coming over the hill to be in charge. All very right and proper he was, but the lads in the troop would be ordinary boys like them, and they could join in, 2nd Walworth. All three, if they could earn enough to pay for the uniforms. And if Itzhak could persuade Mimi he would be fine with all those goyim. Not that he mentioned his mother's concern to his friends.

They began by searching the streets for lost coppers, found a good few too, though their hands and faces were fast as grimy as the road. Then Jimmy had the idea of scrabbling around to collect the fallen winkles from the back of the shrimp man's stall, sell them on once the shrimp man had gone. That worked once, but the next week the old bugger saw them coming and had his belt off to them almost faster than they could run away. Tom knew the man who went all the way up past Camberwell and on to Dulwich to collect the milk, offered to muck out his pony's stall. He only offered once, mind, the threepenny bit he got in return wasn't worth the much bigger bite he'd had from the bad-tempered, tired-out little nag.

Of course they would join all the other kids on Derby Day, hurrying off after school and up to the crossroads by the Horns in Kennington, where all the buses went by heading over to the other side. The children would line the edge of the road, and shout up to the winners on the open-top buses,

Throw out your coppers, give us your mouldies!

The winners swaying with drink and joy and the rolling of the bus as it took the corner heading north, emptying their pockets of over-heavy coins. But Derby Day was only once a year, and months away yet, and Tom was anxious they join the Scouts before summer, keen though he was, he wasn't daft, it'd be a damn sight more fun on a boat in summer than in winter. They needed to make their money now. And so, when all the other options ran out, Jimmy shook his head and gave in, agreeing they could try down the market after all.

Can I help you carry those potatoes, lady?

That crate of apples looks hard work, hold on, I'll take the other side.

I'll take the rubbish out for you, Uncle Charlie, no bother.

You go on home Granny, I'll bring your bags for you.

That last was probably a bit much. Ida's friend May who took in washing and ironing had been carrying her own bags of laundry for the past twenty years, had biceps on her right arm, her ironing arm, the match of any man from down Peckham up to Dollis Hill, and she was only in her early thirties. Tom wasn't wrong though, she was a grandmother, her Enid having fallen with their Alf when she was just fourteen. After a fearful row and Frank calling Enid all the names under the sun, they'd made the best of a bad lot, packed Enid off to the cousins in Kent. A few months later they brought Enid and the baby back home along with half a dozen bottles of new cider, and brought the little boy up as their own. A lovely lad he was now, walking and chattering, happy as the day was long. May gave Tom a hard look when he called her Granny, and then realised he didn't mean anything by it, other than being a cheeky beggar.

What is it you boys're trying to buy, then?

May asked as she loaded them down with her ironing bundles, the three of them fine with the weight from the market to her house by the Baker Street and Waterloo Railway, but staggering by the time they'd made it up the three flights of stairs indoors as well.

Tom told May about the Scouts, and the camping and what he'd heard the Scouts had done last summer,

They've a camp out at Leysdown, right by the sea. My mate's an older boy, was in the company last year, can't do it this year, has to go on to a job his dad says, but he said if they do the same again, go to Leysdown, it'll be sailing all the way down the Thames to get there. Proper sailing, right to the sea. Me and Itzhak and Jimmy'll have a grand time,

we'll be sailors and then we can all join the navy together
and maybe even Mr Churchill—

Tom broke off here to look up at May from beneath the
bundle bending him almost double,

He's the Lord High Admiralty, you know?

May nodded, the boy could talk a hind leg off a donkey,
and he was off again.

So, even Mr Churchill might doff his hat to us once
we're proper sailors. And we're going to learn how to swim,
at the Manor Place Baths.

Your mother will be grateful for that, May said quietly.

How d'you mean? Jimmy asked.

May looked at the boys. She thought of her own
mother, who never got over the loss of her son, the little
brother whose picture May kept by her bed, the young
man who went off to the first Boer War and didn't come
back, sent the three letters of how hard it was, dirty and
rough, and then nothing at all until the death notice. No
glory in that, May thought, and no body to mourn neither. And not just war of course, the sea itself. The dark,
awful sea. She pictured her Frank, an Irishman arrived in
London at sixteen, seventeen when they were married,
the story of his crossing made her stomach turn even now
to think of it. Then only this year, she'd hated herself
for how she devoured the story of that dreadful time on
the Titanic, hated herself and bought the penny papers
regardless, couldn't drag her eyes from the photographs of
the survivors coming ashore in New York, huddled masses
all right.

She shook her head and thought about the wide waste
that was the water, and how lucky they'd been not to have

63

had a war since that last one with the Boers, touching wood as she did so, and – even as she went to the cupboard, even as she questioned her own good sense in encouraging the lads to go to dress in uniform like little soldiers, little sailors – she opened the door and let them see what she had in the cupboard.

And then it didn't matter what she was worried about, because all three of the boys were already taking off their street clothes, Itzhak not so shy now, and yes, the shirts could do with a stitch here or there, but they fit well enough and they didn't half look smart, and that woman up the road a way, off Cleaver Square where they have lovely houses, nice woman, beautifully spoken, she'd be happy about this. She'd given May the shirts a few months back.

My own sons have grown out of them, and they're away at school now, of course, but wouldn't it be lovely if some of your little Walworth ruffians thought scouting might be for them?

May took the shirts and made no mention of the ruffians the woman had packed off to boarding school to learn some manners themselves, she liked to keep her customers happy, far more likely to keep coming back.

There weren't the trousers to go with the shirts, May didn't know what trousers Scouts wore, short trousers, surely, and the boys had those of their own, good ones for school and church—

Or you know, your place, the synagogue on Heygate.

May spoke kindly, with a nod to Itzhak who blushed and went all quiet again.

The shirts looked just the ticket though, as did the hats,

proper Scout hats. And May was pleased she'd bothered bringing the shirts home on a day when she already had more than she could carry, not half as pleased as Tom and Jimmy and Itzhak, who had no care for the uniforms being second and third hand, who were trying out salutes and issuing orders and keel-ho-ing and starboard-froing and all sorts, many of those words made up, May was sure.

The boys paid for the shirts in work, giving May a break from carrying for the next few weeks. They took it in turns to meet her every Monday straight after school to carry the washing to the laundry, then the Tuesday job – the worst of all the days – they helped her carry the sodden bundles all the way back up the stairs, right to the top where May hung it all up in her rooms and the place steamed up good and proper, so you could breathe in lye all the way back down the stairs again. Wednesday and Thursday were easier, carrying the bundles, dropping them off to this house or that block, nicely wrapped in brown paper and string. They were good at taking the money too, each of the boys, not one of them going to cheat May, and Jimmy worked extra hard on his mental arithmetic to be sure he brought back the right change. It was work all right, but Tom took charge drawing up a rota, so it was all fair. And it was well worth it, May let them have the uniforms on tick, and the money they'd saved already went towards their subs.

So there they were, proper Scouts with uniforms and neckerchief ties they had from the Scoutmaster and everything, signed up with the 2nd Walworth. Even Itzhak. It turned out Baden-Powell was quite keen on bringing all sorts of lads together, no matter their background, thought it would be the making of them, according to the Scoutmaster, said it was what the Empire was all about. And Mimi smiled when Itzhak told her this, yes, this was why they had chosen London, *mir hobben à hime du,* this was why they were here.

Eight

It wasn't easy being Charlie Hatch's wife, being Uncle Charlie's wife. Charlie was only thirty-three and he'd been called Uncle Charlie since he was just nine years old and his big sister Lillian had her first boy. Young Charlie had taken the title seriously enough for them all to call him uncle, he had always known his own mind and he wanted everyone else to know it too.

Born bossy. That's what his mother said of him, born bossy and keeping to his own time, no matter that every one of her other babies had come three weeks early, the six more she had in a rush after Charlie, as if he'd kick-started her belly, got her juices flowing she said to Lillian, in a whisper that had them both laughing over their pints.

So Charlie had always been Uncle Charlie, even though there was the big brother who'd left years back and gone out to Australia to make his fortune, barely a peep from him since, a letter that he was married, the one more telling how he'd had a couple of little ones, two boys. With his brother on the other side of the world, Charlie was the eldest boy indoors. A good little boxer he was for a bit, before the flu carried off both his father and the two youngest and his mother lost herself to grief for a while. Charlie stepped in, looked after his ma, and took on her work of running the barrow to provide for the family. No time then for boxing, and Charlie turned the patter of his fists into a sales patter to beat them all. Just fourteen, taking care of the lot of them, and helping Lillian out with a bob or two every now and then, no wonder he thought he was a man long before his time. All of which made him the obvious choice to take on Granddad Stan's pearly crown when the old fellow finally passed. Not that he passed easy.

Stan Hatch, sat in his comfortable chair in the best corner of the pub, a view of the door and a view of the bar, finished his pint of old and mild, tried to get up to go home for his tea and found his legs wouldn't work. Then he saw that his hands weren't lifting from the table either, he looked down and there were his fingers, nine and a half of them like cold fat sausages. The half he'd lost when he worked on the meat barrow, and he never misjudged a cleaver again. He called out, but for once in his long life no one jumped at the sound of his voice, no one turned ready to do Stan Hatch a favour, and the last thing the old man heard was the gurgling of his own mouth trying to call for help, words in his head turning to meaningless noise as they hit the air through blue lips and a tongue that wouldn't move.

For three days the family had Stan laid up in the front parlour, neighbours came to pay their respects, dropping off a rabbit's foot for good luck, a horseshoe wrapped round with red felt for health. When he let out his last breath on the fourth morning, they moved the pillows that had been propping him up, and there he was, already laid out. There were three more days and those who'd turned up with charms and broth were on the doorstep now with pease pudding and faggots, a ham hock, a seedy cake to keep. And then the whole family got themselves togged up for the funeral. Pearly suits were checked over, steamed from inside out to make sure none of the lustre was lost. When they came together as a guard of honour for the coffin being carried out, the combined shine of buttons was enough to brighten the whole house, even with the curtains drawn and the mirrors covered. Young Charlie Hatch led them all, following the coffin up the Walworth Road and round through Peckham to Nunhead Cemetery, where the Hatches were always buried, gorgeous great plumes in the horses' headgear waving ahead, people lining either side of the road round the market to pay their respects.

It was then that Charlie found that he rather liked being watched. In the ring, in the fight, there'd been no time to pay any heed to all that. Behind the barrow, he'd always thought it was just about the voice, the patter, and he was right, it was. But with the weight of the pearls holding him up, Charlie felt he was twice his old self. Twice an already impressive young man.

Rose Smarts did not look as if she was up to the job of besting Charlie Hatch. She came up to his shoulder if she was standing on tiptoe, and that was only because she wore her long dark hair piled up on her head. Rose was as fine, thin and pale as Charlie was broad and big and ruddy. She was pale enough to see blue veins through her skin on the warmest of days, she was black Irish on her maternal grand-mother's side and her skin, alabaster fair, looked as if it had skipped a full generation of the Smarts' hot English blood. Yet for all her fine frame, her soft voice with a little-girl lilt, if Rose called, Charlie came running. Not seen to be running, nothing that might look like kowtowing to the missus, but running he came. Some said it was because Charlie was a martyr to her once she had him indoors, Rose ruled the roost and didn't he know it. Others thought there was a touch of the fey in her, from that black Irish grandmother, and Charlie didn't want to risk a dark charm coming his way. Only Ida knew for sure, could tell what it was from the moment she met Rose, Charlie showing her off to all the family, the little girl from Dulwich Wood that he'd met at the Goose Green fair.

Ida saw that Rose looked at Charlie, really looked. She didn't see just the bluster and the talk, she saw the lad who'd been left with a grieving mother and all those little ones to look after. Rose wasn't fussed that Charlie could run two barrows by himself, or that he'd once won seven fights in a row at the Thomas A'Becket, that he could pull one barrow while pushing another – so they said, she'd not seen it done – she just liked the look of him. The boy under-neath the mouth almighty in the pearly suit. Rose looked at Charlie and saw the kid that Ida hadn't seen since they were six and seven, cousins playing in the yard. There were plenty of times Ida could have wished Charlie further, but on the rare occasion she saw him through Rose's eyes, she was happier to be in his company.

That said, there were times when Rose would happily have given him an earful herself, instead she let Charlie run himself dry, and when he'd finished Rose would still be there, sitting at her table against the window during the day, under the lamp at night, working on another piece of the mending she took in for her pin money. Rose would sew a seam, a pocket, or a fallen hem with perfect, tiny stitches, her mouth full of pins and no option but to nod or shake her head and let him get on with it. Every now and then she'd pull a pin from her lips and pop it back into the pincushion she'd had from her mother Emily, who lived with them, was dying with them. Eventually Charlie would rant himself out and go to bed, sleep it off. When Rose had finished the work, the last of the pins were stabbed slowly, one by one into the old pincushion. In the early morning, long before it was light, Charlie would lean over her and whisper that he was sorry and Rose knew him best, she knew he was hers. He would make love to her before heading off to Smithfields to make sure he got the best meat they could afford for the barrow, pleasuring Rose as she dozed, a slow smile on her moon-pale face, Charlie Hatch in her body, on her body, Charlie Hatch doing what he did best, shutting his big gob with the loveliness of Rose Smarts, the only one who could shut him up.

Nine

Jimmy Hatch was outside in the yard, waiting for Tom to join him. He had the length of rope he carried in his pocket all the time now and was practising his knots. Sheet bend, reef knot and clove hitch were all fine, he had them down pat, and his dad had taught him the two half hitches years ago, securing the summer canopy on the barrows. Not that they called it two half hitches, Charlie had laughed when Jimmy told him the knot had a name, but the boy had persisted until Charlie turned, his face red, not laughing now,

Enough of your mouth. I'm damned if some fancy bugger who's had it easy his whole life is going to have you telling me what I already know. I'd like to see your hero of Mafeking cart a load from up Smithfields and not drop as much as a pig's ear on the way, through rain and fog and God knows what else across the bloody river. The likes of them don't know half of what it is to be a man my lad, not half of it.

Jimmy had known then not to push it, not when Charlie

72

was red in the face, the back of his hand itching to meet Jimmy's head. And in a way, his dad was right, you didn't need to know the names of the knots for them to work, course not, but Jimmy liked the sound of them in his mouth; bowline, anchor hitch, sheet bend – the way they rolled on his tongue. He liked the sailing knots best of all, the ones they were learning now that summer was on the way and they'd the Scout camp to prepare for, sailing downriver to Sheppey, and then camping at Leysdown. Before that even, there'd be the Sea Scout rally at Earl's Court. Tom was patrol leader now, and pushing the lads – Jimmy and Itzhak and three other boys – to learn their knots, get their drills sorted, do well at their swimming. Tom was keen for his patrol to prove themselves at the rally, even though they were the newest in the troop, prove themselves good enough to go to camp. Not that any of the three mates had yet broached the subject of the camp with their parents. Two weeks was a long time from home, even in summer, even with no school, and each boy was waiting for his moment, tracking his prey, preparing the way. Just like a good Scout.

Bowline, anchor hitch, sheet bend, Jimmy whispered again to himself and his fingers worked faster, the rope ran smoother.

The clock indoors chimed, the one in the front room where his sick grandmother slept and, right on time, Jimmy heard Tom's whistle from the other end of the alley. He straightened his tie, and took himself off down the back alley between the houses. Rose looked out of the window from where she stood by the stove, a stew on the go. Three penn'orth of giblets she'd started with that morning, not that she paid of course, not when Charlie had the stall, but he weighed it out anyway, holding it in his hand,

Here you go girl, three penn'orth enough?

Lovely, a few of them sweet onions, couple of carrots and it'll be ready for whatever you bring back to top it up.

Charlie always brought something nice back, something kept aside for their dinner. A fist-sized chunk of stewing beef, a ham hock that'd be lovely with a bit of pease pudding alongside. Rose knew she was lucky, feeding her family on good meat more days than not, many round here made do with giblet stew and nothing added. She popped the stew into the oven now and turned back to the other pan she had boiling on the top, this one full of rags for dressing her mother's abscesses, the bubbling pan stinking out the room. Rose stood sweating under her dress and her old apron, wiped the drops from her face with her sleeve, and waved the boy off. Not long now and Jimmy'd be working long days too, no matter how perishing cold or how stinking hot the weather was. Good luck to him, let the lad have his fun while he could.

Jimmy stopped off at the other end of the Larcom Street dog-leg where Tom was waiting, then the pair of them were scrambling over a couple of fences to the synagogue where Itzhak had promised he'd be on the corner when they let him out. They could have just gone round the road, but there was no fun following the paths, they were Scouts – scout they would.

It was Shavuot, a festival day, important for the synagogue and important for Itzhak who had been inside the corner building all morning with his grandfather, reciting and intoning, listening to the cantor's chant, taking it seriously now he'd had his twelfth birthday and this year was so important, the big build-up to becoming a man. So Itzhak was in synagogue with his grandfather, even though his father was at work – to have his Friday evenings early Lev always worked the half day on Sunday – and even though Mimi was at home cleaning and cooking, whispering to herself how wicked she must have been as a child to have to work so hard now, even though his brothers were out up to G-d knows what, Itzhak was at shul.

Today is the day we remember that the Torah was given to us – and to no other – given to Moses on Mount Sinai, to pass on to us. Today we remember that the law is what we live by.

Everyone listening understood that Rabbi Rosenbaum was an expert on the Pentateuch, the five books of the Torah, respected by all the other rabbis, even the Christians thought he knew a thing or two, the Pentateuch the beginning of their Bible as well. So today of all days Itzhak was there to listen to the rabbi speak, to take what he had to say seriously. The synagogue was even more full than usual with men and a good number of wives, coming back to Walworth from Brixton and Clapham, leaving their lovely new synagogue in Effra Road to hear Rabbi Rosenbaum speak of Shavuot.

Everyone that is, except Shimon who, much as he who loved the Torah, loved the scrolls and the stained glass above the ark, even though he often whispered to Itzhak how lucky they were to have a congregation right here where they lived, even so, Shimon shook his head and sighed, a little too audibly for Itzhak,

Mir hobben es nisht azoy gezingen in der hime.

We didn't sing it like that at home.

Itzhak knew his grandfather didn't mind the new tune, the different tune sung by this Polish chazan here in south London, the man had a wonderful voice – a *herlicha shtimma* – his grandfather whispered. What Shimon minded was that there was no one left to remember the old tunes, the tune he couldn't remember himself, but he knew it didn't go like this.

When, through a quiet moment, Shimon heard the chime of the Town Hall clock, he waited a beat, waited to make Itzhak know that he too must wait, waited to let the boy know that this was a treat, and then he nodded to his grandson's upturned face and the lad backed out of the pew, careful not to let other people see his smile, his eagerness to run. Shimon did not need to see Itzhak's smile to know what was on the boy's face. He had felt exactly the same himself, many times. Felt it even now and forced himself to stay, to pray, to be here in the presence. There was little time and much to pray for. No treats for old men, not even the blessing of an old prayer remembered, sung in the old way.

In the street the three boys met up, whooping and cheering, finally, their day could begin.

Ten

Rose prodded the rags on the stove, the yellow pus had boiled away and all that was left was the scum. She covered her hands with dry cloths and picked up the pan, pouring off the hot stinking water into the open drain in the yard outside and then walked down to the end of the alley to refill the pan. One last boil, this time with a few drops of iodine, and they'd be done. Her mother was sick enough, Rose didn't need to make things worse with dirty bindings. When the second batch came to the boil, Rose plucked out the rags with the old wooden tongs, wringing them out fast to keep the heat in the rags, and fast to keep her own palms from being too badly burned. Twice a day for the past fortnight she'd been doing this, her hands now were red, clean, raw. Then Rose raced through to her mother, waiting in the front room. Emily half-sat, half-lay, pillows wedged behind her, breast bared, and one by one Rose laid the burning rags over the weeping sores, both women talking nineteen to the dozen to hide their pain, to stop the tears, telling stories to make it go away. To make the stench of the illness go away.

These days, Emily had little memory of what happened yesterday, and was wont to forget Rose's name when the pain was too bad, tried to forget her own name when the pain was too bad, but while she found it ever more difficult to be in the body of an adult woman, dying woman, she knew what her life had been as a girl, knew it intimately and fully. And, because she no longer cared to chat about what she thought Rose might do to stop Charlie's slap-happy attitude to Jimmy, or whether Ida from down the way had put on a bit of weight or had she fallen for another baby, Emily Smarts told her memories.

They were all country people, the Wilsons, my father's family. I never was.

Emily spoke proudly of her London roots, no matter that they were shallow. Like so many round here, it was important to her that she was London-born.

Born and bred cockney and proud of it, but my father's family were country. You know that don't you, Rose?

Rose nodded and continued her work.

Tell me about the house, Ma.

It was where my father's mother was in service before she married, and my grandfather worked the land. Huge estate they had, the family. I was eight years old when we all trooped off to the country, that Whitsun, and I saw the big house for the first time. Rosie love, it was so empty out there, put me right off the country. I know they like it like that, them with money, everything green and sheep and cows everywhere, stinking and all, and so noisy, you'd never think, sheep and cows, they don't half go on. And I've never understood why anyone'd want to work in service, if they had a choice. You know me, I'm not afraid of hard graft, but a few years later I saw my school friends in service, seventeen-hour days they did and told to think themselves lucky they had a place. My cousin Phoebe went off to a house down in Herne Hill, just her to do the cooking, cleaning, washing, the lot, the lady never lifted a finger to help, and Phoebe'd to call her 'Madam', curtsey and everything. I'm a grafter like all the Wilsons, but I'd no intention of grafting for someone else and having them treat me like muck.

Rose nodded, she felt the same, her hands got chapped something awful in winter on the stall, but at least she was doing for herself, and her work was different every day. She finished binding the hot rags and poultice to her mother's weeping breast and Emily leaned back against the pillow, relieved to be covered, the shame of sickness hidden between mother and daughter.

Shall I have that tot now, pet?

Rose pulled out the little silver flask she kept alongside the lavender bags in her sewing basket. She topped up her mother's tea with half a dozen drops and waited a moment while Emily took the first sip. The tea was tepid now, and sweet to mask the bitterness she'd just added.

Emily sucked down her drink, a hungry baby, quickly pacified, and Rose went through to give Charlie's stew a bit of a stir. When she came back Emily was more settled, the laudanum and cocaine mix in the flask worked fast, not so strong as to knock Emily out, but enough to ease the pain for a couple of hours. Rose took up her sewing for the rest of the story. She had plenty to do until the light went and didn't mind what story she heard, she wasn't listening for the tale, she listened because she wanted to catch Emily's voice in the room, keep it for when she would need to hear her mother's voice and that voice would be gone.

We stopped that night in the cottage where my father'd grown up, on the estate. They were only farm cottages, but there were three rooms downstairs, all nicely laid out, not that we children went into the front room of course, and another three upstairs – and no sharing.

Emily turned to her daughter with a lopsided smile,

Think of that Rose, those cousins had a whole house to themselves, and ever such a fancy banister running the length of the stairs. He'd made that, my grandfather, one of my father's brothers had helped, the big fellow, what was his name, Simon, Peter, something from the Bible, they like their Bible, do country people.

Emily stopped, thinking for a bit, eyes closed, and Rose put Emily's teacup on the shelf. At the rattle of old china on the cast-iron mantel, Emily pushed herself to open her eyes.

The cottages were all together in a row, but they'd no yard out back or street in front, just a dirt lane, all rutted it was, trees on the other side and fields beyond. Where we'd go into the yard here and you'll always find someone to hand the baby to if you've to head out for five minutes, all they had was fields. Four cottages in a row on the top of a hill and either side just fields and woods, nothing to stop the wind going right the way through from front door to back.

We'd such a palaver of trams and trains to get there, and then a cart at the end, a proper old-fashioned cart with a beautiful great dray to draw it. Don't think I ever saw my dad so much as pretend to care about an animal before, but he was all over that horse, terrifying thing it was. They'd a day off the market, our parents, on account of it being Whitsun, and most of the costermongers weren't to bother with working the Monday either, so we'd three days spare, and we'd been getting there since before first light so the grown-ups settled in for a night of it. There was a ham beautifully done, all treacle-dark in the fat, and a couple of loaves of good bread my father's sister Alma had baked that morning, plates of scones and a ginger cake for after, plenty of barley wine to wash the lot down. Me and my brothers, we hadn't seen such a full table and sideboard since Christmas. Proper prodigal son stuff it was, our dad not having been home for so long.

It was clear from the off they didn't want us kids around, my uncle told us to bugger off over the hills while the sun was still up, we should get some colour in our poor little London cheeks.

We were warned of course, my father was all on about how we weren't to go getting into any trouble or poking our noses anywhere, there'd be hell to pay if we did.

The way I remember it now, he said it with a sort of country accent, slower than usual. I think that was the first time I realised he wasn't really a Londoner, not like us. He'd been in town since he was just fifteen, but it was as if getting a sniff of the old dray when he buried his head in her neck had done something to his mouth, turned his words soft and round.

Those three boy cousins were hard to keep up with, I'll tell you that for nothing. Haring over styles, leaping ditches, testing us, see if we had the mettle to keep up. Course we did, I'd like to have seen that lot try to leap from barge to barge all along Battersea Reach and steer clear of the watchman at the same time. After a bit we were in the woods proper and they were swerving round damn great oaks, just like we'd dodge some docker with a load on his back and ready to thrash anyone who got in his way, but those oaks were never going to take a belt to you, nothing to be scared of there. Then the woods just stopped, all of a sudden, and there it was, the big house.

And didn't the cousins turn to us, all proud faces and puffed-up chests. It was a nice enough house, some lovely stone steps, sweeping round either side to a great big door, a couple of smaller wings leaning off the back of the main building, but it wasn't half as big as I'd expected and it looked dead lonely, sitting there all by itself.

Of course we shouldn't've gone in, they'd have thrashed the living daylights out of us if they'd found out, but the cousins knew a door that was left unlocked, and the view through the windows was so lovely, and everyone was bound to be off at the Whitsun Fair, so in we went.

Emily breathed in deeply through her nose and she smiled,

I can smell it now. Beeswax, rubbed good and hard, day in day out, so all that was left was a gentle shine everywhere you looked. And under that, sharper, bitter almost, silver polish, brass polish, blacking for the grates. I didn't know, then, what those smells add up to, a day that starts before light and ends with cracks in your fingers and those cracks filled with grate blacking or beeswax and the stink of it with you every moment, and how that stink is nothing like clean, not when it won't ever wash from your own hands. But that first day, the first time I actually stood in a proper big house, it smelled grand, like a church, but warm.

We followed John, the biggest of our cousins, all of us hanging on to each other's belts or braces. Our Bob had hold of my plait. I'd a lovely long plait of hair back then, and I remember thinking I was all right as long as I could feel him hanging on behind me, and I could see our Mikey in front, each of us sucking in our cheeks to stop the nervous giggles. There were doors either side of the passage, and at the end it opened out into a big entrance hall, all stags' heads and marble busts and a great vaulting ceiling reaching all the way up with the staircase swirling round into it. The two young ones, Arthur the cousin and our Bob, were all for going up the stairs when we reached the main hall, but John said no, even if there was no one in the house now, what if they came home before dark and we got trapped upstairs? The lads agreed, but not without some grumbling and scuffing of their feet on the floor. John turned to us city cousins, and we could tell from the smile on his face he'd already decided we were the softest lot he'd ever seen.

Here's the game. We each go off and bring back a trophy. Whoever brings back the most surprising thing wins.

Mikey shook his head and said no way, he was off, back to the cottage. John asked was he yellow, and the cousins laughed, and our Bob went all red in the face, furious at the cousins for mocking his hero, our Bob always did worship our Mikey. But Mikey stood his ground, said they could call him yellow if they wanted, he'd rather that than be carted off to face a magistrate way the hell out here in the middle of nowhere and then who knows what, stuck in some country gaol and never getting back to London. Said our ma and dad brought us up better than this, and hadn't theirs?

Well, the whispers got noisy then, our dad and your dad and all that malarkey. After a bit Mikey just turned on his heel and pulled Bob behind him, said having a look around was one thing, but taking stuff, that was another altogether, and if I wasn't to come with them then it was up to me to deal with the consequences. The cousins loved that. They all three turned to me, grins on their farm-boy faces, waiting for the girl to run off after her brothers. So I stood my ground, said I'd play. Wilf almost let out a cheer and John put his hand over his mouth to shut him up. We heard the door at the end of the passage click shut ever so quietly, and then it was just us four in the house, far as we could tell, just us with the smell of beeswax and the ticking of that great big clock in the hall.

Then there was a clunk and a whirr, and the time chimed out and John said,

There's the half hour. Go and find something special, bring it back before the hour. We'll make our choice as to what's best. After that we put the things back where we got them and we'll all be off home before dark.

We split up. The cousins went first. Despite what he'd said about not going upstairs, John went one floor up to the next landing just above us. I thought at the time he was brave, but since then I've wondered if he'd been inside so often before that he knew where the best things were. The

84

younger two lads headed across the hall and down another passage running off of it, and I was left alone, just the ticking clock for company.

I can see that hallway now Rosie, a big old stag's head above the empty fireplace, the mantelpiece too high to put anything on, this was for big men to come in and stand in front of, and never mind their wet coats and muddy boots, they'd not be cleaning up. Afternoon sunshine just tipping through the old windows and it caught on the floor, reflected off the polished parquet. There were two deep leather chairs either side of that fireplace and I was tempted not to play at all, just sit down in the welcome of that room. I've seen a few big houses since, when I did dress fittings for fancy ladies, this house, plain as you like on the outside, was ever so welcoming indoors. The walls were soft lemon and instead of leaving the curtains drawn to stop the furniture getting spoiled by the sun, they'd pulled them right back, and the light flowed in, red leather and soft yellow and sunshine. Lovely. Daft as a brush I was, wasted five minutes thinking myself a lady with nothing better to do than sit around enjoying the colours of my room. Our ma always told me off for dreaming, Dreams are for bed, they're no loaf of bread, that was her saying.

On the way in we'd passed half a dozen doors, leading downstairs John said, to the kitchen and scullery and pantry, to the coal cellar. I turned on my heel, quiet as I could, and went back down that dark passageway, leaving the warmth of the hall behind me.

The first door was locked, so was the second, and I was just thinking, John knows his way around here all right, no wonder he went on upstairs, when I tried another door and the handle turned. My heart was in my mouth but I pushed it open all the same.

Oh Rosie, the room I walked into was all windows, a whole wall full; they had their own Crystal Palace. On the two walls with no windows there were big long mirrors, and even on the thin strips of plaster between the windows they'd slivers of mirror, running all round the window frames. I'd opened the door, head down, scared of what I might see, so when I looked up I saw dozens of me, and in each one of those reflections was a gap-toothed, freckle-faced little girl, and she was grinning, broad as you like. I must've been wicked to smile so broad while trespassing, but it wasn't just the naughtiness that had me smiling, it was the light, so lovely and bright it all was. I stepped in, ever so quiet. Then, as I turned to close the door behind me, I damn near screamed my head off at the body standing behind the door. Bodies. Three of them. Headless bodies. Naked headless bodies.

Now I know they were mannequins, but I'd no idea back then, never seen anything like it. They were shaped like ladies, busts and all, but no legs, no arms, no heads. I had my fist in my mouth to stop myself from crying out. Of course, it was a sewing room, had been made special to let in the light, and my cousins said after that there were four girls in the family, every one of them considered a fashion plate in society. Once I'd caught my breath and my heart had stopped jumping in my chest, I had a look around. It wasn't half lovely. My ma and I, we liked our sewing, but we couldn't afford not to, everything we had we'd made ourselves, and she was good with a needle, what she wouldn't have given for a room like this.

Emily stopped and took in, for the first time in weeks, how grim the room was, how dark this front room that her life had been reduced to. With the big bed taking up most of the space, and the window right on the street, they'd had to close the curtains, nothing to be done. Emily swallowed a sip from Rose's flask, and took herself back to the bright, light room, out of the dark of now.

Then I saw the cloth. Big bolts of it lined up, one against the other. Velvet and satins, all colours, matching some of them, like they'd been picked to go together, a lining for an evening coat, a petticoat for a fine lawn dress. There was shot silk, deep green with blue thread running through, gold organza, so much tulle. My fingers were itching to run over the cloth, my cheek aching to be laid against the smooth, soft folds.

Now, I'm not proud of this, Rose, but I knew then what I'd take to show the cousins. I picked up the scissors from the table in the centre of the room and quick as you like, I cut off an inch or two from the end of each bolt of cloth. I'd a dozen or more strips of material by the time I'd done, a soft bundle folded in on each other. It was stealing, I know, but it felt so good, a rainbow in my hand.

It was only when I'd taken one last look at those silent, headless mannequins, and begun creeping back along the passage, that I remembered John had said we were to put the flaming things back. There was no putting back what I held, so I pocketed those ribbons of cloth and walked empty-handed into the hall. All three boys were already waiting. The two younger lads had obviously met up, for Wilf was holding a walking stick, a lovely piece of turned wood, with a big old dog's face carved on the top, black eyes glistening in its head, and Arthur held a pretty parasol, topped off with another carving of the dog's head, again with twinkling eyes, jet it must have been.

I told them I couldn't find anything special enough, and John nodded like it was just what he'd expect from a girl. He had this big grin and he turned round to show us what he was hiding behind his back. A real dog's head, on a plaque, and that dog had to have been the model for the carved heads the younger lads'd found. Three black dog heads, all together and the eyes in the stuffed head sparkling even more than the others.

We'd have clapped then, or cheered, I know Arthur had his lips pursed all ready to let out a whistle, but we heard the door. Upstairs, two floors above. The click of a handle, the shush of skirts and a tap of feet on the floor, a woman's laugh, then a man's voice, deeper. Silence. The sound of something else, something I didn't recognise for sure, until all three lads screwing up their noses told me it was kissing. John mimed to the boys to put our things on the floor, quietly as they could. We did as we were told, and John, still holding that big dog's head, pointed to the passage we'd come along, to the door that would set us free. The people upstairs were silent now, save for breathing noises and a bit more shush of a skirt, and we walked in single file along that corridor, bubbling with the excitement that comes of fear, hearts racketing in our ribs. I was last to the door, and John pushed the boys ahead of us and then he turned, holding it open for me.

Shall I keep it, d'you reckon? The dog?

I knew he wanted to, and I'd my own pocket full of cloth ribbons from the sewing room, so I felt for him, but I'd heard too many of my ma's stories about those sorts of folk. A big house might blame a drunken guest for the walking stick and the parasol when they found them underneath the table in the hall, but a missing dog's head? A loved dog at that, carved not once but twice on those very sticks, it could only be thievery. And John had the rest of his life to live here, on this estate, in a cottage belonging to the big house.

I took it from him. Lord knows where I got my courage from, but I walked a few steps back towards the hall, sick with every step, the people above were just on the next landing now, and talking quietly. I pushed open the sewing-room door, scared the light would spill into the dark passageway and those two lovebirds would notice something other than themselves.

Not one of us said a word until we were through the forest, over two fences and halfway back to the cottage and then Arthur began first, I thought he was crying, didn't blame him, he was younger than me even, until I realised he was laughing and holding his sides from the stitch, and we all were, laughing and hurting and Rose, I thought I'd wee myself with the relief, the letting go.

I've often wondered what the seamstress made of it when she next went into the room and saw her three mannequins, the middle one with a black retriever's head, eyes sparkling in the light of that bright, bright room.

I never saw my cousin John again, he was off to California once he turned eighteen, made his fortune in gold they said. Or if he didn't, we never heard otherwise. Arthur and Wilf stayed on the estate, working on the land. And I spent five nights that summer turning those ribbons of fabric into my pincushion, that one you have now. Patchworked from stolen ribbons and shaped into a lucky shoe. It's not the fabric as makes it lucky, mind, it's what I stuffed it with, all these years. There's a lock of hair from every newborn in our family, the innocence of the newborn to keep me safe.

Emily sighed, tired from remembering what it felt like to run and laugh, not a care other than a pocket full of ribbons.

Time for you to fetch me a pint, my love, and a few more drops from your flask. That's been a long story of my wicked childhood and my mouth's very dry.

Emily Wilson, just fifty-two and no hope to make another Christmas, settled herself under the eiderdown, her fingers working, seeing again the brightest, lightest room she had ever seen, and a dead dog's shining eyes

Rose didn't tell her mother that the pincushion was no longer stuffed with newborn hair, that it hadn't been for a while, not since Charlie's terrier bitch gave birth to her pups and Rose had been daft enough to leave her sewing on the scullery table and the whelping pups in their basket. She'd been gone less than five minutes, and when she came back one of the puppies had the pincushion in its mouth, pins and all. Charlie reckoned that one'd fetch a good price, must have thought the pincushion was a rat, no matter that the pins would have stuck her something rotten. Poor Rose was more upset about the stuffing, all that precious baby hair all over the room. Now Rose had an almost-new, almost-old pincushion, made of half her mother's wicked secret and half her own, stuffed with hair from when Ida had cut Jimmy and Tom and Itzhak's hair. The boys had been off to their first Scout meeting, they needed a haircut, and Ida kept her scissors nice and sharp, a blade that cuts an umbilical will shear through hair as easy as a hot knife in winter-morning butter.

As Emily slept on in the front room, Rose got Charlie's dinner up for him. A couple of chops, the biggest for Charlie of course, and sat it on top of the stew that had been simmering all morning. They sat down at the little table in the scullery, Rose with an ear out for her mother's slow, strained breathing, and she listened to Charlie, on and on about Jimmy and how he wasn't shaping up.

When Rose had finished her meal and cut Charlie a nice bit of bread to wipe his plate with, she put the kettle on and sat down to her sewing, enough light through the scullery window for another piece at least. She nodded, letting Charlie have his moan and then, taking half a dozen pins from her mouth, she stabbed each one into the pincushion, a prayer to keep the boys safe with every pin she slipped into the softness of their hair. Keeping them safe from Charlie and his temper, and from anything else besides.

Eleven

'What we see, when we investigate the items, the artefacts, the icons almost, in which these people place their trust, is a true reflection of the changing face of modern London, our new metropolis.'

Edward Lovett looked out at his audience, some listening rapt, some taking notes, one or two, sadly, almost dozing, he picked up his pace, this bit would wake them up, 'Mr Booth and his team have given us an exhaustive analysis of our city, but I would suggest that neither Mr Booth nor the Fabians are looking at the depth, the breadth, of the lives of these people.'

Yes, that had done it, the dozers were roused. The people here were the kind who believed that progress for all came simply from understanding the degradations of the present, Lovett believed the story was far more complex.

'These are lives that look not only forward, as many of us do, to the progress and prosperity that must surely come as we advance in industry and growth, these are lives that recall, in their daily existence, the people and places from whence they came. It is this matter, the matter of a past reaching into and framing the future, that I shall put before you this evening.'

Now they were listening and he launched into the meat of his speech with pleasure, 'The denizens of Mr Booth's black-inked streets, in the huddled yards and hovel-lined alleyways, are – many of them – Londoners, born and bred. But in these past years, the iron tracks of the railways have clawed the rural idyll back into the dark heart of the city. Districts that were once towns and villages separated by hills or streams are now part of larger boroughs, we have seen the city creep out to village greens and winding country lanes. While there were similar expansions at other times in history, never before have we had the ability to document, to analyse, the lives of those living inside our city's now-metaphorical walls. Thus, while many of our most deprived citizens are indeed Londoners, it is also true to say that many of them are not. They may call themselves cockneys, those of the slums along the eastern and southern stretches of the river do exactly that, but look closer, and you will find, as often as not, country folk. The accent may vary a little from Hackney to Bow to Walworth, but all are well within the range of what could be termed 'cock-ney'. How then do we know that the costermonger on the barrow or the elderly lady selling posies, the lad fetching river detritus when the tide is out in order to sell it as fire-wood tomorrow – worse yet, the young woman selling herself on a street corner – how do we know they are not Londoners through and through? We speak to them. We go out amongst them and we return with our findings. We – who devote our free days to our collections and our evenings to cataloguing and ordering – we are the guardians of artefact and therefore of the stories of origin.

'The findings I have to lay before you this evening will prove that for every Londoner who believes themselves to be utterly of the city, there is another who, beneath the coal dust and the stink of the factory, the spit and the grime of the public house, has only to reach for his dear mother's necklace, his grandfather's keepsake, the charm he stores in his own breast pocket – 'Not out of belief you understand sir, just because our old mam gave it me, and it'd be wrong to let it go now she's gone' – and reveal himself to be, far from a son of the city, a man of Wiltshire, a Kentish lad, a Sussex man.

'It is these charms, these beliefs, that we study tonight, and in doing so, we will uncover another London, the London beneath, the city that is all England, come home to roost in the muddy banks of our own winding river.'

Two hours later, Edward Lovett sat back in his chair, the leather and wood creaked a little until it found its place, his form, and shuffled his papers happily. It had been a very good evening. While he was not a boastful man, he had his pride, and one of the things he prided himself on was that each speech should be better than the last, more accomplished. Tonight had been such an occasion. Ensuring that each endeavour was more successful than the last was a simple matter of diligence, application, and attention to detail. All three were attributes he had tried to drum home to his two sons, succeeding with the elder rather more than with the younger, but there was time yet, there was time. Lovett was neither an over-firm father nor was he lax, but he did appreciate that the lack of a mother's tempering presence in the home was unfortunate. Therefore, since he and his wife had agreed to live their lives separately – her choice, not his – and since had undertaken to provide the boys with both a mother's love and a father's discipline, it fell to Lovett himself to determine which attitude was required at different times. Raising a son, cataloguing a collection, writing a speech – success in each was a matter of attention to detail.

He shuffled the papers one last time and put them aside, to file later. This was his favourite time of evening, the house quiet, even with the detour to give his speech, he had fifteen minutes yet before his peace was disturbed. Soon his sons would be home, young men, clerks themselves, their youthful vigour disturbing the calm quiet of the house. His own younger brother Walter would not be much later, though his return from work was less timed to the train, clerking for a ship-owner was a very different matter than clerking in a bank. In thirty minutes, forty-five at most, there would be noise and tumult and this peace would be gone.

He could hear, three floors below and very muffled, the sound of his cousin Ettil and the girl, Louisa, making supper. Ettil would no doubt be demanding that Louisa peeled the potatoes in the way she preferred, placed the beef in this pan not another. Louisa would, as ever, ignore Ettil and prepare the meal in the way she saw fit. Both women would do so politely, carefully, in the way that a middle-class gentlewoman and her servants must these days, the distance between the two was not so very great, and while it was still Ettil's place to issue orders and Louisa's to carry them out, his cousin would never be so impolite as to make a scene or insist. And so the rare beef, the lamb cutlets, the Dover sole, the coddled eggs, were cooked to Louisa's recipes, not Ettil's.

Lovett was secretly pleased about this, though he had never said as much to his cousin. It was an unspoken understanding between the men of the family that Sunday dinners at Outram Road, when Louisa was gone home to her own family and Ettil proudly in charge of the kitchen, were the least enjoyable meals of the week. The boys were polite, as were Edward and Walter, but none of them preferred Ettil's cooking to Louisa's.

Lovett shook his head, his cousin was a good and kind woman, her deficiencies as a cook far outweighed by her generosity of spirit. Exactly his own age, and a friend since childhood, Ettil had stepped in when Edward and his wife had come to their agreement of separation. Not only had she stepped in, she had also agreed to stay in a home full of 'the worst sort of tat wrapped into faithless hope' as his wife had put it when she finally decreed she would not live amongst the collection a moment longer. It was the collection or their marriage. Not that she voiced her displeasure as an ultimatum, nevertheless, she returned to her family home in Surrey, the boys stayed on at their boarding school in Honor Oak, and Ettil had come to London from Cheltenham to provide a woman's hand on the tiller of the home.

Then the gate clanged shut, the front door opened. There would be no more work on the collection now, at least not until supper was eaten, his sons had pulled apart the newspaper and dissected the stories of the day, Walter had told them of the best and worst cargos unloading at the docks, and Ettil had complained, quietly, that Louisa had not filleted the haddock quite to her liking.

Haddock. Lovett enjoyed haddock, and Louisa, in his opinion, cooked it rather well. He stood up and pushed the creaking chair close to his desk. On Saturday, after a few hours of work in the morning, he would get along to East Lane market. There was a piece one of the stallholders had shown him last week, and it had returned to his mind several times since. It was not especially unusual, an acorn held in a miniature ivory cup, a charm for a long life the woman had assured him, but the work was fine, and now that it had come to mind again, he thought he might purchase it after all. There were acorn charms a-plenty, but this one had a particular elegance. Yes, he thought he might. Edward Lovett closed the door on his study and considered himself a fortunate man.

Twelve

Ida was getting up Bill's tea when Tom and Jimmy charged in from the Scouts. She'd never seen the boys so happy since they'd started going along to the hall for their meetings, well on their way to being men and Ida wasn't sure she was as thrilled with that as they were. She missed the days when Tom still let her call him Tommy. They ran into the house, feet clattering all the way down the passage and then they broke off, a whistle – forbidden indoors when Bill was home – and handshake, a pat on the back and some whispered secret words no doubt, then the sound of Jimmy clattering back out again, into the street and along to his own place up the road, to face his father. Ida didn't need to be standing in the street to know that already the lad was dropping the skin of cheerful Jimmy, bright Jimmy, and putting on the mask of the sullen boy her cousin complained of, complained that this was his son, his lad always glowering, flinching, holding back.

The wind'll change and your face will stay like that, Ida thought.

She wanted to tell Jimmy to smile, to cheer up, that Charlie might be in a good mood when he got home, he might. Ida wanted to tell him this, but she knew better. And anyway, she had her own whirlwind boy to deal with, rushing on through the house and out to join his sisters in the yard.

Whenever Tom got back from the Scouts now he was whistling or humming, and when he wasn't whistling he'd be singing to himself, practising his knots, his signals for tracking. For all the tracking he'd ever do up this end of the Walworth Road. Bill came in a few minutes after, straight through to the yard to wash up, and she could tell he was about to start as Tom bounced around the scullery, remind the boy they were not the only people in the house, or shout at him for whistling indoors, they didn't keep caged birds in this family. Ida knew that was the phrase Bill used, but she knew too her husband was wary of whistling from some old story he couldn't quite remember, but had taken as gospel from the time he was a babe. Bill opened his mouth, exchanged a look with Ida, and he shut his mouth again.

You spoil the boy.

You do too.

And they both knew that they maybe did spoil him, but he was a good boy even so.

Bill stretched out his tired muscles from a day unloading heavy crates, and gave Ida the hand of lovely ripe yellow bananas he'd brought for home.

All right love, it's soon enough he'll be working all hours himself, feeling as rough as I do at the end of the day. I'll let him have his fun.

Ida spooned up the leftover stew on to Bill's plate, with a chunk of the morning's bread to mop up the juice, and a few greens as well. He ate a big dinner and a big tea, did Bill. He was a hard-working man, he deserved it.

While Bill started on his plate Ida sliced more bread for Tom and the girls, and then called them in.

There's bread and jam for your tea and your dad's brought us a lovely couple of bananas, we can have them in warm milk for after.

The children sat up nicely and Bill winked at his wife, his gratitude that he had such a good wife, that he still loved her, still loved the look of her too, even in that stained old apron, the one she'd worn so many times stirring up those concoctions on the stove she put aside for her ladies, stinking the place to high heaven half the time. He'd offered to fetch her the cloth for a new one, even said he'd get Rose to make it up, but Ida always said no, she liked the apron, stains and all, said each mark had its own story.

Kitty, three years younger than Tom, and idolising him, sat up and ate quietly. They all knew they'd not long for their meal, Bill's sister Ena would be wanting to get into the kitchen to get up her own family's tea at half past. Bill picked up Lucy, the youngest, and put her on his knee, and the five of them got down to it. They ate quickly and thankfully, though with none of the prayer that Ena demanded of her lot. Bill knew who put the food on this table, he and Ida did with their own hard graft, thank you very much. It was good plain food and the bananas in a drop of warm milk went down a treat too, a half each for Ida and Bill and another shared between the three children. Well, Tom heard his mother say half each, but he saw that his dad's half was much bigger than hers. Always was.

When they'd finished, Bill passed Lucy over to Ida and reached for his paper, held it right up in front of his face so Tom couldn't see him at all and he said,

Go on then lad, tell us about it.

Tom, who had been bursting with the news all through their tea, let it out in one long exhalation of breath and excitement,

There's to be a Sea Scout rally, at Earl's Court, and we're putting on a display, on an honest-to-goodness lake, a real one. Me and the lads, we'll be part of it, a competition and teams and the lot. I'll be leading my own patrol, and we might even win, maybe we could, what do you think Dad? Ma? Could we win? Me and the lads?

An actual lake? Bill asked, biting his lip to stop from smiling, That'll be quite a feat, to put a lake up at the Earl's Court.

But Tom didn't see Bill's smile, he was already on with the next part of his story.

I expect we'll do well enough, we're a team now, our Scoutmaster said so. There's a cup we can go up for, a Relay Challenge, and the whole troop is on to win it, honest we are.

Bill put down his paper, reached out a heavy hand and laid it on the boy's head, tousling his hair, pushing up the cowlick that Tom liked to plaster down with water, fearing the curls made him look far too much like a Tommy, like a child.

Sounds great fun, Bill said, long as you've time for helping your mother and the jobs you've already to do, I should say we'd all like to come to the relay, cheer you on.

Bill started to head through to the yard, ready for a smoke and a look at the evening sky as he did every night after his tea, but Tom wasn't finished yet, and Ida's look kept Bill in the room.

The thing is, Tom was saying, his speech a little slower now, a little more careful, There's to be a Scouts' camp at Sheppey, Leysdown, and they've not to get there on the train, but on a ship, a real one, downriver from Waterloo all the way, and then we wouldn't be just ordinary Scouts, we could call ourselves Sea Scouts for real.

A lake won't do that for you? Bill asked quietly.

Tom carried on, Kitty bored now, already out in the yard and singing her skipping song, the old bit of threadbare rope going round and round, thwack thwack on the cobbles in time with her rhyme.

I've learned all the knots and we're going to be really properly sailing the boat, downriver till we make camp and we'll sleep on board that first night. Next morning we'll be out to Sheppey, so I'll be a sailor and Jimmy and Itzhak too, and it's not until August and that's weeks away and school will be out and I'll help at home and in the market if you want Ma, happy to help on the stall, I can do any job you like, you wait, I promise and ... I can go – can't I?

How long is it for then?

Bill asked the question, but he knew already. The lad probably wouldn't have asked if it was only a day trip, or even two, would've just saved the few coppers he'd need for it and been off at the crack of dawn on the day, back the next night and ready to take whatever was coming rather than risk missing out.

Ask your Ma, Bill said, it's she needs your help with the little ones, it's she decides.

Kitty frowned, stopping her skipping for a moment to look up at her father from her skipping, little ones indeed.

Bill stood at the back door, Lucy hanging on to his legs, and squealing as he lifted her to his shoulders, the smell of his hair oil comforting as ever.

Ida studied Tom's face, this baby that made it past the nine months in her and into the world, this boy that had cleared the way for her little girls, out of the corner of her eye she could see Kitty skipping rope in hand, already beginning to pout at the unfairness of it. Kitty forever pointing out what was fair and what not, always on about how being younger than Tom and older than Lucy meant she missed out.

Ida winked at Kitty and she spoke quietly, Of course you must go, Tom. If it means that much to you. The girls and I will do something special, maybe I'll take them up to the Hampstead fair if it's on, usually is that time of year, we can all have a treat.

It's not just a day, Ma, Tom said, his voice less certain now.

Oh?

No. It's two weeks.

There was a sigh from Bill, and he held Lucy a little tighter, stepping out into the yard. Ida took a breath, tried to listen to the odd feeling in the pit of her stomach, was it only that, was it only her being the kind of mother who wouldn't let her boy go? He'd be leaving school soon enough, she'd been out of the house to work at twelve herself. She and Bill were both far more grown-up than Tom at this age, they'd had to be, but she'd wanted a bit more of a childhood for her own little ones.

Bill?

Up to you, love.

Tom was all eyes, all hope.

Ida ignored the sharp stab at the top of her belly, pushed it down, further down,

What about that then, Kitty? If Tom is away for two weeks can you and I take care of your father and Lucy between us? Now you're such a big girl?

Tom beamed and whooped until Bill, bent low enough to poke his head back through the door and not knock Lucy on the lintel, shushed the boy, and Kitty came back in to help with the plates, delighted to be called a big girl. Then Bill lifted Lucy down, took a look at her dropping eyelids, and he carried his youngest child upstairs to the children's shared bed.

He kissed his wife as he passed, saw she had her worried face on and he whispered in the kiss, It's time.

Bill passed his sister Ena in the passage, she coming down carrying one child, he going through carrying another, and they laughed, because they remembered themselves, the pleasure of being carried to bed, a pleasure long gone.

Ida made sure the kitchen was tidy for her sister-in-law, and pointed out the bananas on the little scrubbed table.

From your brother, I'll take one over to Aunty Sarah and you have the other two.

Ooh lovely, I'd eat them both myself if I didn't think he'd smell it on my breath.

Ena didn't say, and neither did Ida, that it was as likely

Ena's Fred would eat both of the bananas when he got in, always later than Bill because he knocked off half an hour later and then spent another hour in the pub on the way back, determined to drink out the creases as he called it, determined to drink them poor was how Bill saw it. Half-cut as usual, it likely wouldn't even occur to him to share the bananas with his wife and child. The times Ida and Bill had sat below and listened to the pair of them going at it, Fred threatening to knock Ena from here to kingdom come and Bill on the edge of his chair, ready to go upstairs and give his brother-in-law what for, Ida saying wait, that's just how they are. And sure enough, the shouting turned to cooing and kissing and then Ena's slap-and-tickle laugh, a laugh that, if Fred had ever heard it directed at another man, all four of them knew he really would knock seven bells out of Ena.

Ida left then, with the banana for Aunty Sarah, careful to give her sister-in-law space in the kitchen, just as Ena did for her. She thought, as she crossed the road, that maybe she'd tell Tom to take the bone angel with him on the trip. Not that she believed it was special, nothing like that, but it'd be nice to have a bit of home with him, away for two whole weeks. Nice to carry with him a piece of home.

Jimmy had hurried on to the other end of the street. As he ran, he practised what he'd say.

I'll work extra hard all the evenings and weekends leading up.

I'll wash down the barrow, proper scrubbing, every night for the rest of the year.

It's two weeks and you always say I'm in the way and so

I won't be, you'll not need to get the hump with me, I'll be off. It's only two weeks. I can earn the money myself, you know I can, I've been doing it all year, for my Scout uniform and the book and . . .

Please can I go?

Please.

Each step was a little slower, each possibility of what he might say a little less certain, each pace closer to his father saying no.

Charlie thought the Scouts were a waste of time.

There's plenty of things the lad could be doing, working on the stall or helping his mother with the younger ones, or boxing if he was so keen on running about, what's wrong with boxing? Made a man of me and I bloody well needed to be. And now the pair of them carting around with that Jew-boy and who knows what they're learning from him. Then it's an afternoon here, a Sunday there, and the three of them studying up on knots, knots I ask you, and trails and woodcraft whatever the flippin' hell that might be. Plenty for a boy to do round here, no need to be running off to look for it, no need at all.

Charlie Hatch, head of this family thank you very much, didn't need some toffee-nosed general telling him how to bring up a lad. People round here had been bringing up their lads well enough for generations and they'd enough of the do-gooders from all over, poking here and there. Now they had the Fabians bothering the wives with questions of how much do we earn and what do we spend it on and how much goes on coal a week? Coal. Charlie spat.

Buy your coal by the hundredweight, my arse. All well and good if you've a coal cellar to put it in and a horse and

106

a cart to deliver, a man to unload it. Buying your coal a hundredweight at a time is a rich man's game, the likes of us can't afford that. Then there was the toff tart came down the market, all kitted up with handouts she was, telling the ladies to give the kids porridge for their breakfast, keep 'em going all day she said. But where's the money to come from for the milk? The sugar? You try forcing a mite of four years old to eat a bowl of porridge made with water and no sugar. The things I'd tell those do-gooders if ever Rose'd let me. But not Rose, she was all her mother's china tea cup and wasting the last of the good milk on that lot. And they took it too, not got the sense they were born with, the rich, not got the sense to know you don't say yes to milk with your tea when a family's got nothing.

Charlie shook his head, time was they let a community get on with itself. Bad enough the School Board checking up on their little ones, let alone this. He hadn't decided if he'd let Jimmy keep on with it. We'll see. We'll see how well he behaves himself.

By the time he was at the front door, Jimmy had taken off his Scout neckerchief, had pulled off the shirt too, folded it up ever so carefully, put on the new pullover that his mother had knitted from an old one of Charlie's, the wool good enough to make a second. By the time he got to the gate, where pots of Rose's herbs stood out vibrant green in a street where most houses had red geraniums at their front windows, by the time he walked into the house, Jimmy had stopped thinking about what to say to his dad. He knew not to say a word.

At night, or when in danger, keep as much as possible to low ground. Walk lightly, always, don't give yourself away by an over-heavy footfall. Find out how the land lies, make a good study of the terrain, and even then, make your move sensibly. Tactics over force.

Scouting had taught him so much already.

Itzhak ran home as quickly as Jimmy dawdled slowly. He hurried to avoid having to eat with his big brothers who would pick on him if he was at the table when they came home from work. He did it too, to avoid having to sit with the lodgers at their later meal, the one Mimi made after she had fed her working sons, but before her husband came home even later still. Mimi cooked and cleaned for the two men who shared the front upstairs room, two single beds partitioned by a folding screen. Nathan said the two men were *faygelahs*, said he knew they pushed the screen back at night, said two grown men should not be sharing a room, it was bad enough he'd to share with his own brothers. Itzhak didn't mind so much that the lodgers might be like that, even his grandfather agreed it was possible, said he'd known all sorts back home, you never could tell. That wasn't why Itzhak didn't want to sit with them at dinner. It was the way they ate their soup. They both slurped, and his zaide Shimon said slurping was a good way to eat soup, stupid to burn your mouth, better to cool it as you went, but Itzhak hated the way Mr Abrahams crumbled his bread into his soup and then, as he slurped it up, soggy crumbs caught in his beard. Itzhak did not want a beard when he grew up, did not want to have to be forever looking for food in his own hair. Nathan said Itzhak didn't want many of the things of a man, that he was too much his mother's boy, too happy to listen to his grandfather's tales, perhaps he too, was a *faygelah*, if he carried on like this he'll never have the luck to click with a girl and take her out walking.

Itzhak didn't know about all that, but he agreed with Nathan about one thing, he wasn't looking forward to being a man. The bar mitzvah yes, people being kind to him, proud of him, that he didn't mind, but everything else that would come with it, Itzhak wasn't keen on any of it. He wasn't looking forward to leaving school, having a job, being out into the world every day, six days a week and only Shabbat to rest on, if he was lucky enough to find work with other Jews. So maybe it meant he was a mama's boy, like Nathan said, but Mimi knew how her youngest felt, she listened when he got in from Scouts, washed his hands alongside his grandfather, made the prayer as the old man did, before the brothers, before the lodger, before his tired father got home.

She listened when he asked, in all seriousness,

Can I please go on the Sea Scout trip with Tom and Jimmy and all the others? Can I go because it isn't long before I'm bar mitzvah and I will be a man and I'll not be able to do anything fun any more. And this might be my last chance to play.

Mimi spooned another meatball on to her son's plate, ignoring her father-in-law's grin, ignoring too the wink he gave the boy, the pair of them complicit as ever. They might be playing her, but Itzhak was right, he'd have to grow up, and soon. Why shouldn't he have his fun now? There would be many years of hard work to come, please God.

Mimi didn't say yes.

She said, I will ask your father, now eat your meal, you

two think I have all the time in the world to serve you? I have three more suppers to dish up, like a fancy restaurant this house is, and only me to work it. I should have had daughters to help me in the kitchen, I should have had daughters for the blessing of their helping hands. Now get on, be glad you have food to eat and finish it before the others get home.

Shimon winked at his grandson again and lowered his head to his food, Itzhak did the same. Later, when Shimon went into the yard to wash his hands after eating, with the prayer of thanks, Itzhak following his grandfather's words and actions, Shimon looked up at the London sky, still light, summer coming on,

Please God you have a safe journey there and a safe journey back. The sea does not play games, unless it is to win. You and your friends will need to be men on the water.

Thirteen

Much later that night, Ida lay in bed beside Bill, listening to the soft grunts and sleeping noises of her three children on the other side of their bedroom partition and laid her hand on her upper belly, the part of her that had felt chilled ever since Tom ran in this afternoon, and then brought it to her beating heart. Her heart that had been rushing ever since Tom mentioned going to the water, going to sea. The heart and the tense stomach that wouldn't let her sleep. She got up and very quietly went down to the kitchen. There was just a little light from the old moon outside, Ida pulled the chair across and stood up to get her medicine chest from the highest shelf. She didn't need the moonlight to see, knew the placing and contents of every vial and bottle and pill box by heart. She took out a stoppered bottle of tincture of chamomile, and yes, it might help her sleep, but she was not moving it to drink the contents. Beneath the bottle was a small folded piece of newspaper, and inside that piece of newspaper was the talisman Victor's mother had given her, the Lord's Prayer written ever so tiny in spiralling, winding writing, the miniature prayer wrapped carefully around a coin.

In the moonlight of her early summer kitchen, Ida held the prayer to her heart. Outside the city continued with its night life, London never quite still, never truly quiet, always a cart rattling here, a can knocked over there, the rumble of a late goods train, an early tram. She held the delicate piece of paper very close and she prayed a mother's prayer, a prayer that was not the words on the paper, but the only words she had been able to think since Tom made his announcement after tea. She prayed to a God she hadn't much time for, and to whatever spirits those who came to her stall believed she understood, the spirits she was supposed to be able to harness as a wise woman.

Please do not let anything happen to him. Please do not let anything happen. Please.

Ida had a knowing about the water, and it wasn't good. She thought of the bone angel under her pillow, time to give it to Tom.

Victor's mother did not write the Lord's Prayer charm herself, nor did the uncle who gave it to her. Every Christmas he'd sit by the fire, making sure to keep his wooden leg away from jumping cinders, and tell his stories to any who'd listen, often he'd tell them anyway when everyone was too busy and a house full of children meant too much work to take the time to listen to an old man. Victor's mother loved to listen. She was eleven years old, the eldest of the five babies her mother had birthed, before she'd turned to her husband and decreed no more. Even at eleven Anna knew that her whole world was Southwark and that for her, Southwark was enough, which made her more interested in the stories that her father and her uncle brought home.

Her father worked on the incinerators at St Thomas's hospital and came home each night full of stories of amputated limbs thrown into the fire, of the dead that no one could save. Anna ran skittish from spiders and mice, but there was something in her father's recounting of the lonely limbs, the organs removed, and the tiny dead babies that drew her in even as she shuddered at the words. So it was that when Uncle Peter came for his yearly visit, leaving the Greenwich Seaman's Mission where he now spent his days, it was Anna who listened, a toddler in tow and a baby happily knocking on Uncle Peter's peg-leg and the old man none the wiser.

I was just fourteen when I went to sea, and old that was, for a ship's boy. My mother wouldn't have me going any sooner, put her foot down firm and hard.

Here Uncle Peter stamped his peg-leg on the ground and the baby and the toddler giggled at the tap tap tap, banging their own stockinged feet in time.

But come fourteen, I was gone. Easy it was, we only lived in Deptford, half of it country then still, if you headed south down the high road there was a field or more not yet broken for houses. But right up by the river were all the ships that ever came into London. You could catch them before they went into the city, or better, catch them sailing away again, bound to be some lad who'd jumped ship the night before, scared of the sea after all, browbeaten by a girl into staying home, and a ship's boy needed right away.

Uncle Peter shook his head at the folly of the men and boys he had known give up the sea for a woman.

Those ships, you'd hear them before you saw them, wind cracking the sails, timbers creaking. You'd smell them too, the tea cutters, sugar ships, spice traders, salt air and tar and something else, something of hot places they had been.

Uncle Peter had told them many times, how that morning of his fourteenth birthday, he offered himself for a year's work, raced back to his mother with the coins the purser had paid him, and then ran off to sea on a sailing ship in that early part of 1812. He didn't come back until he was gone twenty-eight, even then it was only a month before he took passage on another ship and sailed again. Anna believed him when he said he'd seen Napoleon leading his men, and when he said he'd turned down a passage on the HMS Beagle itself, no interest in the beetles and bugs of other lands, they'd enough of their own in a good English ship's biscuit, weevil-ridden and bitter with it.

This Christmas he had a new story.

We were safely round the Cape of Good Hope and on our way back to England. It'd been hard, we'd weathered some bad storms and a few of our men lost to accidents. There was one who'd fallen from the topmast. If you fall all the way and the ship is with you, if it's on a roll and out of your way, then you might fall into the sea and you might be able to swim and you might survive. But if the ship is against you? I can tell you lass, there were many pieces

114

of that young man, and they were scattered to the winds. Another of the lads we lost went with a cough that came from nowhere at all. Racked with it he was, for the space of a night, and gone in the morning, his lips bluer than the Atlantic on a fine, bright day.

The thing is, said Uncle Peter, drawing his stool a little closer to the fire, Once a cough or an ague takes one man on a ship, you're always on the lookout for the next one.

And then? Anna asked, eyes wide.

Then we put the man in the longboat, and tow him along behind the ship itself, with water enough for a few days and a little food, if he's lucky. We wait and see. If he survives, if there's no storm, no bad weather at all – a long boat won't keep you safe in a storm – if still no fever comes, then the man is let back. But if not, well then your man must do the right thing, he steps off the longboat and into the deep. Better to go with honour and your head high, than bring the whole ship all down with you.

Anna pulled herself closer to the fire.

So we sailed on, and we waited, and the next night, I heard it. My own chest rattling and shaking, rubbing and tickling and itching to get out it was. I tried to believe it was just a bit of ship's dust or the spice grains floating in the air that'd caught me, our old beauty had been on four spice runs in her time, she'd fine grains that might catch in your throat and have you choking for days on and off, a cargo of pepper the worst of it. But it was no dust. It was the same cough all right, dry and hacking through the day, and at night I felt it sitting on my chest, like a succubus. Before the third hour of the watch was called, I had a word with the lieutenant and we both knew there was no point calling the ship's doctor. Not that the man was any more than a butcher anyway, too keen by half on the knife and the saw, that one.

Now, sometimes a man might fight his whole way down the rope ladder to the longboat, they'd end up pushing him or hitting at him with stakes to get him to go. Not me, I'd no intention of doing that to my fellow shipmates, not after the nightmares I'd had myself, dreams of a howling man crying for mercy and damning us all to hell, dreams that lasted long after we'd sent him down to Davy Jones' locker for his rest, much rest he gave us.

They were thankful for that, my fellows, and when I'd climbed all the way down and was settling myself in the longboat, what should I do but look above me and see them all saluting? I saluted back, hoping they couldn't see my shaking hands. They lowered down three days' worth of water and my food rations, my rum, for they were mine by right, no matter that I was no longer one of the ship's company.

The first day and the first night were the hardest. When you're used to being on board ship, so close to all your fellows, running up against one man turning this way and another turning that, the snores and the farts and the grumbling stomachs of the night, these things become normal. It's not just the rolling world beneath our feet we miss when we come home to land, it's the breath of your fellow man, close enough to feel his chest as it rises and falls. I missed that as I lay alone, the breath of other men. And then, the sun setting in the west as we sailed on north, I heard them singing.

They're not like pub songs or church songs, Anna, these are the songs of men at sea for their whole lives, men who come ashore only to pick up another passage. They're songs of sailing and whaling and battles on the wave, of women left behind in port, with hidden verses that we never sing to our sweethearts, how glad we are to be gone, on our way again. I lay myself down and listened, not knowing if I'd ever find my place again in that chorus of men.

Yes, Peter said, in return to Anna's trembling lip, I might have had a tear for myself and all. Only one, mind. When a man has only salt water for company, he's no need to be making his own.

The morning of the second day came and I was a great deal weaker, I could feel it, heavy in my arms and legs. I ate my rations, drank my water, but thought I'd save the rum in case the worst came to the worst, better to drink it all down in one go and let myself slide into the sea, than dive in sober, all too aware of what I'd be leaving.

Through the night of the second day I barely dozed, kept awake by a bright half moon, light as a full moon and more strange for it. Just before dawn there came a huge wave, one of those waves that sometimes rise with no warning. One moment I was lying on my back, dreaming of the breakfast they'd be having up above any minute, and the next I was lifted up and over and tossed out, with a mouthful of briny for welcome and then a smack on the back of the head from the longboat for good measure. I felt myself giving in before I even decided I would. Any sailor knows this, knows fighting the sea is pointless, we sail with it rather than against it, swim with the waves, not over them. The few of us who swim that is. I was lucky to learn when

I was a lad, but I've told you before now that sailors believe it's dangerous to be a swimmer, tempting a fate that will want to chuck you in.

So my body was already letting go before my mind woke up to what it was and where I was, and even when I did wake to it, I wondered if perhaps I should go under. I still had the croup, though I'd thought in the night I could feel a loosening, that perhaps the succubus on me was unhooking its claws, ever such a little. And it was that possibility that spurred me to fight. Fight my own urge to swim against the wave, my limbs waking up and trying to thrash out of the water, up to a longboat and a ship I knew must be far gone by now. I relaxed all over, I let go, became seaweed, driftwood, a gull's feather in the wind, but deep, deep in the blue. And just before the liquid already in my lungs gave way to the full flow of the ocean, I felt my foot break free of the water, break out and up. And then I was an old whale, bursting up and free, grabbing at air and swallowing it down, choking and coughing up all the sputum and sickness that was in me. I knew, when I finally caught my breath, floating on a wave as kind as a mother's breath, that the croup was gone, washed out by the clean brine of the ocean. Rubbing my eyes, I knew the ship was gone and all. But not the longboat, there it was, not two hundred yards away, and right way up at that. And sitting up in the boat was the ship's doctor. That young man who'd such a keen joy in the scalpel and the saw. There was no point thinking he'd bring the longboat to me, doctors are terrible sailors, so I cut into the water and I covered that distance with the strongest strokes my tired arms could make.

118

He hauled me on board and pointed far ahead. The ship, our ship, was a child's toy in the distance, a little wooden sailboat that a lad takes to the pond.

I was listening out for you, he said, I heard your cough change in the night. I wanted to speak to you, see if we couldn't save you after all. Then the wave came. I was knocked over.

He smiled. Doctors never make good sailors, but we do make good doctors, he said, pointing down to where my legs were twisted below me.

And it was only in seeing the gash in my leg and the blood coming from it, pouring from it now the leg was out of the water, that I realised I was in pain, and bloody awful pain at that.

He ripped his own shirt, to tie off my leg and stop the blood. I knew that while he was saving my life by tying off the leg, I'd likely lose the leg should we ever get back. Well, I thought I was gone, thought we both were, all I cared about was staying alive for a day, two. When you're that close to death it's not about weeks or years, it's hours, minutes, that count. We counted the night, that doctor and I, in stories. You'd think, in pain as I was, from the gash and the blood loss and the tight strip of shirt tied round my thigh, you'd think I'd want to hear roses and sweet songs. Not a bit of it. I knew then why most of the sea shanties are of death and sorrow, girls waiting on quaysides for men who never come back, and men giving themselves up to the deep. The only thing that takes your mind off what's bad is a well-told story of worse.

He was from the north, this young doctor, joined his first ship on the Tyne and learned his trade at sea, apprenticing one ship's doctor after another until he found himself on our lady. He told me of the lamp worm, a fat serpent that lives in the Tyne, and his story was as long as it was disgusting. In return, I told him of our own river dwellers. The taniwha brought back from the new world, from New Zealand, stolen from a Maori king, a man covered in swirling, whirling tattoos and the creature brought into our London docks as just a little thing, a lizard almost, but not quite. Carted that little lizard over to show off to royalty, see the wonders they have in our far-flung dominions, and then taken about as a sideshow for the pleasure gardens and the zoological gardens. Which it did for a few years, and no worry, plenty to gawp and stare at the taniwha's scales, its ridged back. Then one night, when a storm lashed the city and thunder rolled up and down the river, the cage where it was housed was snapped by a bolt of lightning, two men fried in their beds, and that taniwha, with not a care in the world for lightning or thunder, slipped away into the water rushing off the lane and down to the river, slipped into the Thames itself.

Peter looked to Anna, her eyes wide and ears reaching to hear more, and he lowered his voice to tell the rest of his story in a gravelly whisper.

You know what they say about the taniwha, don't you, girl?

She shook her head.

He smiled as he said, It's homesick, of course, but the Thames is too busy and it can't get by the ships for fear of being seen and landed and brought ashore for our pleasure again. It doesn't like to be looked at, not directly. And it's bigger, much bigger now, grown full on the secrets we tell

120

to the water. That taniwha lives off our whispers, eating up the fears and tears we tell over the side of a bridge. It's grown fat on what we hide from in the dark, beneath the bedclothes. There's no getting away from it either, it will follow you along the Effra or the Neckinger as easy as it rides the tide from Tilbury to Teddington.

Anna shivered and Peter went on,

We laughed at each other's tales, course we did, but we both knew we told truth too. I thought I was gone, Anna, God's truth, and I will always be grateful to that young doctor from the Tyne who kept me awake all night, kept my heart pumping, if only in fear.

Peter didn't tell Anna that he and the young doctor found another way to keep themselves awake, a way of skin on skin, of man on man, a way that all sailors knew, though few admitted, a way that made sure a man in pain and mortal fear might think it was worth staying awake, staying alive another hour, and another, that life might be sweet enough to bear the pain.

He was quiet for a while and when he brought his hand to his own mouth he remembered another man's hand, another man's mouth.

But your leg Uncle? And the ship? How did you get back?

I'm coming to that.

It was not long before dawn. There's a false dawn, far out to sea, when the whole world's a disc of water, nothing more. A dawn that comes from the west, as if the sun sends up a flare, a last hurrah before it begins to climb up all over again in the east. Sometimes people trust that false dawn, trust it too well. I told you he was no sailor, this young doctor. He saw the false dawn and he was so happy that the day had returned, so glad to see the light that it brought him up from the half-sleep we were both in, up on to his knees in the bottom of our longboat. And he took out of his breast pocket a little parcel, a fold of leather, and inside that was another parcel, wrapped round in one, two, three lots of paper. And beneath that was a coin covered in one last scrap of paper, and on that paper was written, in the smallest words I'd ever seen, the Lord's Prayer. He held it out to me and told me it was our safe deliverance, that his own mother had given him the coin and made him promise to keep it about him at all times, but we were sure to be saved now and that as I had kept him safe all night the coin should now be mine.

I started to say not at all, that we were not saved yet, it was no time to cheer as if we were home and dry. I started to tell him this Anna, but I've told you before now, and you know from my story already, that the sea is an unpredictable woman. And she did as she often will, she slapped him down. A wave, just like the one that sent him down to me in the first place, sent him down to keep me alive through that night. This time she took him, he went with the wave.

I was alone for a day more. You know a body cannot survive without water for long. We can live without food, as too many poor folk know, but without water we're nothing. I was nothing and I knew that I was and imagined I was delirious when the ship came alongside me and they leaned over the rail to call down their surprise that I was in the boat and alive at all and was my cough gone and could they safely haul me up and trust me to answer true? I shouted back,

True, the cough has gone, but it is gone the way you all have, and the young doctor too. I know you all to be dead and the leavings of my dried-up mind.

But they laughed and dropped the ladder down, told me to haul myself up, to count myself lucky, because hadn't I been swept along on the biggest wave since Jonah, swept away and then swept back, and now here I was healed and safe. Their language was more salty than that, girl, and then I knew they were no figment. And nor was the pain of my leg. I pointed to the gash and the blood and the strongest of the young lads was sent down the ladder to help me back up.

That night, when I'd drunk all the water I could get down me and gratefully eaten a dry biscuit or three – you should never take in too much food after a big thirst, the guts can't handle it – I asked about the young doctor, did he have a friend on ship who could take the coin back to his mother. They looked at me like I was sea-crazy after all. The young doctor had died the day after my cough had taken me down to the longboat. I was lucky he'd not come down with his cough the same day as me, or we'd've been sent to the boat together and he'd surely have taken me with him, the sickness had killed him so fast. They'd wound him in his own hammock that very day and sent him to the deep.

I took to my berth that night, glad to have the closing walls of it round about me. As I fell asleep I held the coin with the prayer and prayed for him.

Uncle Peter shook his head, I don't pray now Anna, haven't for many years, but that night I gave thanks for the ghost of a man who would never make a sailor. The next

morning I was on with my work, you mustn't lay a-bed
long when you're at sea, you don't want your fellows to start
thinking they don't need you.

Anna frowned, a question in her mouth, but not one she
knew how to ask.

What is it girl?

But your leg, what happened to your leg? Did someone
else cut it off? Was there another doctor?

Goodness me no. The leg I lost in one big bite, a dozen
years later. A shark it was, off the California coast, the
damn thing near took all of me with it. Clean bite though,
right through above the knee, nicely done.

Uncle Peter shrugged, Still, at least it took the bad leg,
the one the young doctor saved for me for a good few years.
I'd have minded a damn sight more had it taken the good
one.

Years later, when Anna offered the prayer to Victor, he
asked, But how did your uncle come to have the prayer?

What's that, lad?

How'd he have it? If the doctor was – a ghost?

I've no idea, I didn't ask and he died the year later.
There's some things best just believed, you believe and that
prayer will keep you safe.

But Victor didn't take the prayer, and he didn't keep safe,
and Anna gave the prayer to Ida who prayed in the moonlight for her own son's safety.

124

Fourteen

Jimmy chose not to mention the trip that first day, or the next, but by the third day he couldn't stop himself, blurted it out to Rose, the thrill of leaving from Waterloo Bridge, the next morning, crack of dawn, up to catch the tide, into the open sea and then camp itself, lads from all over, and learning and camping and scouting all together.

Open sea, is it, Jimmy-boy? Really? Sheppey?

Rose asked her son, hiding a smile.

It is a real island, Ma, and there's only Holland out from Sheppey, Sweden, Russia beyond. That's the North Sea, takes you to the rest of the world it does, come look on the map.

Jimmy found the big map he and Tom and Itzhak had been drawing for themselves so they could chart not only this course, but all the other courses they planned to take, over land as well as water. Jimmy had done most of the work of the map, the other two carefully adding the colouring-in, the pink for the Empire, and then all the other colours for all those other lands. Rose liked that the hardest bit was done by her bright boy, copying from their school books, carefully tracing around the lines at night after school, after his work with his dad, after everyone else was ready for bed, Jimmy would be with his maps. Planning and plotting, and maybe not as interested as his friends in the sailing part of it, but the journey, the getting there, that's what Jimmy liked. How far from here to the Elephant, then how far again to Waterloo, and how many miles, nautical miles he'd have Rose know, downriver to Gravesend, All Hallows, Sheerness, Leysdown itself. Where they'd stop and what they'd sail past, where the training ship would round this bay and that. He was at it with such attention, such care, that Rose began to see it through his eyes.

She saw Sheppey, flat old Sheppey where she'd been just the once as a young woman, back when Charlie used to take her out for the day, courting. Charlie different away from his family, less of the mouth almighty. Sheppey itself wasn't much cop, a flat land and wide open sky, wider sea, was a challenge to her. Rose needed a church spire, a smokestack, a broken-down chimney to mark out the points of her world, but listening to Jimmy, on about the way this bay curved and that beach landed, how these rocks were to be avoided and that port must've been a landing place since the Vikings, she thought that Sheppey might as well be the Treasure Island in the storybook he loved. It was his treasure, for certain.

She pulled Jimmy close to her, feeling his slight twist away. She could see in his half-frown that he was wondering if he was too old for this, if the feel of her arms around him wasn't all wrong for an almost-man of twelve years.

126

She breathed in, holding still, and it was true that his head didn't have the little-boy smell any more, maybe Jimmy's resistance was right, maybe Charlie was right, perhaps she did mollycoddle the lad.

But even as she wondered this she whispered, I'll ask your dad, I'll sort it lad.

And then Rose felt him relax into her arms, and now he snuggled closer, and it was Jimmy wanting to be held and he was all the ages of her baby, her son. He was the newborn and the little one forever falling over his own feet and the child just gone to school, and he was this one here, now, so desperate to be a man.

Summer had been slow in coming, and even when it did, they were such wet and sallow days, that Rose half-forgot she'd promised to speak to Charlie, then it was the middle of June, coming up midsummer, and Rose had got to say it now, had to ask, or Jimmy wouldn't be on the list for the boat.

Charlie had been out in his pearly finery, out for a do, a real hooley, home half-cut but happy with it, and his happiness on the drink was never a promise, so Rose took her chance.

Don't be daft.

Charlie . . .

Two weeks? You're taking the mick. He's taking the mick, cheek of it.

A week later she tried again. And a week after that.

I said bloody no and I meant bloody no, don't tempt me, Rose.

Rose was not used to this. Yes, Charlie liked to play the head of the family, and never stopped it with his lording over his cousins and his siblings, but indoors, with no one else about, Charlie could usually be persuaded to give in, give over, give up to her wishes. He was no pushover and she had to ask, usually more than once, but that was what they'd come to, fifteen years a pair, it was how they worked. Rose asked, Charlie said no, Rose asked, Charlie said yes.

But this time Charlie would have none of it. The boy was on his best behaviour, good as the day was long he'd been, so it wasn't that, and Charlie was happy in himself too, the barrow was doing well, as were the other stalls he had a little invested in. The summer hadn't been a good one so far, but that was better for business. Far better that people didn't pack up and bugger off to work in Kent or Essex when they found the stinking heat of the city all too much. If you were a carman or a porter, working hand to mouth at labouring and no idea if there'd be work next week or not, and if all the way from the lane to the Elephant was filthy sticky with the smoke and stink of the vinegar factory and horse yards and worse, and the weather so hot and tight that none of it was blown away with wind or washed out with rain, then why not get off for a week or two? Pack up and not pay the rent either. If you were earning all you could in a job that would only take you on the books one week at a time anyway, and if the damn bed bugs and lice and fleas and whatever else that loved the summer weather were seeing more of the inside of your home than you were – God knows no one wanted to be indoors on the hottest of nights – then plenty of folk not tied to a stall would just pick up and head off out of the city where the air was at least a bit cleaner. As it had been a bad summer, the hops and apples would be picked a few weeks later, and most people had stayed put, which kept the market ticking over nicely. Charlie and Rose were able to put a bob or two aside and that always made him an easier man to deal with, so Rose didn't understand what all this was about, his saying no and saying it again, and Jimmy's long face was more than she could bear, so she decided to have it out with him.

I've nothing to say Rose, he's not going.

He's been ever so good and we can afford it, you know we can, you've said as much already and . . .

No.

When he turned to her, Rose was shocked. Her Charlie Hatch had tears in his eyes.

What is it, love?

I don't want the lad to be away two weeks, Rose. It's too long.

Rose almost stepped back she was so surprised, but that what he'd just said and the look on his face had her hands reaching out to him faster than her feet could jump away.

You'll miss him?

Charlie nodded, but even his nod was half of a shake of his head, he couldn't get the words out and couldn't get the face to match, so he looked like a little boy trying to hide tears and it was more than Rose could bear to have both of her boys looking like this, to have to choose between a heartbroken Jimmy or a broken-hearted Charlie.

Rose went to her husband, he who hardly ever did any-thing with the lad, never took him out, fishing or to the

129

park or the woods, not any more, it had to be years since he'd done any of that with Jimmy. Concentrate on his work, that's what Charlie did, and yes he was keen for the boy to get on at school, not to waste time in playing, happy enough for Jimmy to take on a barrow eventually, like the rest of the family, but also, maybe, a little hope that the lad might pull himself up, get the learning that would make all the difference. The Hatches had always been coster-mongers, and proud, but a barrow might become a shop, a shop might have a home above it, a shop might even be owned and the home too and no damn landlord to pay, a shop might grow as big as Tarn's up at Newington Butts. Charlie's son might do better than Charlie himself and Charlie was proud enough of himself. His boy might do better. That's why he pushed him, that's why he was on at him all the time, that's why he had a go.

Rose put her arm around her husband's shoulders, stood on tiptoe and pulled him close so they were heart to heart, left side to left side, and she whispered, I bloody love you, Charlie Hatch, I bloody love you with all that I am.

She took Charlie to their bed. Unlike many of their family and friends, Rose and Charlie had a room of their own, no partition, no sharing, no need to keep their voices down – other than for the thin walls between the houses and the uneven window frames and Rose's mother downstairs – and there was no need to keep their voices down right now. It was Sunday morning, Emily was washed, cleaned, and back in the welcome sleep of the dying. One or two of their neighbours might be at church, others were sleeping off last night, a few more getting their dinner started, while over in the pub Tilly and Samson were already comfortable, she with an apron-full of peas, he with a plate to spill them in, a pint at hand each; five pods and a sip, five pods and a mouthful. Charlie thought of a pint and his mouth watered, Rose reached for him again, not for his mouth this time and his mouth watered more for Rose than for a pint, his cock readier for her than he was for a drink. Jimmy was meant to be off at Sunday school, though Rose knew that half the time Jimmy played the wag, running off with Tom and Itzhak to play at scouting. Charlie wasn't fussed about the boy going to church or not, he just liked a little time with Rose. A lot of time with his Rose. Sunday morning was the one time they could get enough of each other.

In bed had always been good for the two of them, better than good. Charlie was a big man and Rose fine and small, yet they fit well together, comfortably and then some. They fit uncomfortably too, when she turned him over so she could ride him and he crooked one knee behind his other leg to brace her back, earning himself a cramp for his pains. But Rose wouldn't let up and there she was yowling above him, pleasuring herself like a bloody banshee she was, and there he was beneath, unable to move either leg, one from the cramp and one that was twisted beneath her tiny weight, but flaming hell didn't she know how to use that weight, how to shift it just right, like a little boxer his Rose was, smart and light and then oh, but the punch she could pack, all of her above him. Anyway, and then, his cock wouldn't let him think of anything else, wouldn't let him shift her now, not now. If Charlie Hatch was the head of the family, then Charlie Hatch's cock was most definitely the head of Charlie.

Afterwards, after Aunty Sarah over the road had tutted

as she fed her linnet, whispering to the little bird how she wished it'd been her under Charlie Hatch just now, wishing it had been her under Rose Hatch and all, but hush now and lucky you're no parrot; after Rose's mother Emily woke from her laudanum-induced sleep, confused and uncertain and sure she'd heard foxes screaming in the yard; after Rose had washed – a whore's lick of flannel and cold water, and washed Charlie down too, washed down the man that threatened to keep her in bed another half hour; afterwards when Jimmy was back from wherever he'd been out with his mates, too damn hopeful and the waiting wince in him that Rose hated, ready always to be knocked back by his dad – after all that, when they were sitting down to their tea, a seedy cake and a bun for the lad, tea and beer to wash it down, afterwards, Charlie looked over at Jimmy and, not speaking as if it mattered, just letting it out of his mouth between a bite of cake and a swallow of beer, he said,

All right then, your ma's persuaded me, you can go to your Scout camp, two bloody weeks though it is.

Jimmy didn't hear his father add that he'd have to earn the money himself, or that he'd be expected to help out before and after school to make up for the time away. Jimmy heard none of this because he was out of the house and up the street and running into Ida's place for Tom and then they were both over the back alley for Itzhak who was helping his mother with the lodger's room, helping her change the sheets and puff up the pillows, and then there were three boys rolling down the street, arms around each other, singing for all they were worth, Play up the Walworth Scouts, i-tiddley i-tie i-tie eye, hit a copper in the eye, play up the Walworth Scow-outs.

Charlie shook his head at Rose. He was the boss of the family, true enough, but in bed, Rose was the boss of Charlie, and they were both happy with that.

While Rose and Charlie were making the most of each other, Tom, Itzhak and Jimmy were making a deal. There was a boy in another patrol, one of the lads from school, and when Tom had brought the bone angel into the school yard one day, the lad had taken a fancy to it, asked Tom how much he wanted for it. Tom wasn't daft enough to consider selling, nor did he think this boy would have money to spare, his people were no better off than Tom's. But it did occur to him that there were certain things his patrol could do with in their kit, and a good penknife was on top of the list. This boy had a good penknife and Tom had a bone angel. They'd do a trade. And now that all three of them had permission to go, it was time to do the deal.

I'll give it back after the camp.

Tom frowned, You sure you don't need a knife for camp yourself?

I'll take my old man's. He's buggered off and me ma has it in her top drawer, in case he comes back.

All right.

All right.

Shake on it, spit.

Witness it, lads.

And they did. Shake, spit, shake again. The deal was done, bone angel exchanged for a penknife with an old stained ivory handle, the deal to last until after the camp.

Down the street, through the alley, and into the back yard of the Ayalon house, where Mimi and Lev were enjoying a moment together. The drizzle had moved on over the river, Mimi and Lev sat on their kitchen chairs in the yard, welcoming a watery sunlight

You could have gone, to hear the rebbe speak, Mimi reached out her hand to take her husband's.

Lev brought her hand to his lips, kissed it, sighed.

Mimi looked at her husband. The fine lines around his eyes were small cracks, dug ever deeper into his skin from long days squinting at tiny watch pieces. When she studied Lev, Mimi saw not just one man, but all the men he had been for her. The shy boy brought to her parents' home by the rabbi's wife. Her mother had quizzed him about his people, making him stutter and stammer in his answer.

When her father closed the door on Lev and the rabbi, he had turned, shaking his head,

Not this one, too quiet for our Mimi, we want a boy to make something of himself, a boy to reach up. There will be others, London is full of young men, how lucky we are to have found ourselves safely here.

And his wife pulled at the fabric of her blouse and whispered p-p-p, tutting away her husband's tempting of fate.

But Mimi had not thought the young man too quiet at all, she'd thought him beautiful. Long dark lashes, wild black hair, heavy brown eyes and a straight look the one time he'd had the courage to glance at her, the silent girl in the corner. She hadn't cared about the stammer, at seventeen she saw that he was lovely, and what she'd felt was a twist in the pit of her stomach, further down, lower,

134

almost between her legs, and she knew this was the one, the boy that made her body want him, made her body want to make babies with him. Not that she said so to her parents.

Instead she said, He has no mother. He has no practice in speaking in a family, no practice in sitting at a table, speaking in English, a father trying to prove him not good enough for your little princess.

You're our only child, of course you are our—

We love you Mimi, you are our—

I know. And I'm grateful. But you didn't give him a chance to speak and you didn't let me speak to him.

That would not have been right.

Mimi frowned, who knew what was right these days?

You and Papa didn't meet until the day before your wedding, and you've made a good marriage. The rabbi and his wife would not have brought him to us if he were not a good boy. He's faithful and he's observant. I'm seventeen, you were married at fifteen.

We lived in such old ways, it was different.

I'm ready. I want him.

Mimi's parents heard her words and knew that their girl was right, it was definitely time.

When Mimi looked at Lev now, in the yard of their house in Walworth, in a thin sunshine that wouldn't last the evening, breathing in the ever-present stink of the vinegar and the gasworks, the horse shit, she remembered the beautiful boy who'd first come to the house, the quiet and careful young man who took her to their bed on the wedding night, and the man she had unleashed in him, the woman she'd freed in herself. She saw the first room they shared, the back bedroom of her parents' house. She saw their second place, two rooms with a widowed aunt who hated them being in love and bitterly snarled when Lev so much as smiled at his pregnant young wife. The third, with the old landlord who sold the house from under their feet and they were kicked out the next day by the new owner who said he'd have no dirty Jews in his house. All those shared houses, until finally they had this home, a place where Shimon could live out his days in comfort and they even had a spare room to let to lodgers. All the hard work worth it, the holy days that Lev had had to work through until he found a place with a Jewish business, and now a mortgage in his own name, a house from which they could not be evicted. Mimi remembered the births of each of her boys, a woman who preferred the company of men, now surrounded by men, and happy to be so. She recalled each boy's brit, her fear and tears, her husband reciting the prayers, his voice never once faltering, no stammer now, as the mohel did his work. Becoming a father had made a man of the shy boy who'd come to her parents' house. She saw all this when she looked at Lev, all this and every worry, every day of headache-inducing, eye-straining work, etched into the skin of his face, the wrinkles at his tired eyes.

What is it?

It will be good for the boy to go away, to this camp. He is growing up. He needs this.

Yet you sigh?

My father's fears are in me. He says we are not sailors, we are people of the land.

136

Mimi growled under her breath, her father-in-law and his stories of what they were and what they'd been and never letting them settle into this new life.

We were not sailors, true. We were also not home-owners. We were dirty Jews they could kick out of this village and that street and our own homes, no matter that the home was a hovel more often than not. Now we own a house, on the corner here is one of the finest synagogues in London where your father is comfortable. Our son is welcomed by the goyim, he said so himself, their Scoutmaster, all boys are welcome. This is a new time, and Itzhak will be part of it. Your father should be proud, not fearful.

Lev nodded, appeased by his wife's words. He settled in his hard-backed chair, his eyes closed against the light.

Mimi, now she had calmed Lev, closed her eyes too, a few minutes more until she must get back to work. With her eyes closed, not looking, not acknowledging what she was doing, not wanting to give this fear any voice at all, she put her hand to her neck and pulled out the silver hand she always wore. It was not the hand of Miriam that had belonged to her father-in-law's mother, worn so thin by the time it was passed on to her that she kept it upstairs in her sewing basket for safety. Her father-in-law had wanted her to have a charm like his mother's, so she wore this hand that he'd bought her from their own market. She kissed it and wished on it, even as she frowned at superstition where she should have faith. Nonetheless, when she let the silver hand fall, she pulled three times at the fabric of her blouse, lightly, quickly, and she whispered p-p-p. Kissed the hand, just in case. P-p-p, just in case.

Come the night, back in Charlie Hatch's house, Emily was moaning as the pain trickled through her morphine dreams. Jimmy had finally calmed enough to go to bed, and Charlie was out having a pint or two or five with Samson and Bill. Rose gave up on her piecework, the lamplight too yellow for the white linen threads she was pulling. She stood up and stretched out her cramped fingers, stepped to the back yard, looking up for the moon. Rose always looked for the moon, was happy when she found it, even just the light of it hidden by cloud, the moon was her constant. Seeing the half moon now, murky through the cloudy sky, she reckoned on her good and faithful calendar, bringing her hand to her lower belly. It wasn't that they hadn't tried to make other babies after Jimmy, but none had come, and she knew it was a sadness to Charlie, a fellow who thought himself such a man had wanted a tribe of lads to carry his name. Rose usually came on at the full moon, so if it was to be any time, this afternoon would have been the moment, this afternoon when her body decided it wanted Charlie. Rose left her hand on her belly a moment longer and breathed, deep down. Wonder, and a little hope.

Fifteen

The boys ran into the swimming baths, hurrying for the changing cubicles. This place of in between, not yet in the water, not yet undressed, this was the hard bit, where they still worried that the water would be cold, their swimming trunks inadequate, that they would be told they were the wrong sort of boy for this place. Yes, they had second-class tickets, but even so, there was always the chance that they might not measure up to someone else's exacting standards. These were local baths, they were local boys, but the baths were run by people from the council, not those they mixed with every day. And beyond that, the greater fear that they would not do well enough at their swimming, that even now, after all the work of persuading their parents, getting permission to go, they would still be found out, told they could not go on ship, could not join the camping trip after all.

The first time they'd come down to the baths they'd felt very out of place. The Manor Place Baths were for their mothers, for washing clothes and yes, they'd been carting laundry for May for a couple of months, it wasn't as if they hadn't stood outside waiting to be loaded up with her washing, but they'd not often been here for a wash themselves, only every now and then, when there was a spare bob and the flannel at home wouldn't do. Lads round this way didn't go a lot on swimming. Boxing yes, when the people in charge covered the pool to make a ring, Jimmy and Tom would often sneak in to watch a round or two. But why pay to go swimming, even on a second-class ticket, when there were ponds and any number of creeks between here and Deptford?

The baths were for old men too, different old men than the ones who sat in the pub corner day after day. These old fellows were leaner, wiry, some of them swam every day that they could, ploughing through the water, up and down, up and down. Tom and Jimmy and Itzhak were amazed by the old boys, couldn't take their eyes off them in the water, getting out of the water. One of the chaps had tattoos that went all the way down his back, and though he wore a vest to hide them, because it was the right thing to do in public baths, Tom and Itzhak had both caught glimpses of the tattoo, and Jimmy was sure he'd seen the sly curve of a mermaid inked on to the man. A mermaid with no blouse on what was more.

Mermaids never wear blouses, nor shirts neither, Tom said, Mermaids have tails on their bottom half and they're naked on the top, all bosom they are, that's why sailors go for them, why sailors get caught out. They're hoping to get with a mermaid girl and then they get in the water and they find there isn't even a bottom half to go with the top half, and then, when the bloke's in the water, the mermaid calls

140

up a wave and it's too late and the fellow drowns. Sailors hate mermaids, terrified of them they are.

So why do they go to them then, asked Itzhak.

Can't help themselves. Once you've seen a mermaid's face, heard her sing, you're done for.

I hope we don't see one when we're on the boat.

Nah, Tom shook his head, all certainty, You don't get mermaids this far north, they're only in the South Seas.

Itzhak was relieved and Tom and Jimmy looked over at their friend, astonished yet again that the little brother of Nathan and David Ayalon, both of them well known round here for their reputation with girls, should be so unaware of what went on. Maybe it was a Jewish thing, maybe after this all-important bar mitzvah he was always on about, they'd tell him the lot and be done with it. Tom knew everything there was to know about all that, with a wise woman for a mother he'd have to, wouldn't he?

Still, as their Scoutmaster liked to tell them, plenty of time for girls once they were men. They were lads yet, and that meant concentrating on their scouting, learning to swim as best they could, showing the other boys that they might have joined the troop late, but they were up there with the best of them when it came to making a good crew for the boat trip. They'd been told the name of the training ship last week, Arethusa. And didn't she sound lovely the way she rolled off the tongue? Arethusa it was, and they'd be worthy of her.

In just five lessons they learned to jump in without question and, in Jimmy's case, without squealing either. They learned to hold their breath without holding their noses, to take a big gulp of air and to let it out slowly while sitting on

141

the bottom of the shallow end, and last week they'd learned to breathe out through their mouths, blowing bubbles and making as many farting raspberry sounds as they wanted, so the water didn't come in to choke them. There had been strokes and slicing through the water, and the crawl and backstroke and breaststroke, but by far the most fun had been the getting in and sinking like a stone to the bottom, holding until their lungs were fit to burst and then speeding up through the water, bouncing right up and out. If Itzhak had known it was this much fun coming swimming he'd have been in the baths plenty of times before now, and Jimmy too.

There was a swimming test the following week, a whole length in full Scout kit, to make sure they'd be safe if anything went wrong. Hard enough for a new swimmer to manage the full length, though their teacher was dead good, but especially hard when kitted out. Jimmy hadn't mentioned this part of the training to his dad, he knew Charlie would thrash the living daylights out of him if he thought their hard-earned kit, and their own earnings and all, was being thrown into the water without so much as a by-your-leave. Jimmy was ever so careful with his handkerchief and his shirt, dead proud of how he looked all togged up, proper smart Rose said. So how he was going to get home and dried before Charlie came back from the market he'd no idea. Still, when he brought his swimmer's badge home he reckoned his dad'd be proud then. It would be the first badge he had earned in the Scouts, first badge he'd earned anywhere, and Jimmy liked the idea of a badge very much indeed.

Today it was training. Into the pool and no playing and no blowing bubbles, just one length after the other.

As many as you can in thirty minutes boys, let's see who's got the stamina for this, any stroke you like, and off you go – the lad or lads still swimming when I blow my whistle gets a treat for himself and for his patrol.

Well then. Tom, as patrol leader, had to go all out for this one, and so did Jimmy who was Tom's patrol second, but what none of them expected, and what he certainly hadn't expected himself, was how Itzhak took to it. Yes, he'd had fun with the jumping and the blowing raspberries and the sitting on the bottom, as much fun as any of the others, but this was different, this was a whole new feeling. It didn't happen right off, there were a good few lengths where he was just pushing on, trying not to hit the lad in front of him, trying not to kick the boy behind in the face, but after a while, when one by one the others got out, at three or four or even seven lengths more than any of them had managed before, panting and puffing and red in the face, and their Scoutmaster told them it was a fine effort for a first time, and good on them for that, Itzhak kept pushing on.

And when the pool was less crowded with Scouts, when there was less pushing from behind or knocking into someone ahead, he found there was a rhythm to this swimming lark, that crawl suited him best, and Itzhak knew he wasn't going ever so fast, knew because Tom was still swimming, only just, and puffed out Tom was, Itzhak could hear the rasping, gasping breath as his mate ploughed on past him one last time, all arms and kicking and splashing, but not Itzhak. Itzhak just kept on.

He hadn't known there was music in the water, had no

143

idea there could be this rhythm in his body. Itzhak was swimming as if all of him was the water, as if the water was all there was. The Scoutmaster was watching him from the shallow end. The other boys stood there too, all covered round with their towels and shivering, and they were looking at the gold watch given to the Scoutmaster by his own father when he'd won his first race. It had been a running race, not swimming, but the young man recognised it all the same, recognised that Itzhak Ayalon had rhythm in his body, not just in his strokes, but inside himself. He saw that the boy was in that place where long races were won, battles fought, where lives were saved that would normally have been lost.

The Scoutmaster was a young man, from the Dulwich Mission, and he knew this feeling had been described as grace by some, a sense of being fully in and yet beyond one's own self. He'd not recognised it as a religious fervour when he'd felt it himself. What he saw in Itzhak, with his clumsy turn back from the deep end, his slightly uneven stroke that nonetheless had him finishing another length and another, was the quality every trainer looked for, someone prepared to sweat lap after lap of a training pitch, length after length of a pool. Itzhak Ayalon had it all right.

Almost three quarters of an hour had passed, the other boys were shivering, the young Scoutmaster shook his head and held up a hand, blew his whistle, and the piercing note got through to Itzhak who finally woke in the water, woke from a place of being with water rather than in water, and he stopped, dizzy, half-blinded from the pace and the water still running, rushing over his face, and came to the edge. It was only now that Itzhak realised his lungs were hurting with the effort of breathing, that his shoulders ached from the round and round and round. And across his usually peaky little face was a grin larger than any he had ever grinned, so big it hurt his cheeks, a smile so wide it cracked his face in two. Then the other lads were cheering him as the master took him by the hand and hauled him out because he was too puffed even to pull himself up and his arms were shaking anyway, proper trembling, too much to hold the ladder. The other lads were crowding round, Jimmy and Tom had him up on their shoulders and Itzhak Ayalon was carried off by a crowd of cheering lads to the changing cubicles.

Not bad for the boy who, five minutes later, stood in the corner, his towel around his lower half as he got changed, even as other boys whipped theirs into twists and flicked sodden flannel at each other, stinging and nipping and leaving little red welts, yelps from the recipient and cheers at every hit. Itzhak, hero of the hour, got on with his dressing, quietly in the corner, hiding his circumcised self from the Gentile boys, hiding himself just in case. In case one of his mates, one of his friends, one of those who thought of him as 'our Itzhak' took it into their head to also think of him as a dirty Jew, a yid. Itzhak knew not to remind them unnecessarily.

Come the day of the test, the boys were all nervous. The whole troop lined up at the entrance to the baths, while the pool itself had been booked out for the boys for the hour, no one else to come in, just the 2nd Walworth Scout pack and their Scoutmaster, a few helpers, one or two dads who'd come along to see their boys, a few nervous mothers. Ida was working her barrow, with both the girls alongside her, Bill had been off to his shift since first light. Jimmy hadn't even mentioned the test to Rose or Charlie, he knew Charlie would never believe that he wasn't about to jump in and swim a length fully clothed just for the hell of it, knew he'd be furious about the waste, spoiling the leather belt. Jimmy was worried about the belt and all, May had promised to take in clothes after and iron them dry, nice and careful, so there'd be no shrinking or spoiling.

Jimmy went along to see her about it himself, didn't take Tom or Itzhak with him, went alone and made her his own offer, all grown-up and businesslike.

Aunty May, I have a question.

Do you now? May smiled at the 'aunty', usually the boys called her Missus, if that. She knew what a boy was about when he started adding the aunty.

I need help with my clothes.

Jimmy explained the problem of the swimming and the uniform and May didn't need him to explain his father's temper.

I'll carry your washing bags for another month Aunty May, if you like. Help out a bit more, in return of course, I'm not asking for any favours.

You'll be dead on your feet, lad. You've no time for your schoolwork as it is, with all these scouting trips and what-not.

Not me, Aunty May, I'm a hard worker, all the Hatches are, you know that.

You take after your mother as well as your father for graft, I'll grant you that. But no son, I don't think so.

May shook her head and then spoke again quickly, seeing a flush come to his ears, the flinch of his brow,

I don't mean I won't help, I mean I'll do it gratis. You and your mates have been a boon to me this year. I'll give you a hand lad, because I'm a neighbour and because I can, and I'll ask nothing in return.

Jimmy had brought a change of clothes with him to the baths and as soon as the test was done, he'd be round to the laundry to wring the sodden shorts and shirt through the mangle, and then over to May's for the heat of her iron. It was a fine day, better than most this month, if he was lucky he'd be home and dry before anyone noticed. Not that his mother was noticing much, Rose had Emily to look after, always Emily to look after these days. When Jimmy woke up in the morning he was never sure his nan would be with them still. He'd never seen a dead body before, but he'd been sneaking a look at Emily when no one else was in the front room with her, and he reckoned she couldn't be far off. He hoped she wasn't to die while they were away at camp. He hadn't been to a funeral before either, and he thought he'd quite like to go to one, to walk in the procession, horses up ahead with plumes flying behind their ears, and everyone watching as you slowly filed past, all solemn and serious, but shiny too, your pearly suit glistening like tears.

Mimi and Lev weren't at the baths either, but it was Saturday and Itzhak wouldn't have asked them, he did ask his grandfather though, expecting a no, and was surprised to see a smile on the old man's face, to hear a happy sigh as he said,

147

To watch you swim and win, better than all the other boys, no?

I don't know about that, Zaide.

But you beat them last week?

This is different.

No, this is the same, but harder. We are good swimmers in my family, we have not been sailors, but swimmers, yes. Maybe I could, maybe ...

Shimon thought about it for a while, a good long while and Itzhak waited patiently for his answer. When he finally sighed again, Itzhak understood and shook his head, It's fine, I know.

I would like to, but if you are not to come to shul with me and your father is at work, your mother looking after this house of men, who will say the prayers for you and your father? Your brothers will not be there, we both know that. So, I will pray for us all, and you will come back from this foolish swimming safe and well.

It's a swimming pool, Zaide, nothing can happen in a swimming pool.

Shimon shook his head, Once upon a time, a long time before you were born, when we all still lived in Russia, my friends and I found a swimming hole in the forest. Deep and blue it was, with clean edges of rock and no mud, just the forest and the pool, so beautiful. We too thought we were safe.

And Itzhak, forgetting he was a boy who was almost a man, recalling instead the years of comfort from the old man's stories, sat on the floor at his grandfather's feet for another story of the homeland, that place that we must never forget that we come from, no matter what your mother says. This story was of the dangers of deep water, and the woman who waited at the bottom of the well, the lake, the sea. The woman who must be Baba Yaga's sister, she was so cruel and mean and old. And you never, ever wanted her to touch your toes, once she had touched your toes . . .

In the water, the test itself.

Tom wasn't pulled under by the weight of the sodden clothes and he didn't come in first but he didn't come in last and that was good enough for him. Tom liked to win and he liked to lead, there was no denying it, but he knew what he was about well enough to understand that trying to better some of the other boys in the water was pointless. Tom wasn't backward in coming forward, but he'd not come forward if he couldn't be the best. He'd won prizes and badges for his knots and his semaphore, and he'd no doubt there were more where those came from. He didn't need to be the top swimmer as well.

Jimmy got himself through, that was all he needed to do. He wanted to be on the boat, at the camp, with his mates, and that's all he wanted. What got him through the test in his own record time was that he needed to get on and get those clothes dry again.

Itzhak gave himself to the water, was in and of the water, and he was awarded his badge with merit. The certificate was pinned to the wall at home and the merit stamp allayed Mimi's worry just a little, perhaps it would be fine for him to sail, to swim, to be with those other lads. Perhaps they would continue to be kind to him after all. Perhaps she herself was right when she insisted to her father-in-law, time and again, that this was their home now. Perhaps the fear that sat in her breast and had her panting for breath when she thought about her boy going off for two weeks really was just foolishness and it was time she let him simply be her son rather than her youngest, her baby. Regardless, she offered a prayer for him anyway, her own hand to the silver hand at her neck. She felt the cool metal beneath her forefinger and frowned, picking up her piecework, there would be nothing left of the hand by the time her sons were fathers with children of their own.

The boys were happy, the camp was under a month away, they were prepared.

Sixteen

An early summer evening in Croydon. The sun slow to set, lighting the city with a golden warmth that had the blackbirds and starlings in the garden dancing around the study window. Edward Lovett looked outside to the rose that had grown, carefully trained to surround the window and he frowned. Aphids. He would speak to the man who came weekly to work in the garden. A bedding planting of marigolds beneath would deal with the problem, at least at the base of the rose, perhaps this high up as well. Lovett liked a full garden, he liked a full house, and a growing garden now meant groaning shelves in the winter months. The household was managing very well these days, there was order of sorts, a natural order, not imposed, but real nonetheless. Perhaps he should leave the aphids to the birds after all.

Lovett was cataloguing. This was the best part of his work. Yes, he had a job at the bank, and worked assiduously, but he acknowledged it was without passion, without any great interest. This was the work he cared for, speaking with people he would never otherwise encounter, trading with them, collecting a piece of this man or that woman's story. He had set aside three charms to catalogue this evening, none particularly remarkable, yet each due its proper place nonetheless.

A piece of amber, wishbone-shaped, worn smooth from years in the soft earth and then further years rubbed for luck by rougher hands.

A hand fashioned in bronze, the size of his own thumbnail, pleasing for its rustic nature. The elderly woman from whom he'd purchased the piece shook his hand as she gave it over, saying, A blessing for you, to ward off the evil eye, one of half a dozen my old ma had on a leather tie round her neck, never let us take them off her, not even when the goitre had swollen to the size of a boxer's fist.

Finally there was another wishbone, this one from a chicken, bound in thin velvet ribbon, once red, now ochre with age.

The collector had no need of more wishbones for the collection, and they were not special, being a charm anyone could manufacture at home after a good meal. And yet there was something about the prosaic nature of the beribboned wishbone that appealed, perhaps more than other amulets with far greater care taken in their finding or their creation. This wishbone was a household magic, a local god, something a suburban man understood very well.

Each charm was allocated a small label, with the date on which he'd bought it and the person from whom it was purchased, as well as the location of its find, and, on occasion, a brief anecdote. There was not a great deal of information imparted to the label, that was not the point. Unlike many of his class, Lovett did not enter these streets to bring about a social change some might consider long overdue. Nor did he hold any faith of his own in the power attributed to the objects by their owners. He took care to simply record. Let the observer create their own understanding, if they would.

While he did not share belief in the objects, Lovett nevertheless allowed them a value, one that history might permit. The objects that only twenty-five years ago had been called country charms, were now wholly ascribed to the city. There were pieces that the parents of their current owners, their keepers, would have called true country charms, now believed to be dyed-in-the-wool London artefacts, with London stories attributed to them. Unlike certain members of the Folklore Society, he was not one to go along with the superstitious folk who placed shoes in their chimneys against the devil, his newborn sons did not wear blue glass beads hung around their necks to ward off illnesses of the lung. Lovett did not collect in order to utilise magic, he collected in order to have collected. This was how he understood his own world, how he held it. And it made him happy to order his world.

Edward Lovett's pleasure was not the raucous happiness of those he met in Walworth, New Cross, East Ham, Shoreditch, Camden. Men and women laughing until they cried, singing themselves hoarse, a pig's trotter in one hand, a pint in the other, and a mouthful of both at the same time. He had witnessed the overflowing happiness of the working class and had, at times, wondered how it might feel to be as wild in his own passions. He had seen their suffering too, and was sure that the belief in efficacy of these impotent charms flowed directly from that suffering, the only hope anyone with so little might possess in times of direst distress.

He did not catalogue the poverty he saw in his walks, nor did he give his opinion on the beliefs he wrote down. He noted simply whatever he was told, with date and location. At the bank he was similarly thorough, with no opinion on one man's debt or another's wealth. In his daily work Lovett was a clerk of numbers, in his study he was a clerk of hopes. The two were not so different.

He blotted the label and tied it carefully and securely to the amber wishbone. Time for supper. Cold chicken.

Seventeen

Mid-July, still damp, horrid sticky nights, with Emily in pain and Rose sitting up with her the best part of the short darkness. There'd been a visit from Ida earlier, to chat over the boys' trip and ask Rose what she thought the boys ought to take with them. Not that either woman had spare clothes for her lad anyway. Looking through the list of this vest and that shirt for best, they could have wished Baden-Powell and his *Scouting for Boys* further, the pair of them. Too late now though, everyone was agreed, and the subs paid, with rather more contribution from both mothers than either woman would admit to her husband, and early tomorrow the lads would be off, soon as the tide was right at Waterloo. Tom and Jimmy were going to sea with their school pants for best and their home ones for every other day, the two shirts they had each, and that was that.

The boys were playing in the yard, as ever, though it was less playing these days and more like taking turns to test each other, this knot and that turn and what does this signal mean, what does that tracking sign say? Ida could hear that

Tom was bossier than Jimmy, Rose heard it too. Charlie Hatch's bark had skipped the fence, jumping his own placid Jimmy and alighting on Tom. Rose didn't say she was glad her son had been spared his father's big mouth, and Ida didn't say she worried for Tom, that his friends might find his manner all well and good for now, but if he wasn't careful his mouth would get him hanged.

They passed a half hour, and it was nice to stop for a cup of tea and a catch-up. Jimmy had told Tom, who'd told Ida, that Emily kept them all up half the night with her moaning, and Ida turned as she left, an overexcited Tom slow to follow her to the door.

Look at the shadows under your eyes, Tommy, there's as much black as blue, you want the Scouts to send you home for worry you won't be able to stand on the ship?

The boys laughed at the idea that they might not be allowed to go, not now they were all packed and ready, and Ida quietly grasped Rose's hand, pushing a bottle into her palm.

For your mother. Two drops, three at most, it'll help. But no more, you hear?

Rose was touched both by the kindness, and the lightness of the small, stoppered bottle. The women held each other then, they rarely kissed, friends because of their sons, because of the street, the family, and then Ida took Tom home. A long night yet to endure before his life's adventure began.

Years ago, when Tom was a small boy, before Ida had had the girls, the people three doors down kept a cockerel. Never one to sleep long, Tom had loved its pre-dawn screech, took it as a sign to be up and out of his half-bed built of orange boxes, to climb in with Ida and Bill and burrow his way between them, nudging Ida until she'd hum his favourite songs. Then Ida would get up, worried to wake Bill who'd often as not been working late in those days, and she'd roll the eiderdown around her and Tom, and take him through to their other room, kitchen and parlour together. They'd sit wrapped up, Tom working his fingers into an opening in the threadbare eiderdown, pulling out loose feathers, and Ida would stroke his back and sing to him. Old songs about men and maids and then Tom's favourite song, the one they sang together, a keeper did a shooting go, under his arm he carried a bow, and Tom's line of 'master' in response to Ida's 'Jackie-boy', calling and responding, almost too big to be on her lap still, but never too big for Ida. By the time they'd sung it five times through Tom's voice would lower and Ida's too, more often than not, and the cockerel would have crowed another half hour more and then Bill would come from his bed, sweaty and hot as the night always left him. He'd stumble through shaking his head at the two of them wrapped up warm and tell Ida she must have cold blood to match her cold feet, and she'd say anyone'd have cold feet with all the standing she did in the market, and then Bill would cut a doorstep of bread and lather it up with dripping for Tom and that would be breakfast and the day would be on.

As she lay awake this night, Ida heard the boards creak in the little room next door, the one Tom shared with his sisters, and she knew he was awake and looking at the haversack, wondering if he should pack it again, as he'd done four times already. She wanted to go in and scoop him up, hold him on her lap, wrap him tight and not let him leave her side. Instead she got up, put her head around the door and watched silently. In the soft light from a sun almost up, Tom was folding and re-folding his one good shirt, the creases she'd so carefully ironed into it all gone now with his handling it. When Tom finally looked up, she brought her finger to her mouth and then curled that finger round, and she and the boy went through to the kitchen, where she made the tea and he cut the bread and lathered on the dripping himself, one for each of them, ready on their places at the table. Tom took the cup of tea through to wake Bill and Ida thought that if her boy was big enough to use his father's brute of a carving knife on the loaf, and she no longer pictured the blade going straight to his bone, stuck in that bone, every time he did so, then he was big enough to go away for a couple of weeks. It might be the making of him. She'd need to bake more bread today, Tom's idea of a doorstep was a sight more generous than his dad's.

Then the girls were up and Bill through for his breakfast and Tom was off fiddling with that damned haversack again. Not that Ida was rude about it to Bill, one of the softest gestures she'd ever known him make, letting the lad take his precious haversack with him. Still, packing a bag was easy work when you'd little enough to put in it, no wonder Tom thought it no bother to pack and repack. Tom loved that haversack. Bill had brought it back from his year in South Africa, that first war against the Boers, and if you held it close you could smell sand and dirt still, time and hard work ingrained.

Bill had joined up aged just eighteen, keen to see the world. It had seemed as good an idea as any at the time, a poor city lad needed to find a new way to make a penny, and the army was recruiting. This was long before he and Ida started courting. With a good ten years on Ida, Bill'd had a bit more life by the time they met, but even so, he rarely spoke of his time over there, except to say it changed him and no more than that. He'd plenty to say on how it had changed the country, how both of the South African wars had set the working man on his way to making England what it bloody well ought to be, a country fit for the working man. Not the war itself, mind, wasn't war that'd made the change, but the lads who came back, eyes open to what having an Empire actually meant – wars fought over dominions already slipping from the old queen's grasp, wars that proved the toffs had no more right to run the country than Bill himself did. No more sense neither, half the time.

And now Tom was heading off on his own with his mates, and already there was the new National Insurance and the Trade Boards telling bosses their thieving days were numbered, and maybe even votes for women, one day. Bill was all for Ida having the vote,

Smart girl, our Ida, no reason why not, if only those daft bints'd concentrate on the vote. Once they start banging on about temperance, they've lost me. And don't tell me half the ladies round here don't like a pint or more of an evening and all.

When Bill came back from South Africa he knew himself a changed man all right, with ears that could still hear the boom and the scream, nose that held the stink of blood and piss and shit if ever he let himself slip into a daydream. Damn good job he worked such early hours and so many days in a row, the dreams that came on his day off were never any fun. No, Bill didn't speak about what had happened when he was over there, but he'd kept the haversack, and he'd given it to Tom for the trip.

Here lad, something to pack your kit in. You take care of it, mind, been with me a long time, that has.

Tom had never even been allowed to hold the haversack before now, he didn't need reminding to take care.

In Itzhak's house, the lodgers had been awake and praying since dawn, washing before praying. The older one of the two, with the cough, racking his lungs since he began to move about, the other, the quieter one, offered sips of water that were turned down, the cough continued. Saturday morning was always an early start. The lodgers worked for Jewish bosses and so, unlike many Jewish workers with no option but to give up the Sabbath for toil, their Saturday was spent in shul. Nathan and David woke up early too, but to Itzhak it seemed as if they woke early only to complain. The bread not fresh enough, the house too hot. Soon they would be gone to work, neither had any interest in finding Jewish firms who'd let them have their Saturdays free, they'd no intention of working Sundays to make up for it. Once the house was quiet, the clatter and bulk of men gone from the rooms, Itzhak and his mother would look under Nathan's bed and take the knapsack he kept there, the one he'd already refused his little brother three times.

Mimi agreed with Nathan, as it happened. They did have a busy household, there was little enough private as it was, and Nathan had bought the knapsack with his own money, so it was his property to lend, or not, as he wanted. She also knew that there was no money to buy Itzhak a knapsack of his own and so she meant to defy her firstborn and put up with his temper later. If she could not teach her boys to share, then clearly she had failed as a mother, she would take the consequences.

What Mimi didn't explain to Itzhak or to her father-in-law, both of whom worried that one day Nathan would follow through with his violent threats, was that yes, Itzhak was her baby, but Nathan was the baby that had made her a woman. The day it became clear, from a twitch in her belly and a fullness in her breasts, that she would be a mother, that was the day she finally felt she was a woman. The mikvah had not given her this, nor the wedding veil, nor the chuppah, becoming a mother was what gave her womanhood. Mimi had not enjoyed being a girl, the rules and regulations were too confining, too demanding. It wasn't as if there weren't plenty of rules for mothers and wives, but for Mimi motherhood also brought a kind of freedom, a widening of her love, of her desires too, an opening of herself. It was Nathan who had given her motherhood.

Mimi knew her firstborn son, held him in her even now in a way she had never held anything before or since. Nathan might rant and shout, but he would never raise a hand to her. And later, a week or more later, after whatever fearsome row they had had, one night when Mimi was up working late, and the house was quiet, Nathan, who never slept well, would come down and sit with her and they would talk, about her childhood or his, the things he remembered, so much he remembered for one so young with so much life ahead. They would talk about his dreams and, with the light only on Mimi's hands, whatever piece-work she was sewing that night, Nathan would also tell her his fears from a chair in shadow. His fear that he might not be big enough to live up to his hopes, that he was not as good-looking as David, as clever as Itzhak, that there was so much he wanted to do and so much he wanted to be and he honestly didn't know if he had it in him. And that was why Mimi knew her firstborn son's threats were all mouth, because she also knew the reach of his dreams and how they scared him.

For now though, there was a knapsack to be fetched, whatever Nathan had hidden in it must be found and not remarked upon, and Itzhak's clothes to be packed for his two-week trip. And this before they went up to Waterloo, a walk together, and then she must hurry home and make the meal for her big boys and her husband and the lodgers, a meal that would satisfy both those who had been praying since five and those who planned to be out on the town half the night. She wished the Scouts had picked another day to begin their camping trip, a more godless day to begin their camping trip.

Eighteen

Where Tom had barely slept for excitement, down the road at Charlie Hatch's home, Emily Smarts also lay awake, in pain. At two she heard a church clock chiming somewhere to the south, perhaps St Peter's, lovely inside, Emily remembered, unsure if St Peter's had a bell or not, it should have had a bell, surely. She used to love popping down there when Rose was a baby and they were first living round this way. Not her local church, but the one she'd picked for her churching anyway.

The priest had been all, Oh you must go to your own church, the chap at St John's is a lovely fellow, I don't want to be upsetting other priests, I have to work with these people.

Emily hadn't liked to tell him she had no intention of being in anyone's congregation, she cared more for the building than the man looking after it, but she insisted, quietly, that St Peter's it was. And the priest took her word for it, his church or no church at all. So there she'd stood, on his steps, a first-time mother and that babe in her arms couldn't have been more than a week old, and the spring weather dreadful. She'd made the effort to come halfway down to Camberwell, it was not up to him to question the spirit that had brought her.

Emily couldn't recall the priest's name now, but she remembered the drop of his shoulders, the surrendering shrug, what could he do but take them in and give them the blessing? Not so much in fashion now, churching, in Emily's day it had been a serious matter, couldn't let more than a couple of weeks go by without getting out of your bed, no matter how bad a birth you'd had, and off to be welcomed back into God's fold. Not that many round here had occasion to lie in bed, mind.

Emily's attendance had been a high-days-and-holidays churchgoing at the best of times, and she'd certainly not been since the sickness got her, but she could still smell St Peter's now, hearing the chime and thinking of it. And she did try to think of it, when she could, the better to hide the stink of her own breath, the rancid sweetness that told her it wasn't long now. Emily bit her teeth down hard to stop herself wishing her life away as another wave of pain hit and she was sweating she was trying so hard not to scream, not to wake the whole street. St Peter's, the church, yes, back there, in St Peter's the light had always felt warm, something to do with the candles and the incense, with the windows letting in more light than most churches. All that sky and there was the open space inside, above the pews, cool white with a place for God in the air and the light. Emily was thinking this as she listened to the distant bell chime the half hour through the summer night, as she willed herself not to wail in pain, and then an animal keening slipped from her twisted mouth anyway.

Rose sat up with Emily for the next while, in the part-light before dawn when the blackbirds and sparrows began their call, and when the light finally filtered down through the thin cloud Rose was surprised her mother was still breathing, heart still staggering against her ribs. Surprised that anyone could withstand such pain, and Emily so thin, nothing of her but the disease now. She'd given her as many of Ida's drops as she dared, just one every ten minutes or so, despite Emily's mewling cries for more, more. Even as she counted them out, Rose knew she'd keep giving, and maybe they'd cart her off and hang her for it, but Rose couldn't stand it, the piteous bleats whenever she made Emily wait a moment more for a drop.

It was gone five before Emily slept, a rasp of breath in the back of her throat the only thing that told Rose it was sleep and not death, despite the grey of her mother's skin. Charlie was up, he fetched a bit of bread and jam for himself and he brought some in for Rose as well, with a cup of strong tea to dip it in. She needed the tea. The end of the loaf it was, Charlie said he'd ask his sister to make up an extra batch of dough for them and pop it in when she took her own bread down to the baker's big oven. Rose was grateful, she didn't think she could face baking today, her red eyes itching from the night awake. Charlie told Rose to make sure the boy knew to mind himself, mind his manners, do as he was asked, but not to forget either, that he was a Hatch and no one's fool. Rose asked didn't he want to kiss the boy goodbye, and Charlie blushed. He'd kissed the sleeping lad already, ruffled his hair and all, didn't say so to Rose but the look on Charlie's face told her she was stupid to have asked.

Rose nodded as the front door closed, she loved Charlie as much when he was gruff as when he showed the soft of him, both sides to the one man. She listened to him heading up the street, through the alley to the lane where the barrows were kept in lockups, off to the market, to his work, to his day and she would rather have been anywhere than here, anywhere than sitting beside her dying mother, and oh what a wicked woman she must have been to feel this way.

Twenty minutes more passed and Rose, who'd been dozing without realising, heard a noise that brought her red eyes wide and she sat up so swiftly she felt a twinge go in her back. The noise was Emily clearing her throat and maybe this was it, the death rattle Rose had been waiting for. But what she saw was Emily awake, quite rested, almost easy.

Your tea'll be cold now love, shall we have another, the two of us? And a bite of that bread, if there's any left? I heard Charlie say there was jam, didn't I? I could just fancy a mouthful of raspberry jam.

Smiling for her mother, Rose got up to the kitchen and cursed herself for having wished the old woman away, for having given in to the dark of the night. Not today. It would not be today.

Jimmy hadn't expected to sleep, hadn't been able to sleep all the rest of the week, nor Itzhak, nor Tom, but in case he did fall asleep, he'd tapped his head six times on the pillow, just like his dad did – though Charlie's head hit the pillow five times – to make sure he woke for six o'clock. And then he lay down determined to stay awake, thinking of sailing and camping, of tying knots and winning badges, stalking the enemy and swimming in the real sea, but here it was morning and he must have missed six o'clock, though he'd had a dream of his father, of Charlie kissing him goodbye, telling him to be a good lad, good man.

He readied himself for camp, carefully packing his few things into one of the big bags his father used to carry stock. The bag was half-knapsack, half-mule-pack and all hessian. It was not old with a story of its own like the haversack Tom was borrowing from his dad, nor was it almost new and very flash like the knapsack Itzhak planned to half-inch from Nathan, but it was a market-lad's bag. To Jimmy, more of a Hatch than Charlie gave him credit for, it was a badge of pride to carry a market-lad's bag. It felt grown-up and proper. The whole trip felt very grown-up, and Jimmy couldn't wait.

Jimmy kissed Rose goodbye, and she gave him a chunk of seedy cake, an apple and a fat crust of the new bread Ida had popped in with, just out of the oven and all gooey inside it was so fresh. The bread was slathered with both jam and marg, unheard of to have both at once, a going-away gift of sweet fruit and fat. The cake was wrapped in paper, and the bread in a clean cloth. Already the marg and jam were dripping through the warm slices, staining from the inside out. They sat in the top of his bag, with another cloth beneath to keep his clothes clean. Charlie was down the market and Rose was to stay with Emily. The other boys, all the other lads from his own patrol, and most of the ones from the troop had someone coming to wave them off, not Jimmy. He accepted one more cuddle from his mother, then left his kiss, gentle as you like, on Emily's head, wondering if his nan would be dead and gone before he was back. He left the front room holding an odd sadness tight in his chest. Rose didn't need him to cry now, she'd more than enough on her plate and he'd not upset his mother for the world. But then Emily started choking again and Rose's only concern had to be for her mother, so Jimmy let himself out the front door.

He waved to a couple of the girls from their school, more a raise of a chin than a wave, but Jimmy Hatch was a good-looking lad and liked, so the girls crowded round and they were all, Ooh, where are you off to Jimmy Hatch? Proper market-lad you look with your dad's bag.

Jimmy took their talk and the glances and felt that he could get used to this, that he might like being noticed. He looked kindly on their hopscotch, just a girls' game, while he was off to sail a real ship, down the finest river in the world. At the top of their street he stepped into the noise and fuss of the Walworth Road, all trams and people, harassed mothers, grown-ups off shopping and children playing and big strong men hauling carts this way and that. Jimmy had never known anything but Walworth, this street, had never known anything but exactly where he stood, at this moment. He turned right and headed north, up to the Elephant, leaving his whole world behind him. He could not have been more excited and more frightened and more thrilled. It would take him fifteen minutes to Waterloo, to walk away from home. He reached behind himself into the bag for his bread and unwrapped it quickly, still just warm.

It's good bread, Jimmy thought to himself, nodding in approval, liking the way the bread had been brought by his dad's sister, to care for his mother's mother. This was how they did it, looking out for each other.

It's what we do, we look after each other, Aunty Ida had said, when she asked Jimmy if he wanted to walk up to the river with her and Tom.

No thanks Aunty Ida, I'm fine to go by myself.

Jimmy Hatch walked away from his home and family for the first time in his life, whistling between bites, a mouth full of soft bread and jam and marg and joy.

Nineteen

Rose sat back now that Emily was sleeping again, knocked out from a violent bilious attack and as ill as she had been suddenly awake just three hours earlier. Rose looked across to the wishbone on the mantelpiece, the one she'd wound about with old red flannel, and had given Jimmy last night to keep under his pillow while he was away.

He'd given it back laughing at her, What pillow Ma? Sailors don't have pillows. Keep it for me indoors, I'll have no bother with bad dreams where we're off, I'll be too tired to dream.

Jimmy had patted her shoulder like he was the man and she the girl, and then Emily had called again, her voice sharp from a new onslaught of stabbing pain and Rose shifted from mother to daughter, from worrier to nurse, as she brushed a quick kiss on her son's forehead.

Mimi stood on the dock, Itzhak was already on board with his mates, with all the other lads. He was not crying, definitely not crying. Not looking towards his mother though either, just in case. Mimi shuffled to the back of the crowd as they gathered, not wanting to embarrass her boy, not wanting to be that mother, the one who wouldn't let him go, and not wanting him to go at all. Her hand tight at her neck, holding the silver hand. It wasn't a real chamsa, like Shimon's mother's, but it would do to hold her prayer, protect her boy from any evil, any harm. She brought it to her lips, edged further back into the crowd, she would not have Itzhak see her tears.

Tom had sent Ida home when they turned into Lower Marsh, man enough to carry his father's haversack and man enough to walk the last few streets up to the river alone. Ida let him go on his way and hoped Bill would remember that he'd said he'd look over from the railway yard, see if he couldn't get a glimpse of the ship. She'd wanted to see the ship for herself, see the vessel that would carry her boy. She turned to south again and she could feel her son's hand in her own as she did so. Ida looked down and her hand was empty, but here was Tom's hand, hot and sticky at two years old; now his hand freezing and too dry when he was five and had been so ill with a fever that left his chest, neck and face burning, his limbs chilled; here was his hand that day he'd come home, palm red with welts from the thrashing he'd taken from the teacher, a big fellow that even Ida was scared to speak back to, but not Bill. Bill had marched up to the school and given the man what for, what did he think he was about? Thrashing a boy half his size, nothing manly about that, nothing big about it at all. And here was Tom's hand now, the hand he'd squeezed hers with as he kissed it,

Don't you worry Ma, I'll be fine.

He walked on to Waterloo, and Ida watched him go, her boy who was not a baby. When she got home she checked under his pillow. Good, the angel was gone, she'd been worried he'd left it at home, had meant to remind him this morning to take it with him. And though she told herself she was daft for thinking it made a blind bit of difference, she felt better anyway.

Lining up at Waterloo, the lads said goodbye to worried mothers and proud fathers, envious brothers and doting little sisters. They boarded the Arethusa, Scouts and Scoutmaster and a few fathers along for the journey, some of them naval men, ready to help out if needed, happy just to sit and watch and pass on old sailing yarns if not. Their gear was stored first, shipshape and Bristol fashion, then they stood at attention for inspection. This handkerchief was knotted a little more tightly, that lanyard placed more correctly, those socks pulled right up to the knees. There was a speech about safety, then one about duty, respect, not just for the ship and for the sea when they get there, but also for the river, our old Father Thames, a different fellow altogether as they sailed out past our London banks, they'd find that out soon enough.

The twenty-four Scouts were set tasks, no matter that they were hungry to be actually sailing, there was the tide to wait on and work to do for now. This patrol was sent to plot their course on the maps, that one to practise lookout, another to go below and learn a few more secrets of the ship. Those looking on from the bridge pulled their summer coats closer as a wind picked up along the water.

Watchers on the dock, finally understanding that their concern for their sons and brothers would not make the tide change any faster, eventually grew fidgety, small children began to ask still-worried mothers for a walk or a drink or a bite of something to eat. It was time to go. Several waved their goodbyes now, waves that were returned by boys who happened to be looking up from one of their tasks, ignored by others already immersed. The sky was dark grey, hanging low, they were lucky it had held off for now, a rotten summer so far and it didn't look as if the rest of the day would bring anything better.

Half an hour more and even the boys engaged in their tasks were fidgety too, was it now? Would they sail soon? When would the tide be right? Was it now? Tom took the penknife out of his pocket, polished it, and put it back a dozen or more times, thinking how much better he'd done on the deal, angel for knife. Then the noon chimes began, each one crossing the other, a deep boom cut into with a sharp chime, and that undercut with an old cracked bell and a broken tone. Notes rang out from Big Ben of course, but now that they were right here on the water they could clearly hear the bells of St Mary le Strand to the north and St John's in the south, its big white portico just like the ones in Brixton and at Kennington, a little grubbier perhaps, so much closer to the centre of the city. Just after the hour, there was a clatter of trains, from the new platforms at Waterloo Station, people heading home to the suburbs after their morning's work in town.

A few minutes later there was a shift. The boys could feel it, their Scoutmaster felt it, and it was confirmed by the fellow from the Arethusa herself, this was the pull they'd been waiting for. The cutter shuddered once, shuddered again and then, creaking as she went, seemed to ready herself. The tide was with them. It was time.

Ropes were untied, loops made, they began to move off, London slid past. The Arethusa rolled gently with the current, drawn into the correct lane of the busy river by a combination of skill and nature, centuries of sailors' understanding of the Thames and the very latest knowledge of tides and weather, forecasts and forethought, Baden-Powell's ever-present preparation. Waterloo slipped by, fathers placed protective arms around mothers, little brothers and sisters longed to be on board. One or two of the more enterprising older children ran alongside, but were soon stopped as the docks became busier, gates and pallets and off-loaded bales, bundles, ropes and fist-thick chains blocked their way. The cutter sailed on, the rolling became more rhythmic, or perhaps the lads on board were already used to it, already loving the pull of the tide. Now there was the rich green of the Inner Temple's gardens beyond the Victoria Embankment, the grass thick and lush from the wet weather. Both sides would be lined with docks soon enough, as the ship passed, busy with work and workers even before they got to Blackfriars Bridge, and so much busier thereafter, but the Scoutmaster saw the green of the north bank and the soot of the south bank as a sign, an approval. A faithful young man, this was why he gave up his free time, why he worked hard at his job, but harder still to bring joy into the lives of these Walworth lads. Their daily lives did not involve walks in the neatly laid-out gardens along the river, afternoons of cricket on well-kept greens. They would eat well in camp at Sheppey, work and play outdoors every day, come rain or shine, and they would benefit from the fresh sea air. In a fortnight's time he would bring back lads unrecognisable from the peaky boys now onboard. He would give them their own green, sea green, wilder and better than any in town. He smiled at the idea and then, as quickly as the smile had arrived it was checked, an arrogance to think he was the one bringing these lads to fresh air and the sea. This was the work of many, and of the Lord, and they would give thanks tonight, in prayer under the stars. The statue of the old queen came into view at Blackfriars as a drop of rain fell on his forehead and he shrugged, they could pray just as well under a damp sail if need be.

All the lads were up on deck now with tasks to keep them busy, polishing and knot-practice and the like, but the adults onboard knew that the boys were more interested in watching what was going by, and they couldn't begrudge them that. Some of the fathers were more interested in the sights too. Two of the men were navy themselves, and one a merchant seaman, but the Thames had changed so fast in their own lifetimes and there was new building work at almost every dock, bigger ships off-loading in deeper docks, brand new container buildings and warehouses going up to replace the old ones, fine new electric lighting in many of them too. Further downriver they saw the works for the almost-finished Woolwich Foot Tunnel, that was progress all right, Mr Crooks was a friend of the working man, one of them himself. The south London working man was always last remembered when the big chaps in Parliament were making their plans, at least now they'd be able to get across to the docks of the East End without going all round the houses, earn an honest bob without it taking half the morning to get to work. Then the working man might have a bit more time for what else there was besides work, like coming away with your lad on a cutter down the river, or taking your wife and little ones up to Hampstead Heath for a picnic. Or maybe even working with the unions, building up the working man. Chances were Mr Crooks had that in mind as well, no flies on him.

They were down to Erith by nine that evening, it was a long slog, but there'd been a light wind with them most of the journey and none of it was dull for the boys. The weather had not let up for a moment, a slow, fine drizzle right into the evening. Spirits were high, and the singing helped, good scouting songs and one or two more lively Walworth tunes thrown in, censored of course, both by the helper dads and the lads themselves, they knew better than to get up a blush on their Dulwich Mission Scoutmaster. They were all fond of the young man, he wasn't one for too much of the holier than thou, and he wasn't even that keen on the sound of his own voice for a toff, a kind of toff at least, so a few lyrics were fudged or sung under their breath when they got to the saucy bits. It was gone ten before two of the older men took over the watch, little red lights from their fags marking their places on the ship, the giggles and murmurs from exhausted lads died out and the last of the boys were sleeping. Or not.

Jimmy Hatch lay under the damp sail on a damp deck and cursed his cousin Tom. He didn't enjoy the roll of the ship and he didn't like lying here and he hadn't meant to let it show, had been screwing up his eyes and face in the late twilight for half an hour or more to stop it, but there it went, a flamin' tear falling down his face and his nose running and all, and now his chest wanted to heave and he was damned if he was going to let out the sob that wanted to come, he was a Hatch and if it ever got back to his dad, he'd never hear the end of it. Jimmy set his teeth, top jaw against lower, and set his mind to stopping himself crying. How could he be feeling rotten now, missing home and his ma, when everyone else was having such a great lark of it? And it was only one night, there were two more weeks of this yet. He was the one who'd walked to Waterloo by himself, hadn't needed his mother's hand to bring him, as much a man as any of them snuffling and farting in their sleep alongside him. Then, through the dark, carefully, he felt a hand on his shoulder, a whisper in his ear.

Who's that?

Me. Itzhak.

What do you want?

Jimmy's voice was gruff, he shrugged away the hand.

I'm just ... it's ... nothing.

Jimmy turned to his mate and he peered at the dark space where Itzhak must be, the late summer light almost gone, darker still with the heavy damp sail over them.

You all right? Jimmy asked.

Thinking about my ma. Hope Nathan doesn't give her a hard time when he sees his knapsack gone.

Jimmy was relieved not to be the only one, and glad of his friend, and rubbed a sleeve across his snotty nose and poked his mate in the ribs.

You're a soft bugger, Itzhak. Course she's all right. Now go to sleep.

And when Jimmy rolled over and when Itzhak heard his friend's breath steady, and felt that the stifled sobs had eased from his mate's body, Itzhak too, allowed himself to fall asleep.

Tom lay awake, last to fall asleep indoors, and last to do so now. He didn't mind, he lay on his back and listened to the creak of the timbers, the shush of the water, the breath of his mates close by, and felt it deep inside, the thrill of something coming.

Twenty

On the watch, in the light drizzle of the dull summer night, nearing the midnight toll, Harold, a naval man, father to one of the sleeping boys, reached into his pocket for his tin of tobacco and felt for the stone he kept there. Just an ordinary stone, but a hole right through the middle. Not for finding by yourself these witch's stones, anyone knew that, did you no good if you went searching for them, but if you happened to stumble upon one, or be given it, then it carried the power of a charm. His mother, may she rest in peace, she'd had this one hanging outside the front door of the old house, when they lived in the country, in Kent, when he was a lad. When the family moved to the city it came with her. No front door of their own to hang it by, no room for him and his four brothers and sisters in the same bed neither, but London was where the work was and so they all came up, his family and his mother's sister's family, and cousins too.

When they finally managed to rent a couple of rooms in Kennington, just behind the big church, she'd hung the stone above the door to their part of the shared house, and no one minded. When the stone did no good saving her against the croup, when she died a week after it had taken their father, that was it, the girls went to service, one brother to the army, the other took himself back to Kent. Left alone, Harold decided he'd had the city up to the back teeth, so he took the stone down from above the door, put it in his pocket and there it stayed, through all his voyages, right to this one. And here he was, at midnight on the water, the time he always felt most alive. He hadn't seen either of his brothers since they went their separate ways, had met one of the sisters and her husband for a drink at their pub down in Streatham, but it was a long way to go to catch up and they'd not found enough to say to do it a second time. The other sister wrote to him once a month from the big house where she worked way out in Ealing, but mostly Harold had felt, and for such a long time, that it was only him, him alone.

He'd survived two turns out with naval brigades, once against the Boers and then again in China, and like so many of his mates, had come home changed. He got himself a job on the docks, took up with a nice girl, and they'd started their own family. All the while the stone stayed in his pocket, rattling alongside his tobacco tin. And then the accident happened. Loading a crane he'd been, and a rotten, foggy day it was at that. Almost time for the whistle, he was hanging on for the end of the shift, and somehow the load had slipped off the crane, the chain holding the load together must have snapped, or never been fixed right in the first place, he had no time to find out which, he was halfway up a stack of china tea chests and had only time to

180

hear the crash and look round before he saw the end of the broken chain whipping back round and coming right for him, he put up his arm to shield his face and turned in to bend his body, small as he could, years of dodging his big brothers' blows had taught him that much, and then the whiplash chain hit him hard, and then he fell.

When he came to he was laid out in the yard office and his mates were gathered round.

They laughed when they showed him what they'd found, Your bloody tobacco tin and your crazy witch's stone stopped the edge of the chain, stopped it going right into you.

Would've had your kidney out, that's for sure.

Or a chunk of spine, I'd say.

You're a bloody lucky man, Harold.

And a hookey one too, keeping a charm in your pocket like that.

They laughed, and Harold pulled himself up, and with a mate on either side they stopped in at the Crown and Anchor for a few on the way home, to toast his health and toast the tobacco tin and toast the stone with the hole in it and all. A few more at the King George and one last pint at the Three Stags and he'd finally been delivered home to a worried wife who only stopped her going on when she saw the look of the whack he'd taken on his back.

The story didn't make much sense when she put him to bed, but the sight of the bruise next day, and the one that flowered across his lower back, all down his right buttock and leg, growing deeper and darker over the rest of the week, showed he'd had luck on his side. The errant chunk of snapped chain, moving faster and sharper even than the hook itself, had punctured the tobacco tin, and gone straight through into the stone behind, taking the edge of it at the centre, but no further. It didn't puncture him, and Harold and his wife both believed the broken chain would have gone straight through to the kidney without the stone to stop it. Yes he could have thanked the tobacco tin, but he thanked the stone. The bruise had been a sight for weeks, and his shoulder gave him trouble even now, a couple of years down the line, but here he was, on the Arethusa, and in another few hours it would be time to cast off again. Lovely for the lads to be out of the city. Lovely for them to come home to it too, they were London boys after all.

Harold felt the stone as he put back the tin and brought the cigarette to his lips, maybe it was time to hand the stone on to the boy. His lad loved to play with it, giving it on would be a nice thing to do, if only the little beggar didn't manage to lose it. He'd give it to him when they woke the boys up, they'd be setting off by four at the latest, just before dawn, the tide'd be with them then, off on the last leg round to Sheppey. The lad could put it in his own pocket and may it keep him as safe when they left them at the camp. Though he'd tell his son not to mention it indoors, his wife already thought he was far too soft on the boy, couldn't believe it when he said he'd miss a day's work to come along today. Best to keep it between themselves, man to man.

Three thirty and the boys were wakened. Come four o'clock everyone was ready, what little bedding they had was rolled away, packets of bread and marg handed out to hungry lads, the Arethusa set sail.

Sunrise was at four twenty-nine and the boys smiled through the continuing drizzle, as they sailed into the east and the wet sun and their camp, a strong wind with them and their songs ringing out to wake any sleepy fishermen still in bed. Out past Canvey Island to the north, All Hallows on Sea to the south. It was a long morning but a good one for the boys, and Tom and Itzhak and Jimmy sang their hearts out, nodding heads and tapping feet in time to the shanties. Then they rounded Warden Point and came right into a rough rain squall and quickly, lads, look smart, get a move on, all hands to bail out the water that came in for a good while. Two o'clock came and the boys were wet through, most of them, with no fancy oilskins like their Scoutmaster and that chap from the Arethusa, but it didn't matter and they sang louder still because now they could see the sea, the real, proper sea. This was it, opening wide before them, the North Sea itself and they really were sailing now, rain and waves and obeying orders and quick to and on with it. What did a bit of rain bother them? They were Scouts and they were sailors and camp wasn't far away now, not far at all. There'd be a fire and hot food and warm drinks and tents to sleep in and a good kip tonight, a fine kip tonight. If this rain would only clear they should be able to see the camp, and perhaps they could, perhaps that was it over there, the darker patch there, just where the squall squared off? Yes, perhaps it was.

Twenty-One

There is a way that the wind can change, a catch of the breath, a hiccup almost, nothing more than a hiatus and then, it comes back at you faster than it had been going in the other direction, knocking down anything in its way, comes at you as if it is doing so with intent and purpose. As if the wind itself has a mind of its own, a mind to slap you down. Every experienced sailor knows this wind, the one you cannot fight, the one where your best bet is to hang tight, see it through. Every experienced sailor knows the only thing is to hang on for dear life, work with your mates, maybe, if you can get to them, work with them into the wind, with the wind. If the wind will let you. The sailor hears that in-breath, the way the world sucks itself in before letting go with a furnace blast of a wind that has whipped around and attacks from nowhere. The sailor hears it and knows there is nothing he can do, no way to be prepared. Every experienced seaman knows the time will come when that wind gets him or his mate, when leather-tanned skin and calloused hands are not up to the task of holding the ship to a wind-beaten course, when the best-built boat gives in, gives over. Every experienced sailor knows it is only a matter of time. Some you win, others you lose, the elements and the sea are not to be fought, they are to be ridden out. And if your number is called, then down you go.

The boys of the 2nd Walworth were not experienced sailors.

They'd had their swimming lessons at Manor Place Baths and their swimming badges to prove accomplishment, they'd done very well in the Earl's Court Sea Scout rally just the month before, even though they weren't actual Sea Scouts, even though the sea in question was a man-made lake. They were not experienced sailors.

Tom didn't know what had hit him. He was sitting with Jimmy, the pair of them enjoying the passing of the squall, their clothes wet, their hair dripping, the grins on their faces bright as they sighted the camp.

There, see the white-painted cones? That's us, that's our camp.

Other boys stood up to look, their Scoutmaster came along to say yes, they would put about in a moment, ready to run in, close to shore.

Itzhak joined his friends, making up Tom's patrol of six. Other lads got into their own patrols.

Here we are mates, here we nearly are.

And there was a bubbling joy in their hearts, boy hearts wanting to be men, lads who were pleased to be with their friends. Jimmy wasn't saying so out loud, but he was pleased too, to be getting off this damn boat. He'd found it harder than expected, the wind and the rain, the way the movement of the ship drove the rain down his back, up the frayed cuffs of his third-hand sleeves. He hadn't known how much he minded being wet, there'd been plenty of afternoons on the stall when he'd stood helping his father or some other family member, Charlie had him always ready to take a stand behind a stall if needed for another Hatch. Jimmy hadn't ever minded it much, not even though East Lane was a wind tunnel in the dead of winter, an alley of lashing rain often as not. But at least the ground was firm beneath his feet. Ah well, nearly there, and no one but Itzhak had seen he wasn't having fun with it. Tom still didn't know that Jimmy would happily have chucked the whole thing in at five o'clock this morning, when they'd cast off and he got another eyeful of wind-belted rain. Jimmy was pleased with himself, he'd kept his mouth shut and there Tom was, still going on about what great sailors they were, the lot of them, not one in his patrol seasick or complaining. Jimmy reckoned he wasn't the only one who'd kept his mouth shut, but they all liked Tom, they wanted him to be proud of them. Right enough too, it'd be over soon.

The ship went belly up, turtle up, up and over, up the wrong way, no right way, the squall smacked into them, it was the squall they'd already sailed out of, maybe another, the wind was hard south-west, sharp about from the more gentle south wind, and this new wind smacked them over and now there was a rough lop on the water, the tide pulling strong and then there were lads in the water, lads under the capsized, upturned boat, lads all about and none of it made sense and

they couldn't see the shore and

some of the lads were under the boat, they must be under the boat, here was a Scoutmaster, barely in his twenties, crying out for his boys, and here the young fellow from the Arethusa, only a year or two older than the Scouts himself, he could see lads clinging to the overturned ship and

under the boat was pitch black, the ship a midnight sky of sails and tangled ropes and bare deck raining down and

how could they tell what was under, what over, what under

hang on, here's help coming, the coastguard has sounded the alarm, he'd been waiting for the boat, waiting all night as it happened, and then he'd seen this, dear God, seen it with his own eyes and in sight of the shore, in sight of their camp too, mother of mercy, save the lads, and the alarm rang out and

they came running to the lifeboats

hang on and

how much longer under there? Pockets of air and pockets filled with water, penknives and gobstoppers and an old stone with a hole in it and string, so much string – why do boys always carry string in their pockets – fell out, fell into the sea, down in the sea

and heavy boots full of water pulled him down, pulled him down, and him, and him, this one too and

then there were big hands, strong hands, a father's hands – not mine, my daddy, I want my, want my – but big hands nonetheless, pulling him out of the water, up and out and into a lifeboat and there, here was air to breathe and the

187

black sky that was no sky turned to grey again, a good, grey English sky on the good, grey English coast and

under the boat, under the ship, which was it? Which was she? Which was he now? Dead or alive? and

then the turn, she righted herself, the Arethusa, right up, upright, standing in the water in which the boys were sinking, pockets filling, she was made for this, made to turn upright again, a training vessel, she was a good girl in the water, a better girl on the water, so many boys in the water and

the lads who'd been hanging on, just hanging on, to the upturned hull, were thrown off. Up and off and back and down, so far down, and

drown

don't drown

breathe, you're safe now, in the lifeboat now, here you are lad, there you are boy, spit it out, there's a good lad, that's the way and

salt water and bile spewed from his throat and it burned, a good burn, retching up the sea he had swallowed and

the sea was swallowing them

one

after

the

other

the man was in a heavy coat, too heavy for the water, he tried to take it off, to pull his arms out of it, eventually his effort was rewarded and the old greatcoat floated free, leaving him able to dive for boys, small boys, small south London boys with not enough good green vegetables and rich red meat and strong fresh air to make them big and robust like the country lads he was used to working with, the seaside lads who swam this coast nine months out of twelve, he was diving for lads, an oystercatcher, catching boys, lost boys

and

it didn't stop. The wind, the sea, the waves, the grey, the water, the sky and the sea together, the water, it didn't stop, flowing into eyes, ears, nose, mouth, the water flows and pulls, tugging at the shirtsleeves, let me in, can I come in? Please can I come in. I'm coming in

hungry water, angry water

and

it didn't stop

Twenty-Two

It was not the falling off that hurt, it was hitting the water.
This was not the falling – jumping – from a city bridge into
the hard, fast-flowing Thames. This was not the deliber-
ate – accidental – drop from life to no-life that a long fall
might create, turning gentle water into a moving wall. And
yet, hitting this water did hurt. It hurt the boyish pride,
that almost-man pride, the belief, foolish as it turned out,
that had insisted, I could stand here, stay here, survive.
Tom had been so proud, of his uniform, of his patrol, of
bringing his friends to the Scouts, of bringing the Scouts to
his friends. He had taken both pleasure and pride in these
accomplishments, in his ability, in his sea legs. Tom had
neither sea legs, nor tail, nor fins. Tom was a swimmer, yes,
but a baths-swimmer, a creek-swimmer, a pond-swimmer.
Tom was not a sea-swimmer in a squall, when a rough
wind hit and their ship was upturned, overturned, Tom's
hopes overturned.

And even then, all was not lost, because others could
swim, and swim well. Scoutmasters and fathers and other

boys had ability, were possessed of badge-worthy proficiency, and there were hands to hold, ropes to hang on to, and the water that was so very different to the river, or the pond, the water that was far saltier than Tom had expected, saltier as it slapped his face again and again, the water was still below his chin. Tom could have whistled if he wanted. He thought of the mermaids and of whistling sailors and he feared that this was not the South Seas, there could be no mermaids this far north, there was no reason to be afraid, no reason to be saved. This was England, this was home, we have no mermaids in British waters. This was not home. Now the sea was a salt-lick at his lips, his father had told him of the salt-cake the men were given to eat when they were working on the engines, stoking coal into hungry fires, and the sweat running off them and salt pouring from their bodies, so they had to lick salt-cake, harried to lick it by the bosses, lest they pass out and the fire be untended for a moment. Lick, lick, licking his lips dry with salt.

Below his eyes. The water was below Tom's eyes. It flowed over his mouth and his nose, once, twice, three times, but then suddenly he was up high again, and the water was down by his midriff. How did his midriff come to be bare? To be naked? Why was his shirt undone? Had the sea done that? Tom thought this and then another thought darted across his flickering mind, a mind confused by the lack of a shirt, and thinking about mermaids and how they too were bare-breasted, Tom wondered about being prepared. What was the preparation for this? He was not prepared for this, and he had not prepared his friends for this, and if he could lift his head above the water that was almost covering him now, suddenly covering his chest, neck, mouth, nose, the cold cold water on a day that had been so soft, so calm, if he could lift his head out of the sea, lift his eyes – lift mine eyes unto the hills, was that a song? a prayer? Had he learned it in Sunday school? He hadn't been often enough to Sunday school – Tom thought he might see those friends. But he could not and he could not and then. Then there were hands holding him and it was good, it was going to be all well, all well and good as he, they, were still in the water, in the sea, still choking and swallowing and choking again on brown twists of sea water, but even so, Tom was breathing. Tom was alive. At this moment Tom was still coming home to Ida.

It was a wish, a hope, a possibility. There was still enough wind in his lungs to make a wish. Right now, Tom was alive.

There were other boys who were not alive. They were being pulled from the water, dragged into lifeboats, turned over, their backs slapped, slammed, beaten by hopeful coastguards, hopeful helpers, hope that was giving up the ghost, transitioning already from boy to body.

Ida was down the lane, at home in the market, in her place, on the barrow. She was looking along the lane at the work and the weft of her life, the threads that were family as Charlie boomed from his own barrow three up from hers, and the seams that were friends, Tilly rushing, no time to stop for a natter, a pint later. After Tilly was Samson, just coming into the lane, on his back a clattering clutter of pots all tied together, their clanking announcing his coming. Ida smiled at the sound of the man and thought of her Bill, this heavy day ahead of him, they'd both shaken their heads at it first thing this morning, a half shift on top of his own, covering for a friend and sharing the extra with a mate, but better to take the extra work in summer if they could, winter with them soon enough and they'd need the extra for the coal. Maybe there'd be enough to put some aside and still leave over a little for a treat. High summer now, if you could call it that, and school starting soon enough and Ida knew they ought to buy the boy some new shoes, but Tilly thought she might have some right about Tom's size, only been worn the few times, and Ida hadn't wanted to ask, but were they dead man's shoes? Dead boy's shoes, worse.

Ida felt a shiver, across the top of her back. No, it wasn't felt – she had, had a shiver, her body had it, her body shook, was shaken. Not up and down like a usual shiver, but right across the top of her back, as if an arm was laid across her shoulders and then ever so slowly taken away.

She looked up into the cloudy sky and down again along the lane and couldn't for the life of her think why she'd shivered, but she had, and it had been very real. Then before she could think any more of it here came a young woman asking her for a tincture for the spots, awful lot of them all over her nose and chin she had. Ida knew exactly what she needed, and set to with dried rosemary and a sprig of fresh thyme, the two ground fine, poured into a paper to weigh out, and the paper tipped into a little glass jar. Then she took her funnel for a tot of cider vinegar, a squeeze of lemon, a drop of sandalwood. That was the girl all set.

Ida shrugged off that feeling across her shoulders and got down to work, one customer – as ever, thank God, thank the way all markets work – attracting one more, and each one adding to her pocket of coppers, so perhaps they'd have a couple of chops for their tea tonight. She was happy for Tom, he'd been wanting this for so long, she was glad she'd got over her silliness and let him go.

When she was packing up that afternoon, not long after two it was, no point working late on a Sunday, most people already off home for their dinner, the shiver came back, crept back, and Ida found herself going through her little boxes, faster now and less careful, sure she needed it, wanted her hand on it, where the hell had it got to? There, the pink glass seahorse. She took a breath, a deep one, she'd been biting her lip that hard there'd be a bruise tomorrow she was sure. Well then. Here was the seahorse, an old sailor's mascot it was, all the way from Venice. Was that right? Ida laughed at herself, unsure. The Venice story was something she'd been telling customers so long, maybe she believed it herself. Was it truth, had it ever been? Ida breathed on the glass, rubbed her thumb across the pale pink ridges, polishing it up with the soft fabric of her old summer work skirt. She'd give the seahorse to Tom when he came home, a reminder of his trip. And she'd keep it beside her for now, in her pocket, under her pillow tonight. A rose pink to wash through her dreams of her boy, keep him safe. She was a wise woman, was Ida, and knew that half the time what she had to sell was a tot of hope and nothing more, but even so, tonight, she'd keep the seahorse close.

Itzhak was out of the boat, he was on the water, he was in the water. He was smacked across the face, and his lip split, eye blackened, and then, trying to hold on though nothing would stay still, hanging on with any part of him that could, his leg was ripped all along the calf by a length of cold, hard rope. The wet hemp and the speed with which it ran across his leg turned each strand of rope to a sliver. But nothing hurt, nothing hurt, even when the tip, the trip happened, the trap of the sea-mouth pulling him down and in. It did not hurt then, it did not hurt now. Itzhak knew he had been hurt and there was a part of him, somewhere distant – *mir hobben à hime du* – that understood he should be in pain. Maybe he was in pain, maybe he was not here, in the water, maybe this was the other place, the hell that Christians spoke of. Maybe the only thing they'd got wrong was that it was cold water, not burning flame. This might be their hell, he had seen pictures from their Sunday school classes, the souls crying out in torment, arms reaching up and no succour offered, the bodies, those many mangled bodies, writhing entwined. There were cries, such loud, long, fearsome cries. He turned and pulled away, pushed himself away. Now. Fast.

Itzhak was swimming, hard against the current, hard against the tide, swimming fast and furious, one eye bloodshot with salt, the other almost closed now, dark purple and swollen, water and tears and blood flowing from the gash in his leg. Itzhak swimming, blinking back tears and murky water, and he wasn't looking where he was going, swimming in no direction. All he could do was swim away from that boat, away from Baba Yaga's sister, ready to grab him from below, drawn by the blood that tasted warm on her cold lips. Itzhak was swimming away from the other boys too, his friends in the water and this time they were not there to see how long they could float, heads down in the water holding their breath and about to burst up, to spit out mouthfuls of water, to pump themselves up to the surface, all the way from the bottom of the pool, up with mouthfuls of bubbling air and water and that was a good laugh, that was one over on you Itzhak Ayalon, thought I'd drowned did you? As if I would, as if I'd drown. What kind of a mate are you, don't trust me not to drown?

Itzhak couldn't think what kind of a friend he was, he'd heard cries in the water, thought he heard a whistle in the water – was that Tom? Was Tom whistling? – and Itzhak could not think what kind of a friend he was, as he swam on, away. And the cries behind him were from Baba Yaga's sister, or a South Seas mermaid here in the cold, furious at finding herself so far from home. Or maybe they were his own cries and the fear was his own and the tears pushing from the swollen eye, from the cut in his leg, flesh parting over bone every time he kicked against the water, pushing away, all his own cries.

Mimi was working, Sunday afternoon, what else should she be doing? And while she worked she prayed. Not the prayers her lodgers made, morning and evening and all times in between, the devout prayers they offered in shul, the devout prayers they prayed in her home. Nor were her prayers the kind her husband and father-in-law offered, pragmatic prayer that fulfilled tasks, completed days, answering the demands that a Jewish man must ask of himself, devout or not, faithful or not. Her sons, the elder two boys, did not pray, not that she knew of. Mimi shook her head, shook out a sheet, maybe one day they would pray. Or not. They were happy, had nothing yet to pray for perhaps and she would not wish unhappiness on her boys just so that they might have a reason to pray. Perhaps it was good fortune that they had no prayers. Perhaps it was better that she didn't know. Her baby, Itzhak, he prayed, Mimi knew. May I be a good boy. May I swim fastest in the test. May I make the other boys laugh with my new joke at the camp. May they be kind to me. May they not pick on me. May I be a good boy.

Mimi worked and as she worked she prayed. And as she was always working, piecework, housework, caring for her men, so it was that Mimi Ayalon was always praying. A prayer for her big boys as she cleaned their room. Let them not get any of those girls into trouble, please God. Let them not get a bad girl into trouble if they do get a girl into trouble, please God. If they do get a girl into trouble, whatever sort of girl she is, let her be a Jewish girl, please God. If she is not a Jewish girl . . .

Her work was not concentrated, on one place, one prayer, it was scattered throughout the house, throughout her day. Mimi began in one room, realised there was a shirt there that should be in another room, a dirty boot here that Nathan or David had worn upstairs, no matter that boots went on the back step, always on the back step, a cold cup of tea, left beside the bed, such good fortune – touching the chamsa at her neck – that she had not kicked it, no time to wash the floor, just the cleaning and the beds and the washing, just time for that today. Before her piecework, before her cooking, before she began again. Five men and one boy, one boy becoming a man, six men, it was a great deal of work. A great deal of prayer. Mimi took the sock back to its rightful owner, the boot to the back step, the cup to the scullery, her prayers followed behind, tumbling down the stairs after her.

Lev was working too, of course. Mimi didn't know if her husband prayed at work, she thought perhaps not. Lev was a serious man and, unlike his own father, he was very clear about the lines he drew between this activity and that, home and work, here and there, now and then. Lev was grateful that he had a job, Mimi didn't think he would risk his work for prayer.

Nathan and David were out somewhere, spending their day. They worked full days on Fridays, had never yet dared, or bothered, to ask English bosses for the half days off that most men in their congregation took on a Friday or a Saturday, did not want to mention Shabbat to the bosses, and so Sunday was a free day for them, a day they lived to the full, and never at home.

The lodgers were in shul or studying with the rabbi. Mimi remembered asking her mother why she had to help in the house when her brother was allowed to sit with the men, all of them around the table, arguing, the books and scrolls between them, why he did not have to help with the housework, or even the yard work. Her mother explained, some people are men and some are women, some meant to pray, some to work. That was just how it was.

Mimi never did find this a satisfactory answer, which was why she now combined prayer and work, but she did not begrudge the lodgers. They paid a fair rent and were good men, quiet, kept themselves to themselves. In a small house, each one of those attributes was a gift in itself. And they were always at prayer, which must be a blessing too, a mitzvah for the house itself, surely, to hold two such devout men?

Shimon was sitting in the front room. Why was he in there? Old man, old bones, always too cold for him in the front room, he sat as close to the kitchen range as he could, needed the warmth, even in the dead of summer, not that this was much of a summer, not that they'd had real sun for days . . .

Mimi stopped in her tracks.

She turned to Shimon, the old man was reaching out his hand and she couldn't hear the words he was saying, couldn't hear a thing because the silver hand at her neck, the one they had bought from Ida, the one to replace the chamsa given to Shimon's mother – not a real chamsa at all, but this was London, what could you do – was burning against her skin, hand reaching out, hand burning cold, and she wavered, stumbled, Shimon rose to help her, slowly, old-man legs unsteady in an always-cold room, they reached for each other, each one about to fall, holding the other. Something had happened. They both knew it, father-in-law and daughter-in-law, something had happened. The hand burned her skin, silver burning cold.

Jimmy was pulled on to a lifeboat, quickly, he was barely in the water before he'd been grabbed out, so lucky, they kept telling him he was so lucky. Plucky fellow too, good on him, little carrot-topped lad, good on him. The men who were saving boys from the water, doing all they could to save boys from the water, keeping the words coming, talking to remind themselves they were alive, fishing up boys, one lad after the other.

Jimmy was pulled in and his little white face against his shock of red hair were all the lifeguard saw at first, good on you carrot-top, good on you red, good lad now.

And then the old man, too old to be in the sea itself like some of his mates, better he sat in the boat here, held it steady, held it waiting, then he realised it wasn't red hair he was looking at, but red blood, where the lad's head had been split open, dear God, split to the bone, and more. How could the kid not feel it? Why wasn't he screaming?

Jimmy was not screaming. He was silent.

Jimmy was grey-white and losing blood at a fearful rate, but he did have a pulse and he was there, in the bottom of that boat, beside one breathing boy and one too-still lad, the blood pouring from Jimmy's head testimony to the beating of his heart.

Grey sky, grey sea, red hair, white bone.

A hand clamped down tight on Jimmy's head and another pulled him close to a warm man, heart beating fast, they were full now, this was all the boat could take, the men knew this, another lifeboat would come, for now this was the best they could do, save those they had already aboard, take care of those they could. They turned about and pulled for shore.

Row the boat ashore, alleluia.

Twenty-Three

Rose was enjoying this, a little bit of time on her own, her feet up and a nice piece of ginger cake, all to herself. Well, to herself and the baby. She patted her belly, barely there, barely risen, but she could feel it anyway, feel how it had made her tummy draw down, her breasts rise up, feel that beginning twinge in her lower back. She loved it all, this feeling of new growth. And nothing like when she'd finally fallen for Jimmy, sick all the time and dog tired, Rose was doing well, so far at least, only this morning Tilly had remarked on her bloom, her skin, she nearly had to shush Tilly saying it aloud, pointing it out like that, so anyone might guess.

She'd told Charlie at dinner time and he just laughed as he wiped his face and got up to go back to work, a big hand on the small of her neck, warm as he leant in to kiss her forehead,

Down the lane? Our lot? Don't be daft love, they'd reckon you and I were at it all last night, that's all the blush in a girl's cheeks means round here. The lad's practically a man now, and we've not had any others since, no one'll think we've another on the way. Don't you worry. What they think is that Charlie Hatch is a one, and they're not wrong.

His kiss moved down her face from her forehead to her mouth, lingered there, on her lips, then Charlie was gone to his barrow and Rose was back looking after Emily.

Astonishing what a day could do. The night before last Rose had been sure they were going to lose her mother and Jimmy would've had to stay behind for the funeral, not go off on his camp after all. Then yesterday, early afternoon, Emily woke up bright as a button and cheery with it. It had tired her out of course, a good day like the one she'd yesterday, she'd slept most of today, but proper sleep, deep and restful.

Rose was no fool, she knew this was the last rally, that it might go on one more day, a week, a month at most, knew the disease had gone too far and it wouldn't be stopped now, but she was glad of a chance to truly rest while her mother slept. Maybe her mother might die more easily now, maybe having a few days or even a few hours without too much pain, with some spirit in her, maybe that would make letting go easier.

Rose didn't know what made death easier, but she knew that a nice bit of cake and a cup of tea in a quiet house made a picnic of a Sunday afternoon.

When Charlie walked in fifteen minutes later he saw his wife sleeping, a teacup balanced on her lap. His mother-in-law, still breathing, lay thin in the big bed filling the front room. Charlie stood there, his boots still on, his face red from running, red from an anger that was more about his fury at the tears that wanted to fall, than it was about anything specific. He had nothing to be angry about. Not yet.

(He was furious at the boy, waste of bloody time, stupid lad, waste of time and money and what the hell did he want to go off and spend a fortnight away from home for, eh? What kind of a kid wanted that in his summer break from school? Didn't he want to work, earn a bob or two? He was a Hatch, he should be on the stall. He should be here. Home. He should be here.)

Not yet, Charlie would not be angry yet.

Nor would he wake his Rose. He didn't want her to hear this. Let her heart beat steady for now, let her sleep five more minutes in peace.

He stood in the doorway of the front room on Larcom Street and outside was a damp summer Sunday and inside all was stopped. Waiting. Charlie Hatch, that mouthy Hatch bloke, stood a small man in a small room, dwarfed by the words he had to say. Waiting. He stepped forward quietly, Rose would be amazed that her Charlie could be this quiet, didn't know him to stand quietly, sit quietly, to do anything with care. Another step. He stopped. In the room where only the clock was ticking, only Emily was rasping a liquid breath, only Rose's chest rose and fell. Charlie stopped still in the front parlour of his own home, placed himself between his pregnant wife and his dying mother-in-law. Stood between them, in a room full of life and of death, saying nothing. If he didn't say it, if he didn't tell her, perhaps it hadn't happened yet, perhaps there was no need to feel this gut-fear, yet.

When Rose opened her eyes she assumed Charlie was telling her that Emily had died. When Charlie told what had happened, she wished he'd been telling her that Emily had died.

Twenty-Four

Lads who were saved, lads who were drowned alongside the young fellow from the Arethusa, the turned-turtle training vessel that had now added loss to its curriculum. Necessary for any sailor, lessons in unnecessary loss. Still in the water, coastguards pulled at the belts of boys, smacked their backs, trying to drain young lungs full of sea, saturated breath, hoping to bring light back into dull eyes. Lads whose mothers also grieved, boys whose fathers were also broken.

Two boys huddled in the bottom of the coastguards' boat, grey with shock. There was another with a compound fracture to his arm, a dirty white shard jutting from his forearm, the bone ripped through his flesh and had been almost ignored in the shock of now, until now. The scar would heal, the loss recede, slowly ebbing. One day, twenty-eight years hence, a man who never spoke of his youth, who had become a sailor after all, would set out for Dunkirk to bring them home. And as he loaded his own little boat with broken soldiers, exhausted men hauled aboard in carcasses of sodden uniforms, he would cry out at a sudden sharp pain in his forearm. A pain that was barely registered when it first happened, just a couple of miles off the coast at Leysdown, too much else to feel, too much else to try not to feel, would return with full force. And a grown man who had always called himself lucky, would stop and cry out, chest burning, shoulders heaving, sobbing on another grey afternoon. No time to cry when it had first happened, no time to cry at Dunkirk either. Never a good time to cry.

The young Scoutmaster was in the water too, freezing and not giving up, hands chilled and still reaching out for his lads, his eyes sea-blind, he grabbed at anything he could to haul up, haul out. Guilt saturated his own pain, not much more than a lad himself, he was doing his best, trying to do good, to make a difference. He had already made a difference.

A father who had only come on board to support his two boys. Both of them keen Scouts, they'd begged their dad, a naval man, to come along. Both Saturday and Sunday off work had been hard for a working man to agree to, hard for his wife to agree to, but they had, good for the boys, a chance to show off their dad, a man who knew all about the sea, with his own stories and his own battles fought.

Come on Dad, you'll show them all.

His wife shook her head, knew him too well. Never able to say no to his lads, always wanting to be the hero in their eyes, in their hearts, she watched him agree to their begging even before he'd said the word yes. No matter, she'd work an extra shift herself.

Now here he was, the sailor father, both his boys lost to the sea. Both. He'd dived in after his lads, shucking off his old greatcoat in the water, two wars he'd worn that coat, stayed with him all through, now it was a dirty great thing, weighing him down, pulling him under. The helpful sea ripped away the coat, drowned it fast. Then he was free to swim, to save, to pick up. He didn't only make for his own lads, he was grabbing any boy he could, lifting them to safety, lining them up on the hull of the upturned ship, the keeled-over Arethusa. Then there was his own boy, the elder of the two, calling out. So many voices calling, screaming, but he heard his son in the roar as if it were his own voice, his son's lips and tongue chilled and tired, but the words were forming and that was good. The father knew that keeping awake in the water was half the battle. He loaded his big boy on to the upturned boat with the half-dozen others already there and swam back out, looking for his other one, the younger one, his wife's favourite. He shouldn't have known that, but he did. Shouldn't have thought it there and then, in the water, but he did. She was half his life, his wife, and he felt her grief already. There, there he was, his younger lad. Four, five, a dozen strokes over and through the waves, the boy was gone again, the father pushed on. Now, this time, one last overarching reach and he'd grabbed the collar of the lad he thought was his, prayed was his, begging forgiveness from a God he didn't believe in for praying the boy was his and not another mother's son. No words came from this boy's mouth, too cold, too chilled, but alive, perhaps, a little light in his eyes, perhaps. Good, good.

Holding the lad close to his chest, keeping the boy's head out of the water, one-arm swimming, he turned to bring his younger son to the safe harbour of the upturned boat, to bring him to his elder brother. And as they turned, the naval man and the bone-chilled boy, the upturned Arethusa righted herself. That bitch, that bitch of a ship set herself to rights and all those boys, the lads who had trusted that they were safe now, saved now, were swept right off and back in, back down. One wave, another, a third. The father couldn't see any more. Too grey, too sodden, so much salt. Bloodshot eyes in too much salt and no eyes to see what he had just seen. He was exhausted and he swam on, the coast-guard's boat was there, just there, just here. And the little lad, his little lad, his wife's darling, slipped from his grip, his hands couldn't hold, the child was an exhausted dead weight and there was no fight left. The lad slipped away and down, five, six fathoms deep. The father lived, and both his poor boys drowned. His watch stopped at five to two, and he left it stopped, hands ever askew.

Twenty-Five

Coastguards' wives have always understood the loss of the sea, it was the lure that was harder to comprehend. A woman might marry a man who had the sea in him, in his blood, and she'd be from a fishing family or a coastguard family herself, brought up with a father who had the sea in him, brothers the same. She'd have seen her mother waiting late nights, looking through a darkening window, seen the lines laid on her skin in the hours it took for a boat to come ashore, the men to be counted in, each one safely home. When one of those girls married a lad from the same kind of family there was at least an understanding. As if passed down with her own mother's wedding linen, she would take on the waiting, wear it as she might wear an apron handed down, waiting to grow into it, just the way it was, what you do, what we do.

Other times a girl from town or the country would fall in love with a boy from the sea, and it was harder then. Town girls knew dirt and grime and hard work, yes, but they couldn't comprehend hours soaked to the bone and loving it regardless, didn't understand that the stink of fish would never leave the skin, sticky scales sticking to him to the end. A country girl might know that there were dangers in any work, would have seen plenty of accidents herself, a big horse and a kick to the gut that could kill a man with a ruptured spleen in half an hour. She'd have heard of bull horns in the back, trees felled on to foolish woodsmen, and she'd know the dangers of iron and leather. A farmer's daughter might know that a man – and a woman often as not – was expected to work all night in spring, lambing, calving, birthing livestock, dead stock and all. She'd know a farmer must tend to his crops from dawn to dusk with a few hours' sleep a night, if he was lucky, in the height of summer. Any girl from town or country would come with her own understanding of the life of men, of men's work, but a girl who grew up away from the coast could never be fully prepared for the life of the seawife. The land does not shift in shadows, the land does not slap back, the land does not swallow a man whole.

The seawife's role was to wait. Days if her man was a fisherman, whole weeks if the ship was large and the crew willing, months or years if he was a sailor. A seawife knew that she was not married to the man alone, she was married to the sea on which he sailed and that she had better know the water as well as he did, better know the tides and turns the way he told them, from the moon and from a feeling in his bones, his gut. He'd not be at home to teach her for long, and when he was gone she'd want to know where he was. If she learned the sea as well as her man knew it, she'd be able to reach out to him in the dark, in the hours before dawn, those nights when the waves attacked the sea wall, battered the shore, when she was most scared. And she would hold him better because she understood.

The coastguard's wife was a little different. Other men might love the sea, work the sea, live on the sea some of them. The coastguard had a different task, he fought the sea for ships, for bodies, for life. The sea would hand back broken men and wrecked hulls, but the coastguard wrestled that water for breath. And the coastguard's wife waited, knowing that one day the fight would prove uneven. When he brought life home with him she took it in, warmed it up, dried it off. When he returned with death she made her husband a cup of strong tea with as much again of rum, forced him to swallow down a stew or a broth, rolled him in warm blankets and she would hold him until he thawed. There was a chill that came with bringing in the dead ones, a picture of the body broken, grey, an image stuck behind the eyes, hard to shift. She would hold him until that chill moved off, hold him in whatever way she could. Sometimes she held by not speaking of it at all, other times it was a way of being, until the man went out again, in another storm and this time he brought home a live one. Only a live one could shift the cold of the dead.

That night, the Leysdown coastguard brought in twenty live ones. Chilled, shocked, sick. Boys were wrapped into grown men's clothes and given the coastguards' own beds, blankets piled on top of them, and they were held by other boys' mothers until they slept, each woman whispering thanks that it wasn't her boy who had been through this, her boy's teeth chattering in his head. In the morning the seawives were up at first light, rinsing sodden clothes, hanging them on the line to dry, salt wind licking at London shirt sleeves. Inside the little cottages the lucky lads who had been able to sleep, slept on. Others strained their eyes staring into the dark of strange rooms with small windows, looking for their friends. Coastguards got up after a rest of just an hour or so and started again. They headed out knowing that there would be no more live ones to fetch in. They headed out now to pick up whatever the sea had thrown back.

And the seawives watched their men go, each woman turning to her locket or precious shell or lucky stone, each one offering a wish, a plea, a prayer that had nothing to do with God, that knew the sea to be the only deity, praying her man home safe.

Twenty-Six

Rose sat quietly, making bargains. Her mother for her son, a fair enough trade, no one would say otherwise, least of all Emily, who'd already said as much herself, bony hand beating her breast when she heard the words Charlie had to say. Rose shook her head, wicked bitch she was to think it and she couldn't but think it. And there, quieter than a whisper, was another trade, darker still. This baby for that baby. This new life, no life at all yet, for that one, the one she felt hanging on to her by a thread, felt him alive still, willed him alive still. This baby for that boy. Anything for her son. And no she didn't mean it, how could she mean it, how dare she even think of meaning it, but oh yes, she did. On and on.

Rose had set up a little altar at the side of Emily's bed and stared at it now, the bits and pieces that were her boy. Here was Jimmy's first baby tooth, she'd never let Charlie throw it out, kept it in a small bag at the bottom of a drawer. The rag book he'd loved, each of the letters in it embroidered for him by Emily, traced and learned by heart. The first piece of string he'd started practising his knots with, hopelessly tangled and left in his pocket to become still more mangled come next wash day.

Rose lifted her apron to her eyes, then brought her hands down again, firmly. Not yet, no tears yet.

That's right, Emily said, voice constricted with pain and speaking anyway, every word clear as day, We cry when it happens, girl, if it happens. When there is reason to cry, then we cry. Not until, you hear me? Not until. Don't you be giving those bad dreams any power with your tears.

Not yet.

Rose's eyes were raw with wiping away tears she wouldn't allow.

Jimmy's things. A farthing. One of those with the old queen's head on it still. He must have been five or six, had just started to understand about birthdays, and that his own birth year mattered, what with it having been the turn of the century and all. Rose had been counting out her change from the shopping and Jimmy was trying to count with her,

Four farthings make ... two ha'pennies make ... add tuppence to that ...

Rose knew it was important to Charlie that the boy be able to help on the stall, sooner rather than later, and counting out the change was one of the first things his father would expect of him. Poor Jimmy could never quite get the hang of it, found himself confused and then he'd get upset, but this time he'd grabbed up the coin with the old queen on it, thrilled to see the number, count it out.

Look Ma, that's me, that's when I'm from.

Rose was so pleased that he could read the number and

understand what it meant that she let him keep the farthing for his own, even when Charlie told her she was soft on the lad. Other boys might spend theirs on a bit of cinder toffee, or put it towards something bigger, one of those toy sailing boats his cousin Tom was so keen on, but Jimmy never did. He kept it by his bed, even as he got older, the coin that marked his year.

There was the wishbone Emily had given her to hang over his cot when Jimmy was just a baby, the bone wrapped up in fresh red cloth, the one he'd said he didn't need this week. The bone itself was broken beneath the ribbon, it bent if you gave it a little tug. Jimmy always swore blind it wasn't him who'd cracked the bone, but Rose knew that when he was smaller he'd take it off the wall at bed-time, make a bird of the bone, flying it across the pillow, or a plough, for digging up long trenches of the pale blue candlewick bedspread. He was too old now for such make-believe games, but for years she'd smile as the night came on, listening to the lad prattling on to himself. Charlie was always on at him to shut it and sleep, morning would be here before he knew it, but Rose didn't mind, she liked that her boy had his own stories.

Rose built an altar of her boy's precious things. One hand on her belly, one on her dying mother, making her trades.

Mimi stood in the back yard of her home. Inside there were beds to be made, meals to be cooked, pillows to be pummelled, the passage to be swept, front step to be scrubbed, dishes to be washed. For now she stood, swaying a little, perhaps she was praying. Mimi had watched men all her life, her father, her brothers, husband, father-in-law, watched them davening, swaying as they prayed, as they were taught by their own fathers. Now she didn't know if she swayed to pray or to find her balance. She could not find a balance. When Ida had come to the door with the news – Ida, bringing the news herself, as if she didn't have enough to worry about, as if she could walk and talk quite normally with half her soul floating above, watching, waiting – when Ida brought the news, Mimi felt the floorboards shift beneath her, and now she could not right herself. Ida had taken her inside, along the dark passage and down to the scullery, these houses were all the same, Jew or Gentile, the scullery at the back, opening on to the yard, Ida knew where she was going and had taken Mimi through and sat her down, fetched a glass from a shelf – no cups, they drank from glasses? – and poured Mimi a cold tea, opened jars until she found sugar and dug in two big teaspoons.

And all Mimi could think was, Two? Such extravagance. It must be bad.

Ida stayed with her until the swaying stopped a little, until Mimi shook her head and, apologising, sent Ida home, back to wait herself, back to pray it might not be her boy, might be another mother's boy.

Someone must have told the rabbi, because not long after there was the rabbi's wife, in Mimi's house – and so much work still to do, the beds to be made – asking if she wanted more tea, water. What Mimi needed more than anything was to be alone. Alone in the yard, alone in her home. The men were in shul, even Nathan and David had gone with the older men. Shimon said the cantor would be rehearsing and he wanted the cool of the wood-panelled room and one voice, carrying light. So all five of the men were gone, half a minyan for Itzhak. It was good that her elder boys should pray. It was about time. Mimi could have gone with them, could be sitting in the women's gallery, watching from above, but she would rather be alone at home. She and Itzhak were often alone in the house, the two of them together. Mimi was trying, and failing, to feel that Itzhak was with her now. Dear G-d, please don't let it be my boy.

Bill's sister Ena had been sitting in the scullery with Ida for hours and she wouldn't shut up. She was talking about Tilly's teeth, what a caution Tilly was, how she was refusing to get false ones, but soon she'd be left with nothing in her mouth at all, just gums to suck her tea through and what would Samson say to that?

Ida looked up, unsure. Of course Ena didn't mean it, Ena would no more make a dirty joke than fly to the moon. Ida frowned, what kind of a woman must she be? Couldn't seem to stand and make a cup of tea, couldn't do a thing for her girls who were no end of upset and frightened themselves and had been bundled off out of the way, and yet an unintentional joke about Tilly and Samson made a nasty kind of sense. What sort of a mother must she be to hear something like that in her sister-in-law's words, at a time like this? Ena couldn't have meant it, Ena was innocent as a lamb, poor thing, too damn innocent, if Ena were more worldly she'd have known what Ida knew. That it was already too late. That whatever they were waiting for had already happened. The tragedy had been and gone and all there was to wait for was confirmation. Ida felt it in her marrow, deeper than her bones, far deeper than the stupid heart that pounded in her chest, refusing to stop when by rights it should have given up the ghost the minute she'd been told. Given up. Ghost. Dear Christ, no.

Ena put the kettle on for tea. More bloody tea. Ida did not want tea, Ida wanted a pint and another pint and another, she wanted a barrel of gin to pickle herself in, she wanted to drink herself into a rotten-drunk sleep so she could be somewhere else, anywhere else, so the picture she had in her mind from the day she'd watched the Albion stumble into the Thames, the screams she'd heard then, over and over again, so those screams inside her head would leave her. Bill had dropped the girls off with his cousin in Kennington and he'd gone with Charlie down to Leysdown. That was daft and all, Ida had wanted the girls close by, safe in their beds was fine, waiting up alongside her would have been better, but no, they'd all taken one look at Ida's face and quick as you like, Bill and Ena had said the girls shouldn't be here for this.

What was this? Had there been news? Had they said?

Until Ena answered her, Ida hadn't known she was speaking aloud.

They're not back yet, the men, we're still waiting.

Waiting.

At least the girls would get a good night's sleep at Bill's cousin's place. It was for the best. There was no best.

Someone had done a whip-round in the pub and someone else came over with the pot,

Here you go, Bill, Charlie, go on, get the train, find out what's what. You need to see for yourselves. Get down there and bring the boys home. Off you go.

218

It had been meant kindly, Ida knew that, and Bill wanted to go, so did Charlie, the pair of them were breaking their necks to get off, anything other than this awful waiting, but Ida could have done with Bill here, holding her hand. He'd have been able to tell Ena to shut up, had never held with his sister's prattling. Ida shook her head, no, no more tea. No more. And Ena made a pot just in case.

Ida turned inside and listened. Heart beating, blood washing through her veins, she could hear it clear as day, the way she'd listened to her own blood when she put her fingers in her ears as a kid. Ida listened inside and found only herself. Tom was no longer there.

Someone was knocking at the door, the heavy brass knocker, a fat ring held in the lion's mouth, knocking even though the door was open, Ena had left it open, unlocked at least, hadn't she? Why'd she lock the door? Thieves round here, course there were, same as anywhere, but they'd not a thing worth nicking, and everyone knew it. Why would anyone knock? Unless. Unless. They were not from round here. Ida jumped as she had done at every call from the threshold and Ena smoothed her hair even as she walked down the passage, smoothing her hair like it mattered who she found standing there, holding out a cake, a loaf of bread, a bit of boiled beef. There was no room for the cakes they'd been given already. They should have a sale. Give them to the church, a bring and buy.

A cake for my son? Cakes on the sideboard, like birthday gifts for a special birthday, or a wedding. Ida wouldn't think of a wake, wouldn't let herself think that, they were just gifts. A party for the lad. You wouldn't think people round here had two bob to rub together, and look at the amount they were bringing to her home. She should be grateful, Ida knew, ought to get up herself and go to the door and thank them,

Don't you bother about me, take that back for your own little ones, give them a treat. Thank you thank you anyway, you're kind to think of us, we'll be good as gold once the lad's home.

She ought to get up, but leaden limbs pinned her down. If she stayed here, in the dusk of the scullery, if she didn't see the looks on their faces, if she didn't let the clock tick one more minute, not one more minute.

Ena said it was May at the door, a lovely treacle sponge she'd brought, didn't want to come in, not to disturb, just to bring a little something. Which was daft, when did May ever knock, when did May ever not just troop on in, dropping her laundry bags and demanding a cup of tea and some gin to top it up, if there was any going. Well.

Very kind, people are so kind, Ena said.

Ida shook her head, pursed her lips, shut herself up. They were there though, the words, filling her mouth, the curses, the damn them all to hell for bringing their kindness to her door, their fucking treacle tarts, what did she need with treats when there were ashes in her mouth? Ida was a wicked woman and she couldn't think a single kind thought. And then there was a cup of tea by her hand and she brought it to her mouth anyway, something to do, and as it came to her mouth Ida found herself thirsty after all, and she drank down the whole cup, just like that. All gone so fast. The tea was sweet and salty at the same time. Why was there salt in her tea? She would ask Ena but her sister-in-law had another look on her face now. Or maybe the look was cast by the shadows, sudden light making shadows all through the scullery, where had that light come from? When was it morning?

And now here was Bill, walking down the passage, good thing they'd left the door open, best to leave it gaping, bring him in, bring him back to Ida. Here was Bill with his arms by his sides, nothing in those arms, no son in those arms, what the hell was he doing here with no boy by his side? How dare he come indoors with no lad running ahead of him? And Bill was old, when did he get so old? Had the journey been so long, so much time gone?

It was Monday, long past tea time, and here was Bill home from Leysdown to tell Ida that their boy was drowned.

They had told Bill that he would not be able to bring Tom home, not yet. They told him that there were plans being made for bringing the boys home, plans other men were making, decided in offices and grand halls, they said this gently but firmly, and they gave him the rucksack. Bill was allowed to bring the rucksack home.

Bill stood at the door of the coastguard's cottage, other fathers inside behind him, tall men bowing their heads to avoid the beams in the low cottage, bowing their heads to cover broken faces. The air inside was thick with tobacco smoke and steam from the drying clothes hanging all around the fire now that the drizzle outside meant they must come in off the line. The young man at the cottage door, on the other side of the threshold, was soberly dressed and over-polite. He was from the Scouts. They had been out since first light and the searchers had found this rucksack on the shore. They'd found many items on the shore, precious things that the saved lads and the lost lads had kept with them, the young man began to explain this to Bill, and then he stopped. Bill was grateful that he had stopped, thanked him for the rucksack, for his wishes. No, there was nothing they could do.

Inside, in his chest, in his head, in the fingers he held paddle-stiff to avoid making a fist, Bill was shouting in the young man's face, spittle flecking the too-red, well-scrubbed cheeks,

Haven't you done enough? Didn't you do enough? Can you not just shut up, stop now, you've done everything you could. There is nothing more. You have done the most, the worst. Just bugger off out of it, go back to the great big house where you belong, back to some country park, you damn do-gooders and your fresh air and sea air and all that rot, all that god-awful rot. My boy was not meant for any of that. My boy should have stayed home. My boy should have been with me. My Tom.

Thank you, no, we'll do all right. We've our own at home, they're looking after us, they're with us. Thank you. Yes, we're sorry too, we are.

Bill's voice was held, soft, careful, his vowels rounder than usual, even now, speaking slowly, carefully to the polite young man, trying his damnedest not to speak out of turn, out of sorts and despising himself for it. He closed the door after the young man and leaned against it. One of the many women round about, he'd been introduced to her, heard her name, not spoken her name, she'd been kind, careful, and she stood before him now.

I'll take that, shall I? You don't want to bother with that. I'll pop it away, I've a clean flour sack just the right size. You can take it home to your wife.

Her hand was on the rucksack, reaching out, a slight pressure where she was gently pulling it from him and Bill wrenched the rucksack back to himself, to his chest, wrenched her hand as he did. The woman stepped back in shock, a touch of fear crossed her face and then she was calm again, quiet.

Of course, love, as you will.

Bill could not bring himself to apologise again, thought he might choke if he said sorry one more time, and barged past the woman, pulled back the door, through the throng of heavy men, out to the yard. Not even a proper yard, this, just a space behind the cottage, open to the wind and the incessant bloody roar of that damn sea. Bill held the rucksack in his hands, in his arms, and the rucksack was a little boy, a screaming baby, a lad. Just a lad.

Bill held the rucksack and hated himself. Hated that he'd made a fuss about the stupid thing, hated that he'd told Tom to be careful, gone on and on about it. What kind of a man was he, what kind of father, that he hadn't wanted to share this piece of himself, of his own youth, with the boy? How could he not want to share it? Bill damned himself and the sea and the smartly dressed young man who had come to the door and the gentle woman and all those other men in there, the ones with boys alive and those still waiting as he was, and he damned his Tom for being so keen, so full of it, so all-consumed with his flamin' scouting and his hunger to get out and do and see, to get on and into the world. And Bill knew exactly where he'd bloody well got that from because Bill had felt it keenly enough himself back then, before South Africa, before the heat and the flies and the stench of dead men and broken bones and what for? Queen and Country all over again and none of it for the likes of them, none of it ever for the likes of them.

Bill had had enough of the seaside. They would not let him bring his lad home, so he would go home anyway. He was a working man and he knew better than to hang on for the permission of the toffs, they'd do what suited them, always did. And God knew, Ida needed him more than poor Tom did now.

The water wasn't blue. Tom had found himself surprised, even a little disappointed, when they were on the Thames. He had hoped his old brown river might pick up some sea blue, sky blue as they headed out to the coast. He had been hungry for the blue of the picture books at school, blue of the stories, the deep dark blue of the toy boats that sailed the pond that was every ocean of the globe. But even when they were well past Bexley the river was still the same old Thames that he knew, wide then wider, rushing on the current, on the tide, but it was not blue. Tom had dreamed of a blue or perhaps even a green sea. But the Thames was brown and the river mouth was rich brown and rough, and even when they rounded out and back into the coast itself, the water was still brown. Brown like the firm clay of London, flecked yellow in the sudden light before the squall, flecked grey when the wind and rain hit, white wave caps the only change to the swirling, sodden brown.

Tom had hoped for blue. He did not see, but his lips

were blue, even as they whistled, whistling for a mermaid to come fetch him and hold him warm. His toes were blue too, and his fingertips. Tom did not see, but his open eyes were blue, looking up into a grey sky, looking deep into dark water, staring blind at the soft seabed.

Twenty-Seven

The news began to filter out to the rest of the country. Eight bodies pulled from the water or washed up on the shore. Seven of them Scouts from the 2nd Walworth, the eighth the young fellow from the Arethusa, not much more than a boy himself, only fourteen. Worse still was one of the Scouts missing yet, presumed drowned. Nine of them all together. Dreadful, dreadful. People whispered to each other, touching wood or crossing themselves, lucky there'd not been more loss of life, though they knew they didn't mean lucky, even as they said it. In brighter voices they said what a blessing the coastguard was, but such loss, such sadness. Mothers hugged their own boys tighter. Not my son, thank God, not my son.

Edward Lovett sat in his study and listened to the sounds of his sons in the room below. They were debating, voices raised, the elder lecturing the younger about something, the younger not paying attention, long past deferring to a brother just two years his senior. He pictured himself wrenching open his study door, running down the flight of stairs, grabbing both of his sons and crushing them to his breast, pulling them to him as he had when they were small boys. He saw himself holding them close even though the scent of grass stains and cricket leather was long gone. He listened to their argument, now turned to laughter, one lowered voice, then another, then a second shout of ribald laughter between the two. Boys who were truly men now, who did not need him to hold them close. He turned back to his desk and his catalogue, a mole's foot to note, a cure for cramp from the ever-curled foot of the digging mole.

Lev had brought Itzhak home on Monday morning. He'd have brought him back Sunday night if he could, if there were a train or a cart to travel on. Even now Itzhak had still not stopped shaking, the doctor in Leysdown had advised against moving the boy at all.

The boy should not be moved, the cut to his leg is deep, the stitches could rip.

His mother needs to see him.

Your son has been kept as warm and comfortable as we can manage, yet he is still shivering. It will do his heart no good to take him all the way back to London just now.

His mother needs to see him.

He should not be moved, his leg . . .

To see that he is alive.

She knows that now.

She needs to see him.

A telegram had been sent, the Scouts had taken care of everything, Mimi would know that they were lucky, blessed. But

Lev knew his wife, knew his father too, neither would rest until Itzhak was home with them.

The doctor sighed, he was used to dealing with country people and fishing folk, used to being paid in pig meat or fresh-gutted fish as often as coin, he was not accustomed to a patient, a patient's loved one, speaking back. He held his tongue. He was an Englishman, and would take it in good part, foreigners simply did not know our ways, the unspoken hierarchies.

Then take him home, but it is against my advice.

Thirty years later the doctor would still wonder what became of the little Jew-boy, shivering under layers of coarse grey blankets, his black eyes shadowed as if he'd gone half a dozen rounds with the local champion at the May Fair. He wouldn't wish it on anyone, what the lad must have seen in the sea, the screams he must still hear. They said that those standing on shore could hear the lads calling for help, crying, voices held in the wind and whipped back to the helpless people on shore. Dreadful business.

Still, no use dwelling on what was. He was off to see another boy in another cottage. And another, and another.

The journey home was slow and tiring, two different trains with a long wait between, and Itzhak sat on his father's lap the whole way, Lev could not afford two seats. People looked at them, stared openly at the boy wrapped in his father's arms. The other passengers knew, or they guessed, what they were looking at, and Lev couldn't shake the feeling that everyone who saw them must be thinking how lucky he was. Yes, he was grateful to have Itzhak back, grateful now to be taking his son home, sitting up on his knee, whimpering in fear and pain. He was grateful not to be Tom's father. Grateful, of course, but not lucky. Lucky would mean never to have heard of the Scouts at all, never to have agreed that Itzhak could learn to swim, go to the camp, travel at this age – so young, a child still, what had they been thinking to agree? Never to have allowed the boy to risk his life following those friends, that would have been luck. If none of this had happened at all, if Lev did not have to feel this guilt, a thin and burning bile in his throat, right down into his gut. To not have known himself blessed that he was not Tom's father, and to not have been disgusted with himself for that blessing, that would have been good luck. This, on the other hand, this was just a long, slow, and painful journey home. *Mir hobben à hime du.*

Far worse than the gash on Jimmy's head, the strip of hair shaved off, the stitches standing out stark against his white scalp, was the problem of his arm. It was broken, and badly, and while it would certainly heal eventually, it would not do so easily or well. The doctor said it might never grow properly now, not as the boy would grow. Jimmy would be in pain for weeks, likely months, he would need care, Charlie and his wife must stop him playing too boisterously with other lads, they must keep an eye on him. Jimmy would be well, after a time, but he would always be broken, a little.

Charlie Hatch was the big man filling the dark front room of the cottage, tough man bowed with the fear he had carried all the way down from London, fear he could not shift, even though he had seen his boy, heard Jimmy's shuddering breath, the tears the lad held in a drugged dream. He nodded politely to the doctor.

Thank you and yes of course, and no, we won't move him for twenty-four hours and of course that's the right way, yes sir, thank you. I have money here, please, thank you.

Charlie didn't know where this new voice came from, the careful whisper from his mouth, Jimmy was sleeping off the effects of the laudanum they'd given him when they'd sewn up his head, before turning to the harder task of setting his arm, the rasp of waves on the pebble shore outside matching the grate of bone on bone.

He found some coins for the doctor, grabbed from this pocket and that and another, probably not enough, but Charlie had not thought to bring much with him when he rushed from the house with the pub's pot for his train fare. He had not considered that Jimmy might be hurt and a doctor need paying, all he could think was drowned or alive, alive or drowned. All any of them could think, Charlie reckoned. Well, a broken arm wasn't much, not good, but not much, not when he thought again of all he'd pictured on the way down – pale Jimmy, broken Jimmy, Jimmy washed on a wave, Jimmy in a coffin, red hair bright against white white face. Charlie rubbed a hand over his jaw, his teeth set solid against each other, his neck muscles tight with holding it all in. Enough with the images of his boy gone, his boy dead, he'd see a future for the lad now instead. If Jimmy couldn't lift or carry, if it turned out as bad as the doctor warned it might, in the long run, then Jimmy would still have a stall. Nothing would stop a Hatch getting behind a stall, taking his place. Charlie'd had an old uncle, his legs long gone, sell from a stiff-backed chair, tied into it with rope by his willing sons. The old man couldn't walk, but they'd found a strong boy to help with the fetching and carrying, and his uncle still had his mouth for the patter. Being on a barrow was as much about the talk as it was hard graft, always had been. Jimmy'll be all right, he'd do all right, they'll get him home and he'll do all right.

Charlie sat beside his boy for another day, in the dark cottage, slept the night on the floor beside the lad, didn't touch him, did as the doctor had said, obeyed orders. Charlie Hatch was as meek and mild as they come, but when the twenty-four hours were up, he'd had enough. Jimmy was awake and hurting now and he wanted to be home and Rose, poor bloody Rose, would be beside herself wanting to see the lad with her own eyes, hold him in her own arms. Charlie knew she wouldn't believe the telegram, she'd need to touch the boy herself, feel him alive. And not just that — mostly that, but not just that — being here, being off the stall was costing him. Yes, Jimmy would be taken care of, and Rose too, the family took care of its own, always had done, but that wasn't the point. Charlie wasn't himself away from the lane, from his barrow, his people. Charlie Hatch needed to be about his work, he only knew himself when he was about his work.

The coastguard's quiet wife changed the bandage on Jimmy's head and the splint and the dressing on his poor arm, whispering that she'd seen plenty of breaks and sprains in her time, he'd be mended well enough come Christmas, there's a brave lad, there's a good boy. Then Charlie wrapped his son tight in another fisherman's blanket — there'd be no bedding left in Leysdown at this rate — and carried him home. Jimmy mewling in pain the whole way, and Charlie Hatch didn't care who heard his boy cry. This lad had saved himself from the sea, wrenched himself back from the whore sea, this boy was man enough.

Ida was indoors with a friend, Tilly perhaps, Bill couldn't be sure, the names that belonged to faces he'd known for years eluded him now. Ida was with Tilly, or another friend, a kind woman who would let her sit quiet, Ida wanted only silence, and Bill walked out into the yard. A proper yard this one, their own yard, with walls and a wooden door to the alley, a hinge he needed to oil, must get around to oiling, and here were solid paving slabs that led down to the outside drain, slabs laid by Bill himself with his own father when they first rented the house, when Ida and Ena had despaired of the mud outside and Bill promised his wife a real home. This proper yard was closed-in enough for Bill to feel safe, held to the earth, for now. Bill was worried that once he started to feel what this was, this pain, he might spin out of his place, never stopping.

He had one hand on the salt-sticky rucksack and the other in his pocket. He pulled out the little knife he had been given by his own father, the knife he'd meant to give to Tom, had planned on giving to Tom for the camping trip and then decided it was better as a homecoming gift. He'd planned to leave it on the boy's pillow the day he came home. The plans of a stupid man who believed everything would go on as it always had. Bill was no longer that man.

The knife was plunging into the rucksack and tearing, stopping, sticking, ripping jagged chunks in the thick threads of the fabric, matted now and solid, sticky and

232

damp with salt water. Damp, still? Plunged and ripped and torn, tears to rhyme with fears, tears to rhyme with there's my boy, there, cold and still, there's my boy, there, there. Rip. Rip. Wrench.

When the rucksack was broken threads and shredded leather and Bill was finally still, Ida came into the yard. Ida had no words, Bill had no words. Sticky, still, salt water. She held out her hand and Bill, who now understood that he was lying on the ground, had been beating bloody fists into the ground, the paving slabs, pulled himself up without her help.

Ida and Bill stood together, not touching, while released scraps of fabric and thin strings of thread floated and spun around them in the yard. Summer had arrived this afternoon. It would not last. It was already muggy, would be a sticky night, and the city that was London, sitting in a basin of hills all around, was spinning, eddying, in a warm, wild wind.

Twenty-Eight

The First Lord of the Admiralty frowned, he hadn't been in the job a year and already there had been too much death and precious little glory. Now this.

The British people will have had enough of seafaring by the end of the year.

Sir? the clerk asked, not sure if the words were meant for him or were simply the young First Lord speaking to himself.

The First Lord wasn't actually that young, the clerk corrected himself, though at a year shy of sixty himself, anyone in their thirties seemed young. He waited for his superior to answer, for a response to the news. Eight bodies found, seven of them Scouts, the other the lad from the Arethusa. And another boy, still lost at sea. A funeral to be arranged and already the papers gearing themselves up for national mourning.

We can't have it.

The First Lord was speaking aloud again, speaking to himself the clerk decided, and waited anyway, in case a response was needed.

We are a naval people or we are nothing, we cannot have

234

them frightened of the sea, of ships. We will honour these boys.

Yes, sir.

Where are they from?

From, sir?

Where do they live? Their families . . . ?

Walworth, sir.

Walworth?

Near the Elephant, sir.

Ah, the Elephant and Castle.

The First Lord's voice bounced back from wood-panelled walls, his lisp slipping on the *s* of the castle.

We shall honour these boys and do it well. Everyone agrees, and agreement is in short shrift these days as well, so, step to it.

Sir?

What do we have in the way of ships, what do we have available?

Sir, I believe the Fervent . . .

Splendid. They will return home on a destroyer. His Majesty's navy at its finest, carrying our finest home. We'll bring her up the Thames and the people will come out in their hundreds. They always do. It will be both sign and signal, that we trust in the ships and we trust our men in charge of them.

An order was given, a letter drafted and approved, a signature added, blotted, it was done. Winston Churchill was bringing the boys home on HMS Fervent.

The First Lord of the Admiralty paused for a moment to think of the boys, and of the one still not found. Then he got on with the job, much to do, much to do.

Edward Lovett was taking advantage of the long summer evenings to get on with cataloguing his collection. He carefully handled a child's shoe, left for many years in the chimney flue of an old cottage, part of a row recently demolished to make way for a new terrace, wider, smarter, running water inside each of the houses to replace the standpipe shared by a dozen or more. The collector had seen many of these shoes, left inside the chimney, on the ledges that might have been built there for this purpose rather than for the efficient escape of smoke. Placed there to stop bad luck entering the house. This find was more rare, instead of one made for the purpose, this was an actual child's shoe, worn down at the heel, the beginning of a hole at the toe, found in the chimney stack when the demolition men came to take it down. The collector shook his head, thinking of his own sons and those poor people down at Walworth who had lost their boys. He wrapped the shoe in tissue and laid it in a small box, noted the catalogue number and date, the builder's lad from whom he had bought it, and how much he had paid. He put the box away with the others. A shoe for luck, an acorn against lightning, a wishbone for hope. What charm was there to protect a child against the sea?

Eight coffins were loaded on to HMS Fervent. One last coffin, ready, white-painted, awaited a body, a boy. Scouts stood at attention, locals alongside in their hundreds. At first, the men supervising the bringing home of the boys had been worried, what if there were not enough people to farewell the lads? A small place, Leysdown, not easy being the centre of attention, not used to the pressing questions of journalists, not sure how to answer when the London accents asked who and how and why.

The people of the Kent coast well knew that there might be reasons to explain a disaster, a carelessness, a foolishness, inattention to this detail or that, so much of seafaring about the detail. But they also knew that all too often the sea would have its way with you, the sea and the sky together, and whatever you had done in preparation, studying charts and almanacs, all that careful planning could be swept away as the sea decided whether you lived or died or found yourself a cripple for life. The people of Leysdown, and Sheppey as a whole, were circumspect when they gave their answers to the press, and although they usually spoke proudly of their lives on the water, beside the water, their answers now were quiet, and brief, and they were the same.

It's no one's fault.

It's the way of the sea, she will turn on you.

There's no accounting for it.

That young man has nothing to reproach himself for, he was doing right by the boys.

That young man will find it hard to forget.

That young man nearly lost himself trying to save these lads.

I wouldn't be in his shoes.

I wouldn't be in his shoes.

It was no one's fault.

There'd been no need to worry about the turnout, they were there in their hundreds. The coffins were taken out to the destroyer in boats, not little boats by their own standards, yet they were dwarfed by the Fervent. White coffins, silent boys. And on every tongue, in every heart, was a mixture of hurt and relief and guilt. Hurt for the lads and their families, relief that it was not their son, their brother, their friend, then guilt for the same. And pity too, pity the only word for it, for the young Scoutmaster who'd brought these poor lads to the sea. Such pity for the young man who had brought them to this.

Eight coffins lined up on the deck of the destroyer Fervent. The lad of fourteen from the Arethusa and seven young Scouts stopped in their tracks. One last Scout still out there somewhere, not yet found. At least these ones were going home, these mothers could bury their sons. A few boys from the 2nd Walworth, those who had stayed on at the camp, stood to attention alongside all the other Scouts who had come down to Leysdown for two weeks of summer fun. The lads of the honour guard were stoic, others unable to stop the tears, especially not when a few of the grown men around them broke down, proper adult sobs the like of which most of these boys had never heard before, a rip from the throat, a spat-out cough that sounded as if it were made of blood. They held the salute, the Fervent began to move off, silent, no bugle, no fanfare, just the waves and the shore and the wind.

Twenty-Nine

Charlie went up to Bermondsey to meet the ship, meet the boys, bring Tom home. Not that he could get anywhere close at first, so many people, all sorts, behaving as if they thought the lads were theirs. Perhaps they were, it wasn't just the Hatches with big families, plenty round here would consider their cousin's kid their own. Plenty round here might have brought that lad up themselves, if he needed help. Even so, that didn't account for the crush at the dock, the push of them all at Cherry Garden Pier. Charlie knew the ship had stayed off of Gravesend for the night, might have wished for a better name for the town. There was one family, he'd heard, had stayed all night at Gravesend, on the shore, not wanting their lad to be too far from them. Charlie understood it, thought he might have done the same had it been his Jimmy. Dear God, the luck of it that it wasn't their Jimmy.

He'd come up to Bermondsey for Ida. Ida couldn't seem to stand, to speak even, Bill had his hands full, looking after her and the girls, so Charlie was here for the Hatches, for the family, all togged up in his pearls he was. Let them see who the boy was, that he was theirs. Their boy, lost. And then there he was, Tom, found. He was in the hearse, horses pulling the boys back to St John's. Charlie walked alongside in his pearly suit, bringing Tom home.

Ida had no idea how to dress herself. Ena had helped, the frock was laid out in the bed, black of course, with a lovely lace cape to go with it, the woman, Itzhak's mother – Ida was forgetting names, losing words – she, the mother, Mimi, that's her, had brought it over last night.

I don't mean to bother you my dear, but I thought you might . . .

It was a lovely piece of work, very old, clearly precious. Ida took the piece and nodded, no words, the words clogging the back of her throat, tickling there, itching to come out, as if she might pull one word from her throat, a thin hair of a word and then pull and pull and it would be like the dirty stinking drains she'd had to clean as a child, her job to clean out the drains twice a year. All that muck clinging to one hair. Ida was scared that if she let out even one word, the others would spill from her, never stop, and so she kept her mouth tight shut, lips clamped, and the closest she came to speaking what was in her heart – no, not her heart, she shook her head, not there, lower, her womb, the burning there that wanted to speak, corrosive words made of bile – the closest she came to speaking was in the cold dark thoughts she held inside.

Mouth shut, a sigh nevertheless escaped from her shoulders, the back of her bowed neck. Ena, who was still trying to make Ida get dressed, put out a hand.

Ida? Please? They're waiting.

The girls and Bill, down in the front parlour, all dressed up to the nines, ready since first thing in the morning. Bill had been up even earlier, getting out of bed with a sigh that became a stretch that shuddered back into a swallowed sob. Neither of them had slept, nor spoke either, just lay there breathing, astonished to still be breathing, side by side and not touching, throughout the night.

The girls had talked about the funeral until late, Ida had heard them whispering from the other side of the thin wall. They'd made her angry in the dark, their whispers just a little excited, what would it be like and who would be there and all the people, the way everyone was talking about it. She'd wanted Bill to tell them to stop it, to shut up. She couldn't say it herself, could barely bring herself to speak to the girls, she was a wicked mother, she knew that much. You have to go on for your girls, people kept saying, but Ida would have stopped breathing if she could, no part of her felt it necessary to go on, she wanted to slap those who said, kindly enough of course, there's the girls Ida, don't you forget your girls. Ida wasn't forgetting her girls, but she had no intention of forgetting her boy either. And it was Tom who mattered right now, not the girls, nor the nasty little thrills of excitement that neither of them could hide.

People said she had to be strong for Bill too, that she needed to be his rock.

Men take it harder than we do, Ida, they don't know what to do with themselves.

Ida hadn't noticed that, Bill seemed to know what to do all right, how to speak and who to talk to, who to avoid.

Perhaps it was the practice, Ida wondered. His mother, his father, both gone when he was just a lad, a few years older than Tom was, is, was. Then those friends in the war, picked off one after the other. Seemed Bill knew all about mourning and stupid Ida had never thought to get used to it, never thought to get the practice.

She knew the church would be ready too, the vicar who'd come calling quick enough, scooping up souls, asking did she want him to pray with her and could he do anything. None of it badly meant, and every word another stain she'd never be able to rinse from her memory. Good, good, forgetting this would mean forgetting Tom. No.

They'd told her about the people who'd come to the church to visit. Ida couldn't fathom it, didn't understand why so many strangers wanted to get close to her boy, why they didn't understand they were in the way. They took her to the coffin, said perhaps it was best not to look, that the sea, even in such a short time, was damaging, but she couldn't bear the idea of not kissing him goodbye, and so she had insisted and she had looked and now Ida wished she hadn't. She'd never have forgiven herself if she hadn't, would have known herself a rotten cow of a mother if she hadn't wanted to kiss him that one last time, but still, she wished she hadn't. He was her boy, even though the water had done some damage, as they'd said. Not a lot, but enough. That was the problem, he was too much her boy. Ida thought it might have been better if he'd been as damaged as they'd warned, if he hadn't looked quite so much like Tom. But he did, just like her Tom and also not enough. Not alive like her Tom.

Ida had steeled herself to get to the church for the

viewing, to walk round the corner and in the big door, past plenty who'd wanted to get a gawp of her and all. What were they doing there? It made her furious to have to nudge past, seeing first their angry looks at the woman who was pushing to the front of the queue and then, when they worked out who she was, why she was being led ahead, then she saw the other look on their faces – dread and pity and something else, interest or, surely not, but maybe – envy? Envy, perhaps, at seeing someone else given such attention? Queer, that's what people were, dead queer.

She had managed to get herself there to see them laid out, the lads in their coffins, lifting one foot after the other, feet she could barely feel as she'd been bustled down the road. Too close to the house, this damn church, she'd have had that walk take a lifetime. The quiet inside, all of a sudden, was shocking, and a little sickening, sudden quiet and the scent of too many lilies, too many candles and all that incense. The stink of it, of the dead sea, dead salt, dead boys. Ida got herself up to his coffin – all those poor little coffins, laid out in a line at the altar – and when she did, she forced herself to look in, and dear God, there he was, her Tom, and it was all she could do not to scream out, because he really didn't look that different, didn't look dead, not dead enough to bury, surely, not dead enough? And that was what was clawing at Ida's insides now. How could she put him in the ground when he still looked so much like her boy?

And yet she was, today, now, she was doing it, readying to bury her boy. Bill had tried to talk to her about the funeral, when they'd lain in bed in the dark and neither would give in to sleep, neither would let sleep steal those hours from them, precious hours where their boy was still just up the road, not in the ground, not yet.

I know you think you can't, love. I think I can't and all, but we can, we will. We'll do it for Tom, and for his mates. We'll show the girls how to stand beside their brother, by doing it ourselves. You can't make head nor tail of it, neither can I, but it doesn't need to make any sense. That's why we have all this, the church and the funeral and those same old words we know. We don't have to believe what the priest says, but it's a guide, isn't it, love? Eh? It's there so we know how we do this. So we don't have to think about it, we just get through. And we do it for the boy. You'll see. I promise, Ida. I promise love, honest. You'll see, you don't need to know how to do it, but you will. Like in the war, none of it makes any sense, and it's bloody barbaric, it's fucking absurd. And we do it.

Ida didn't think the girls wanted the funeral any more than she did, certainly didn't think Tom's mates did, the ones who were going to have to stand to attention and be a guard of honour for all their dead friends, poor little buggers. Ida didn't think they needed to do it at all. But she didn't say so, not in words, and she let Bill tell her how it would be, because Bill had always wanted to look after, and there was nothing he could look after now, nothing to fix, nothing Bill could do. They were both lost and she might as well let Bill believe he was taking care of her. She might as well leave him whispering into the dark of their bedroom.

244

Ida sighed and looked at the dress Ena had laid out on the bed. Her arms, separate from her body, separate from her will, picked it up and pulled it over her head. Her fingers, no fingers of Ida's, began to do up the buttons. Ida looked down from a long way above and watched herself get dressed for her son's funeral.

Thirty

The smell of incense and lilies was closest at the front of the church, worse even than yesterday. Now the warmth of so many bodies cramming in, the hundreds more pressing up against the brick and stone outside, had all the flowers fully out, fully in bloom for the first time this summer, and the scent was a solid wall as Ida walked down the aisle. The families of the dead boys were jammed together into the front pews. Despite Bill's promises that it would make sense if only they followed the pattern, it was nothing at all like a normal funeral, where the hierarchy of grief made sure everyone knew their place and what to say, what to do. Here the families were all bunched up next to each other, immediate family only and woe betide the grandmother who wanted to hold her grieving daughter's hand, a little further back please, parents and brothers and sisters only.

They'd come into the church just as a storm broke outside. Thunder had been rolling up and down the river for the past half hour and the day was warmer than it had been, sticky with it. Samson and Tilly, standing outside along with all the market people, were drenched in minutes. No room inside for them, no matter how togged up they were for the occasion, all sorts of folk turned out in their pressed suits or their best hats or their dear old boots, buffed and polished for the occasion, to be told at the door that it was family only. They were trying to make sure there was enough room inside for all the families of our dear dead boys, and that other family too, the ones still waiting for their lad to be given back by the sea, praying he'd be given back by the sea. That was a lot of mothers and fathers and brothers and sisters, not to mention the cousins and aunts and uncles. Thing was, round here, saying it was family only would fill up the church anyway, this lot pretty much all thought of themselves as family. Samson would have gone in too, but that Tilly put a hand on his arm and spoke softly,

Stay out here love, stay with me. It's going to be rotten enough for them to come up to the church as it is, we should wait here. A friendly face for when they round the corner.

Samson nodded, Tilly was always right when it came to these things. When they passed, the best Tilly could offer had been a hand held out, fingertips crossing, as Ida and Bill and the girls were hurried through the downpour. Ah well, at least Tilly would get to the house sooner, the better to get the tea and things out for when Ida was back from the cemetery. At least she could be useful for her mate. More damn useful than she was standing here with all the press and the gawpers and God knew who this lot were, thousands of them it looked like, right up to the Walworth Road they went, stretching in both directions, back through to the Old Kent Road, Tilly wouldn't wonder.

When the mothers and fathers first began to arrive – walking up to the church together, all of it carefully planned, hoping to avoid too much of the crush, hoping to steer clear of the newspaper men standing around trying to get their best story – the locals were lost for what to do. Unlike the newspaper people, they did not hold cameras or little notebooks. Some of the women who knew Ida from the market, who knew others of the mothers from church suppers or chatting at the baths, over the shopping, on their way to work, had brought little posies, flowers they now twisted in their hands, perhaps they'd meant to give them to the mothers, or lay them down for the boys, but now, in the front of grey-faced grief, the flowers seemed foolish. What good was a bunch of violets? The men took off their caps, and the women found themselves bowing a little, half-curtseying almost, something, anything to acknowledge, to show yes, we are here, we're standing here for you.

The parents and the brothers and sisters of the dead moved forward a few steps, the crush of the crowd edged ever such a little way back. Forward, back, forward, back. The families were no keener to get into the church and the crowd no keener to miss their chance to have a gawp. Honour, respect, but also to look, to get a good look.

Then the crack came, thunder smacking into the clouds directly above them, and right on top of it an almighty slap of lightning, and the rain, pelting down. The crowd swayed back at the deluge and the families were rushed inside. Ida's face, Tilly would never forget that, the poor bitch's face. The vicar was less patient now, it was time, they had to get in, time please – like he was behind the bar, time please gents, calling them in, sending them home. Ida reached for Tilly, and there was just a glance, and Tilly knew her pal would have done anything not to go on in, not to have the next hour pass and the next.

Mimi had never been inside a church before. Itzhak had, sometimes the Scouts went into St John's to polish the brass, help shine up the altar rail. Not that Itzhak had ever told his parents. He wasn't sure they would disapprove, but he didn't want to give them cause to comment either. He knew, without being told, that there was an uncertainty about the Scouts, their Englishness, their 'duty to God'. And that being the God with Jesus attached, not the G–d whose name must not be spoken. So he'd never said he'd been in the church before and now he stood beside Mimi, squashed in at the back, allowed in because he was one of the lads. Itzhak felt himself marked. He stood close to his mother and recognised in her his own wonder at the violent images on the walls – the Stations of the Cross, the curate had called them. Itzhak wanted to tell Mimi, to share his knowing, but he didn't want to let on that he knew, so he held her hand, glad to stand beside his mother.

Mimi had been holding his hand since he got back from Leysdown, sitting beside him in the dark when he couldn't sleep for fear of finding himself back in that water, lost in the water. Itzhak had not told Mimi why he could not sleep, why he chose not to sleep rather than risk a dream.

The first night home Itzhak was exhausted from the preceding days, from all the questions thrown at him, the coastguard and the Scoutmasters and the other boys all asking what had happened, what do you remember?

What Itzhak remembered, and what he did not have words to say, was that he'd seen Tom in the water. He'd heard Tom's voice, and he had stopped and turned and been slapped in the face by a wave as he did so, but still he'd stopped, waiting for the wave to pass, feeling the cold sink into his skin, his bones, feeling his heart slow even in those few seconds that he had stopped, and when the wave passed he saw Tom. Itzhak saw Tom twenty, thirty feet away perhaps. Tom was still, but his eyes were open, they were looking. He wasn't calling, or if he was the sound was carried late on the wind and any call for help was lost in all the other shouts and cries and screaming wind and roaring sea and rushing waves. And when Tom bobbed up, ever such a little, he whistled. Itzhak heard his friend whistle to him. Then another wave slapped Itzhak down, rolling him on to his back, tumbling him under the water, round and round until he thought he'd be left in these rolling waves for ever and when he finally came up, coughing, choking, Itzhak began to swim, no matter that he had no idea where he was going, no matter that the waves kept slapping him down, he just kept on swimming. He did not look back and he swam for dear life. For his own dear life, not Tom's dear life. He swam away.

That was what he didn't tell them when they asked. That he had swum away, Tom's whistle ringing in his ears.

Itzhak stood at the back of the church and he watched his mother studying the Stations of the Cross, appalled and intrigued by the depiction of a half-naked man, bent beneath a post of wood, his head bloody from a crown of thorns, his back red with welts. Itzhak held his mother's hand and she held his.

Mimi knew Itzhak was upset in a way she could not help, and she understood that the funeral might make a difference. It had for her, when her father had died, and then her mother. It had helped to hear the men recite the shemah, to hear the rabbi say the prayers she had heard for her grandparents, for other elders in their little village. It had made some sense of the impossibility that she would never hear her mother's voice again. Mimi hoped that this service might make a difference for Itzhak, but as the choir sang of lost lambs, and the rain smashed down outside, and the heat of the bodies all around closed in tighter and finally, finally, the families of the dead boys came inside, she questioned her wisdom. The choir were singing of dear little lambs, but the images on the wall were of a broken and bloody man.

Outside, the closer friends and neighbours stood right up against the church, trying to hear inside, trying to hear the words, the prayers. Beyond them were so many others. Some said the crowds stretched all the way down to Camberwell, which was a bit daft seeing as how the cortège wasn't even going that way, would be heading over through Peckham, but maybe they were toffs or folk from outside London, all sorts, high and low, the lot of them come to say goodbye to the lads.

Almost the lot of them. There were always some would take any chance to make a bob or two, hawkers selling nuts, plain or roasted, a twist of salt if that's how you like them. There were others with souvenir maps of the route to the cemetery, round through Peckham Rye, the proper route. Half a dozen or more selling penny chocolates, cinder toffee, barley sugars. Well, it was a long wait and there were more than a few here with their little ones, the kids would need something to keep them quiet when the coffins came past, didn't want a small voice piping up with a silly question.

Where are the boys? I can't see any boys Ma, that's just a box.

Nothing like a penny gobstopper to turn out children who were quiet and well-behaved.

There was one enterprising soul must have spent the past few nights up sewing, lovely handkerchiefs she had for sale, each one carefully appliquéd with the Scout emblem, the date embroidered in fine black thread, and the stitching ever so neat. Most of the hawkers were given short shrift by the locals, not the kind of thing a Walworth person would do, disrespectful it was, but plenty of folk from further afield, across the river, or up town to judge by their accents, thought nothing of handing over a ha'penny for a bite of toffee, a penny for a card with a verse of remembrance and the date in a smudged copperplate across the top.

Tilly shook her head and Samson, seeing the lift of her shoulders, the intake of breath, put a hand on the small of her back.

Not now pet, takes all sorts.

Tilly twisted her waist, shrugged his hand off her back, but she held her tongue.

Years later, Ida would try to remember how it had been in the church. The coffins in a row. The singing. The occasional sob ringing out from the back of the church, the muffled crying from the front. Funny that, she wasn't sure she could trust her memory, but it did seem as if the ones making the most racket had not been the families, not those of them up at the front. Maybe it made sense, maybe they'd done all their ranting indoors. A few years later she felt herself less alone, every mother it seemed, with a son gone, a husband lost.

Even later still, Ida would try to piece together the day, aware that in doing so she was hanging on to those moments for dear life, the moments while her boy was still within touching distance, the coffin just a few feet away, Tom still inside, his hair still soft.

She had thought, that morning, about taking a dose of something, a little laudanum, a spot of valerian perhaps, something on her hankie to breathe in, to hold herself up, but in the end she decided against it. She knew Bill had a flask in his pocket, had brought it to his lips more than once, and she didn't grudge him that, not at all. The girls had a twist of barley sugars each. A nice idea, one of the neighbours had thought to bring a little something for the girls. It was going to be a long day and they'd need something to keep them going. The girls had looked at Ida as if she was going to tell them no.

Of course you must have it. Say thank you and wrap your twists in a scrap of the black crepe. Then if anyone sees they'll just think it's a bag of ... of ...

The girls nodded, careful, quiet, too damn quiet.

Years later, Ida still could not remember the name of that

thoughtful neighbour who knew her girls would be starving for something just for them, starving in a home stuffed to the gills with cakes and pies and stews and more cakes. Just in case, for the visitors, because you have to keep your strength up. You mustn't go to pieces.

Years later, Ida thought that was it though, it was all bits and pieces. Her memory of what happened that day jumped, backwards and forwards, sounds and images broken apart, disjointed, barley sugars here, dust to dust there, Bill coming through the door and telling her the news, a night with no sleep, another night pacing the back yard with Bill, the two of them trying to walk away the nightmare, Tilly's hand, just before the rain. All of her memories slap bang up against each other and no thread to pull them straight.

No. There was one thread. Tom. Tom in his coffin, Tom going into the ground up at Nunhead. There was always that. Years later, Ida could still remember that.

It took a long time to get up to Nunhead that afternoon, over an hour some said, so many people all along the way, and the clouds low over the city, low all the way out to the green of the cemetery.

That night Itzhak sat at home with his parents and grandfather. He'd placed himself closer to his mother than usual and neither Nathan nor David had teased him for it, the lodgers were taking tea with the whole family, everyone together, a rarity and yet no one talked about what had happened, the words about death and drowning, honour and memory, were too new to fit in their mouths, the pictures in their minds still too real. Itzhak thought how tired his legs were, how long it had taken, the walk. He didn't really understand, because he and Jimmy and Tom used to run up there in no time at all, up to Dulwich Wood, or round the dairy farms, up to Nunhead, down to Clapham just the same. He thought how the whole of London seemed to be just a run away, but this afternoon, with so many people pressing on all sides, the walk seemed to go on for ever. And oh, didn't his legs ache now. He didn't tell his mother of the aching, he'd enough of her fretting that he would catch cold, that his time in the sea must have damaged his chest, damaged his bones. He didn't want to be given any more of those dark and stinking oils she kept for such times. He was tired though, and sore, and he didn't protest when his father carried him up to his bed, and although Nathan dug David in the ribs, and although the big brothers exchanged a glance, neither spoke a word.

It took a long time to get to the cemetery, and not long enough for Ida. Sitting in the funeral carriage she kept her eyes on her boy, her gaze trained on the coffins ahead, the Union Flag and the matching flowers making his coffin look just like all the others, her determination never to let him out of her sight. When they turned the corner from Choumert Road into Rye Lane and another big crowd got in her way for a moment, Ida almost giggled, felt sick as the half-laugh tried to rise from her chest, it was like the old three cups game, she didn't mean to laugh, but the absurdity of burying her son alongside half a dozen other boys suddenly had her thinking of the trick that Charlie's dad had often played on his customers. Often played, and always won. Three cups in a row, a coin asked from a customer, the promise that if the lady or gent could tell him where the coin was after he'd shuffled the cups, then they could pick anything they liked on the stall, take it home gratis. Anything at all. If not, Charlie's dad would keep the coin. And even though everyone knew the trick, and most knew it was impossible to win, people fell for it time and again. This time they'd get one over the trickster, this time they'd win. The giggle turned to a retch and Ida brought her hand to her mouth. Bad enough to lose her boy, bad enough to have to share his funeral with all these strangers, so hungry they were to get a look at her, but she was damned if she was going to let him go to his grave – another retch – and not know exactly which coffin held her lad.

Bad enough too, that the boys were all going in the grave together. Ida had not said this to anyone, she knew it was meant to be an honour, understood the generosity of the Scouts and the church, taking care of it all, just looking at those uniformed lads lining the way from the church, lining the road to keep back the crowd, she appreciated the effort. She understood that today they were making an important person of her son, now and always. Ida knew this, and it still hurt that she knew there would be no one place for Tom. If she came up to see him at Christmas or on his anniversary – dear God, that her boy now had an anniversary – she'd always have to share the day with the other parents, the other families, other mothers. Ida did not want to be united in grief and she did not want to share. She couldn't say this to anyone but Bill, and so she kept her mouth shut and fixed her eyes on the red, white and blue flowers above the red, white and blue flag on the white box that held her son.

The coffins were lowered into the ground, London soil, London clay, magpies and crows calling out over the vicar's words, the dust and the ashes and the hope of eternal life. And then there was the Last Post and then it was too much. The suppressed sobs, silent screams that had been swallowed down all day, kept in and bitten back and turned to acid in the backs of throats, came out anyway, each one forced free letting out another, encouraging its neighbours. A line of Scouts, bugles in hand and mouth, playing as the coffins were lowered, it was too much.

One mother fell. Another wept openly, enough of stoicism and pointless pride. One woman wailed, a keening, moaning wail that had the crows wondering where their new leader was. And Ida felt her face become the mask it had been threatening to turn into for hours, the music tore apart her resolve. Her mouth turned down at each corner, then her lips were pulled apart by the lower jaw slowly wrenching downwards as that long, low moan came from her, splitting the sides of her mouth and twisting her neck, turning her face up to the sky. Ida heard the deep, guttural sound come from far within, felt it lift up and out from the belly of her, and she knew she had heard it many times before.

Ida, the wise woman, had heard that same moan, the same shift in tone, in her birthing mothers. That change to the heavy animal groan that signalled now was the time, here it was, a bigger pain and a deeper wrench and now, now the time to push, now the time to fully give in to it, to

257

become only birth, only giving, only opening up. Ida had held so many women in birth, worked with them to bring in the new life, she knew exactly what to listen for. And now her own arms wrapped tight around her own body, as if she might draw her son back into her, as sods of clay were dropped on top of the coffins and the sky began to drizzle again and the buglers played and the birthing cry came from far inside her and, finally, she did nothing to hold it in.

Thirty-One

They were crammed into the pub, back to back, shoulders and elbows jostling, feet touching feet. Children hung around the door, hoping for a bottle of lemonade to share, the bottle to return for the penny. Dogs found safety from dangerous feet in the corner by the cold fireplace. On the bar were plates of sausage rolls and ham sandwiches, juicy with glistening fat, chunks of fruit cake and buttered currant buns, boiled eggs and pickled onions. Every now and then someone reaching for a fresh pint would pick up a plate and pass it on behind him to the others crowding forward. And as soon as that space was made another plate would take its place on the bar. Fresh sandwiches, egg and chives, new cakes, a good sticky ginger cake, sunk in the middle, the best way. Drinks were passed back, food passed back, and the women behind the bar, all neighbours, Aunty Sarah with them, worked on, baking half the night before and all of the morning, assembling sandwiches, cutting cakes. Plate after plate, pint after pint.

Edward Lovett carefully folded his newspaper, laying it on the walnut table. His sons would want to read it when they returned from work. They always caught a later train from the City, travelling together, happy in the overcrowded carriage that he preferred to avoid, either by heading straight off to the market, to the lanes, to add to his collection, or by leaving work that much later and avoiding the rush altogether. He had come home early today and he was not the only one, several of the men at the bank had left twenty minutes or so before the usual time, made their way across London Bridge more quietly than normal. Even for these men in their sensible City black, umbrellas furled, there had been a sense of what was going on across the river.

Lovett glanced again at the newspaper, the headline announcing the funeral of those poor boys. He wondered if he might have met one of those young Scouts, in the market perhaps, with one of their parents, trading charms for a few coins. A dreadful thing to lose one's child.

He was waiting when his sons came home, ready to open the door for them.

Father, asked Francis, is something the matter?

Lovett shook his head, No, not at all. I simply ... well, here you both are.

He stood aside to welcome them into the hallway, and they followed him into the drawing room. Lovett turned and reached out a hand to both of his boys, men now, men as tall as he was, taller in Edward's case. His sons, not sure what their father wanted or needed from them, reacted characteristically differently. Francis moved a step closer, Edward a shorter step distant, and Lovett was left in the centre of the room, astonished that he was trying to embrace his sons, and uncomfortably aware that none of them knew what to do next.

Lovett pointed to the headline, and now he noticed that his hand was shaking,

The boys, those young Scouts . . .

Francis stepped closer still, a tentative arm around his father's shoulder.

Edward nodded, Dreadful business. Would you . . . care to join us? We were discussing the series, Francis and I might head along to the test against South Africa.

Cricket?

Yes, the triangular, at The Oval.

A chap in Francis's office has tickets he can't use.

Three?

No, but I'm sure we can get another. Or you and Francis could go, I shouldn't mind.

Lovett looked at his son offering up the place beside his brother, knew it was a gesture of both generosity and of fear, neither was fully comfortable now, when it was just the two of them together, they hadn't been since his wife left. Something had come between them then and none of them now knew how to bridge the gap.

No, really. I should hate to be the cause of one of you missing out. Kind of you . . . both, to think of me.

Lovett stepped away then and went back upstairs, to his study, to the glass of watered whiskey that he swallowed in one long mouthful, the sound of his sons' hushed, bemused, and not unkind laughter rose up from the room beneath.

Then he addressed himself to a particularly lovely find, a

261

wishbone-shaped piece of coral, smooth from years of trust and handling.

After a while the feeding frenzy in the pub subsided and the eaters settled into drinking more heavily. Now plates of left-over sandwiches and the ends of the cakes were made up into parcels for the children and passed high over drinkers' heads to the children hanging around the door. The dogs made for the door as well, more likely to snaffle half a sausage from the hand of an unsuspecting toddler than from the adult mourn-ers who had started the session famished in the way only a long walk and a good cry and a love of life could leave them.

Samson and Tilly stood together.

Did you see her face? When Bill asked if she wanted another drink?

Tilly shook her head, Poor bitch. She didn't even want that drink, only did it to toast the lad. I don't think she's managed even half a cup of tea in the past week. Tom's a lump in her throat and she's frightened to swallow in case she loses him. Better not to eat, not to drink, better to feel it all the time than not feel it for even one moment and then hate herself for getting on.

Samson nodded, Not his fault though, Bill's not wrong for wanting a drink, it is a wake after all.

Tilly agreed, Yes, but it's different burying your old dad or an aunt you half-loved, half-laughed at. Or even the old bastard you hated, the tartar who kept at you when you were little. Then it's all about the stories, isn't it? We eat and drink and talk them out, all night if we have to, that's the remembering, that's the point.

Samson took a long mouthful of beer and nodded. He liked the way Tilly talked. Samson had plenty of thoughts in his head, but he often left them there, to stew, not so with Tilly, half the time he'd swear she opened her mouth and then find out how she felt, what she thought, only when she heard herself speak it.

But see, with Tom, Tilly was saying, No one's telling any stories at all, are they? Everyone was too scared to mention a word of him to Ida or Bill before the funeral, or since. It's not a proper wake because we daren't speak him. So poor Tom doesn't get to live the life he should've had and he doesn't get to be remembered now he's dead, not properly. Damn shame, I call it.

Bill would've had another though, Samson said, lifting his tankard for the girl behind the bar to come and fill it again.

Tilly nodded, draining her own glass and lining it up alongside Samson's for the refill.

True. And Ida would've collapsed if they been here another minute, edge of herself she was. Bill'll get his drink, don't you worry, Charlie's gone over, took a bottle of good whiskey with him, Ida's dad went too. They'll finish it off tonight, I don't doubt. Won't make a blind bit of difference though, the lad's still gone.

Still gone, they nodded.

Tilly turned to Aunty Sarah, her work done for the day and a place in a hard-backed chair made for her, Samson turned to his mate Percy. Even as they turned apart, Samson and Tilly continued to hold hands, as they had done all day, in the church, walking up to Nunhead, walking back under the overcast sky. They held hands as they would

263

do all night, Samson holding on for dear life to Tilly, his second woman, his not-wife, and all the happier for it. She, in her turn, thanking God for bringing him to her when she'd given up hope of a good man, and thanking God too, for bringing him to her late, when there was no chance of making a child they might one day lose.

In Clapham, a boy asked his nanny to take him to the park. He had two boats to sail and wanted to take them to the pond.

It isn't fair that Charles is away and I have to stay home and play alone.

Charles is going to school after the summer, your mother and he need a little time to themselves.

That's all very well, said the serious child, But I have no one to play with, so it has to be you, Nanny.

The middle-aged woman looked over her glasses at the boy, a sailboat in each hand. She looked at the clock on the nursery mantelpiece and set aside her newspaper, carefully placing it with the front page facing down, I expect we could get in a quick sail before tea.

They set off for the pond and before he launched the boats, she said, Take care, George, we can't count on strangers coming to our aid today.

They were nice boys, weren't they, Nanny?

They were very helpful.

May I play with them, if they come to the pond?

I don't suppose they will.

But may I? If they do?

The nanny frowned, There'll be plenty of lovely friends when you go away to school, George.

At the pond they were alone and George played happily with his boats until it was time for tea. The common was particularly quiet, the nanny told George it was probably the earlier downpour that had kept the other children away, and under her breath she whispered an old prayer, watching the blue and red boats, floating on the water.

Ida was lying down, curtains closed, the old eiderdown over her legs. Her mother's eiderdown, dark blue with a gold ruffle, hand stitched and leaking feathers at a rate of half a dozen a week now. Ida's hands were sifting the fine fabric, her ma had been so proud of this old eiderdown, the real duck feathers. Ida might have slept, she wasn't sure, she hoped she had, she hoped she hadn't. She wanted today over and she wanted it never to have happened. She could hear Ena through in the scullery, getting up tea for her own boy, and for Ida's daughters as well, shushing all three of them, telling the children to be quiet.

Ida frowned, she and Ena had always been careful of each other, hard work for a woman to share her kitchen, hard enough with your own mother or sister, but with your sister-in-law, it could be even worse. They'd both stepped around each other ever since they'd decided to take on the house, two families, and they'd done so lightly. Now Ida lay on her bed, incapable of getting up and furious with her husband's sister.

Bill pushed open the door, she could smell the whiskey on his breath from here.

You're awake?

Not sure I slept, not really.

Ena's getting the kids their tea.

I know.

Love . . .

It's fine Bill, I don't mind you having a drink with Charlie and my dad. It's fine. We should all have a drink, it's a wake isn't it?

Ida . . .

I mean it.

Bill sat on the bed beside his wife, setting himself down ever so gently. Ida thought how this big man, her husband, was so light now, had been soft-footed since they'd got the news. Two weeks ago he'd have slammed himself down as he sat and the bed would have groaned and she'd have told him to take care and he'd have said he couldn't help it. Not now. Even half-cut, Bill was all careful and low-voiced near her. Ida understood he was scared she might break, she was scared herself that she might break, all the while astonished that she hadn't – yet. But she hated that Bill felt the need to be gentle, hated that everyone was careful with her, hated that Ena was looking after her girls when she couldn't. She knew only too well that Bill cried himself to a stupor, not a sleep, at night and had done since he'd come back from Leysdown.

What is it?

Ida shook her head.

You've got the hump about something, Ida. I saw them do it, those blokes who came back from the war, shut their mouths the minute we landed on the south coast. Went mad with it, they did, mad with not saying whatever it was they had to say. You have to tell me.

I can't.

Ida was crying now, again, crying slowly.

You can.

Bill stretched out his arm, pulled her up to him, big arm, strong man, big arm holding her tight to him and never tight enough, never enough strength in him to squeeze out all that hurt.

I'm a bitch.

You're not. Why?

I am, I'm a right cow. It's Ena.

What's she done?

Made breakfast, dinner, tea. Done my shopping and my cooking, looked after the stall twice last week, loaded and carried the damn thing for me though she's half my strength and I've always said how I wanted someone to pull it for me, but God knows I can't bear that she's doing it now. She took my dad his dinner, and then brought him over here when she was worried about him, indoors all by himself. And she's not said a word. None of Ena's usual carry on, not a word. And now she's making tea, for my girls, feeding them, holding them, being good to them. She's doing what I should be doing.

You can go sit with them while they eat. Ena wants to help and the girls would like you to sit with them, they miss you, love.

I know. And I can't, and I damn myself for it, Bill, honest I do. I should go to hell, I let him go, I had a bad feeling and I let him go.

You don't believe in all that, love.

No, and more fool me. Selling charms and tricks from the stall and so sure I know better than those so desperate to buy them, don't believe in fate at all. Now look at me, what's this but fate, eh? Why didn't I listen to myself? To that voice I had, scared and worried, way inside?

267

You couldn't know. And we were all of us worried. We let them go because it was good for them, we hoped it would be . . .

I damn me Bill, and you should too.

Oh love, come here.

Ida wriggled from Bill's hold, not letting herself give in to his comfort, not letting herself get away with anything.

Not just that, but I'm such a bloody awful mother I don't even want to be with the girls. I can't sit with them while I know Tom's not coming back, but I don't want Ena with them instead of me.

She's only trying to help.

And she's no end of help. I'm the one who's wrong, I know it.

Ida was standing now, unsteadily pacing the room, feet cold on the carpet, the threads worn from years of her own feet, and her mother's feet before. An old Turkey carpet handed down from mother to daughter and Ida sick to her stomach that she didn't want to be with her own daughters, that she only wanted to be up at Nunhead.

His funeral Bill, the day of his funeral and I'm such a cow that I leave my girls to get on with it for themselves, poor little mites, but I don't want your sister looking after them either.

Bill sat on the side of the bed, watching his wife spin in grief.

An hour later, when Ena had helped him put Ida to bed again, given her a couple of drops of her own laudanum and valerian mix, Ida in such a state she didn't fight them this time, let Ena dose her up, let the girls come to lie beside

268

her, one under each arm, when all three of his girls were sleeping with wet lashes, red raw cheeks, Bill went back out to the yard and Charlie poured him glass after glass of whiskey, his father-in-law drunk enough to be stone-cold sober, slumped in the corner of the yard, lamenting his own guilt at being an old man, having lived so long.

They cut the bottle that night. And the next night, and the next.

Rose was alone in the front room, carefully washing Emily's face and hands. For five days now, Emily had been more lucid and in less pain. She was thinner than ever, her skin a translucent grey, and both she and Rose knew that these were her last hours. Emily couldn't drink, hadn't eaten since before the boys went away, so washing her mother was easier now, no shit to wipe, no piss since she'd stopped drinking last night, not even any bile, the washing was merely a gesture, a cool cloth to soothe her skin, to give Rose something to do. Emily took in nothing but air, excreted nothing but the foul-sweet smell.

Emily clean and her skin, at least, fresh again, Rose opened the window to lean outside. The heavy rain of the storm had washed the city, the sky was clear and a soft air flowed along the street. A nightingale began a trill, stopped, began again, cats yowled, and from the end of the road Rose could just hear the sound of the wake, the last dregs of the drunk and the drinking, singing into the night. She closed the window and took up her seat again, by her mother, waiting.

Emily died just before five thirty. The sun was up, pushing through low cloud. Rose had been straightening the

269

pins in Emily's pincushion, placing the higgledy piggledy pins in neat rows, just as she'd loved to do when she was a girl, with each push adding a prayer for Tom whose hair was part of the stuffing. She felt the change in the room, looked up to see what was gone.

Rose closed her mother's eyes and opened the window to let Emily sail free. Then, a little later, when the body was very still, very empty, Rose closed the curtains, covered the mirrors, and she cried.

Thirty-Two

Two days after the funeral, after the pomp and circumstance, after the toffs had gone back to Kensington and Highgate Hill, once the Walworth Road had been swept of the mess left by so many thousands who'd come to pay their respects and gone home, to their own children sitting around the table, funeral cards and lollipop sticks trampled into the dirt behind them, Ida pulled herself from her bed. Bill was back at work, of course, they might have a scullery full of food, turning fast in this weather, but they still needed to pay the rent, put aside a little for the Christmas pot, a little for the children's – she corrected herself, for the girls' – school money. They still needed to work.

Ida got out of bed and as she put her feet on the floor she made herself offer thanks for her life. A thanks she didn't feel, to a God she had no faith in. Not that she'd had faith in Him before, but now, well. Now. Here she was. She laid out doorsteps of bread for the girls, and a mug of sweet tea each, poured tepid already from the big pot Bill had made earlier, bringing her a cup in bed, as he always did, always had, before he went to work himself, giving her a blissful ten minutes more each day. None of her moments were blissful now, nor did she want them to be. Or did she? Ida pictured the table, her girls and Bill and she around it, eating, laughing, Bill with Lucy on his knee. Then she felt the bile flow up again, sick at herself for daring to imagine a table without her boy at it. She put both marg and jam on the table. Let the girls have it, let them gorge on it, what she wouldn't do to offer Tom both marg and jam today.

Ida poured water into a bowl in the big sink, and washed her face, her underarms, the sweaty line beneath her breasts. She washed her cunt and would not think, could not but think, that this is where she birthed her firstborn, right in this scullery. When Tom finally began to push through there wasn't even time to get to the bedroom, Ida had him hanging on to the kitchen table and crying out that if Bill thought he'd be down the pub celebrating tonight, after all this, he'd another think coming. Ida was crying now and she barely noticed. Crying, not crying, they were all the same to her now. No. Not today. She sluiced her face, rinsed her eyes. It would not do to have red eyes, puffy cheeks where she was going today.

Back in her bedroom, Ida put aside the black dress she had worn for most of the past week, and found another from the half-dozen her women friends had brought over. Cakes and pies, yes, but also the right clothes. No one around here could afford to have more than one mourning frock, however many people were turning up for the funeral. Even with a seamstress for a friend, the fabric had to be paid for, and there were weeks, months of mourning to go yet. The women round here took care of each other. She pulled the dress up over her hips and then over her shoulders. Not a bad fit, she'd just need to nip it in at the waist with a sash and it would do nicely. A good plain mourning dress to visit the mother of the other boy. The boy still not found.

Ida closed the front door behind her and kept her head down. Partly because she didn't want to talk to anyone, and partly out of the awareness that so few of them would want to talk to her. She'd done it herself in the past, seen a mourning friend on the other side of the road and wondered should she cross to them or not, wondered if mentioning the dead one was helpful or not. They'd been brought up to be open and honest, forthright in Charlie's case, but Ida had always wondered about it, bringing the grief right to a person, perhaps out in the street for the first time since a funeral, their skin a little more raw, their bones still unsettled from seeing the truth of death, of ashes and dust. So she kept her head down, she didn't want to talk, and she knew anyone who bumped into her would be worried what to say.

Ida didn't want to talk but she was going to talk anyway. Up to the Walworth Road, across by the Town Hall, down Amelia Street to the Pullens Buildings. She walked quickly, not looking up. In five minutes she was outside one of the big blocks that made up the buildings, and her hands were fists at her sides.

Ida and Bill had tried to get a flat here, a place of their own for the two of them and Tom, on the way. The flats were fairly new and the rooms big enough that there'd be space for another child if they were lucky. But they couldn't manage it, the rent that little bit more, and not making enough between them to stretch to it, so it was sharing a house with Ena and her lot, and learning to live with a new sister, the only sister Ida'd ever had. Not a bad learning either, no matter how fiercely she'd wanted that flat of their own. Ida didn't envy the woman she was going to visit now, not her flat nor the reason for her visit, not one bit.

Lying in her bed last night, cried out, and knowing there were still so many more tears to come, Ida had realised what she needed to do. She'd turned to Bill and told him so.

I'm going to go and see her, the one whose boy ...

I don't know, love, Bill said. You're in a right state, no one expects you to put yourself through that. And she might not thank you.

They both knew which woman she was talking about, the mother who was still waiting, the mother who'd been at the funeral service on Tuesday, but hadn't come with them all up to Nunhead. No point, no body to bury. She'd left the church and been helped home by her own people, her mouth a thin line to keep in the screams of injustice, so unfair it was to know her boy dead and have no funeral for him. Unfair too, that her boy would not get a funeral like this, he was a bright, outgoing lad, he'd have loved all this fuss and attention. Unfair that her boy was still not found. That she was waiting, no promise, no nothing.

You're in a bad way yourself.

I won't be when I visit her, Bill. I know my place.

Yes, but, she's bound to be ... you've had, we've had ...

The funeral. Yes. And the body. Much good it's done us.

274

More good than her waiting, I'd think.

That's why I ought to go. We've had people not know what to say to us, so they say nothing, or others who can't help talking daft, folk throwing drinks and food at us because they want to help. Everyone wants to help.

You want to help? Bill asked.

I want to do the right thing, Bill. Paying my respects is the right thing.

Now Ida stood outside the block of flats because she believed it was up to her to make the effort, if she couldn't make the effort now, perhaps she'd never be able to do so. She was going to visit, one neighbour to another, and it felt like she was spanning a chasm. Bill had been right, it was a bad idea, a wrong idea. It made her sick to her stomach to think of where Tom was now, what was happening to his body, what must be happening to his eyes, his guts, and at least she had the earth to blame. This woman had only the sea to curse.

Ida stood outside the flats, the door open, the staircase yawning up ahead of her. A curtain pulled back at the window right on the street, an old lady looked out, frowned, saw the visitor's mourning and quickly dropped the curtain.

Ida climbed three flights of stairs and double-checked the number on the door before her. She knew she was making a mistake as her hand reached for the door knocker, dropping it down again, slam slam slam echoing down the empty stairwell behind.

A child, a boy, younger than her Tom, opened the door and then it was too late to run and Ida was led along the passage through a flat where the curtains were closed and mirrors covered. The boy, younger than Tom, clearly expected Ida to follow him. She did, and they went into a bedroom where a woman lay on a child's bed. This woman, this young mother, was known round here, remarked upon whenever she came down the lane, shopping basket on one arm and such a smile for any and all. They might not have known her name before, or that of her older boy – though everyone knew the missing lad's name now – but they all knew her. Golden hair piled up, long fine neck, perfect skin, lovely even in her work clothes she was, heading through the market on her way back from the vinegar factory. A beautiful young woman. And now grief, the midnight tattooist, had left his mark. The gorgeous hair was dank, scraped back, no colour and her pretty, round face was all lines, ancient with waiting.

Ida stood for a moment breathing hard. She offered a hand, but the woman's own hands were full, in the dim, curtained light Ida could not see what she held. Several long breaths later the woman sat up, smoothed the pillow and brought it to her face, breathing in. Ida understood the gesture, knew that it was to catch the scent of her son, and that it also held the possibility of giving over her own breathing once and for all. Ida had tried and discovered the impossibility of smothering herself.

There was a dance of gestures where Ida offered her hand again, the woman leaned up and in as if to be held, and Ida did not know what to do. Both women waited a second, and then it was up to Ida to bend. In the strict hierarchy of grief, there could only be one leader. Ida sat on the end of the bed and the woman spoke, no greeting, no thank you for coming, no hello even, she spoke as if she had been talking already, as if Ida had been with her in this room where her two sons slept, her one son slept, for hours, as if they were mid-conversation. As she spoke she twisted her hands around the object she was holding, Ida could not get a word in, not condolence or platitude or any of the other stupid things people had stupidly said to her. And she knew that no words would not do.

I've always hated the sea, the woman said. That wide open grey space, the wind, the waves rattling stones like old bones, dragging back sand, eating away at the land. So much loss in it, all those bodies, fish bones and dead dogs. I love the river, the river's another thing altogether. You can see the other side of the river, can't you? Even when the fog's that bad, when it's dark and thick, you can just about make out the lights on the other side. Or if you can't even see the lights, you know they're there, because they were before and they'll be there again. But with the sea, that's all there is, just water and nothing beyond.

Schooling herself to stay still, Ida nodded. She reminded herself that even though she had forbidden Bill and the girls and anyone else who came into their home to mention the sea, to speak of the water, she reminded herself that this woman's grief was bigger than hers, her loss unfinished. She sat still and she listened.

I cross the river every bloody morning, first thing, to get to my cleaning job, the one I go to before the factory. I haven't stopped, can't stop. There's always someone here, indoors, in case they call by, you know, in case they bring him back, someone waits here. But I'm on my own, I've three other children and I need the work and I'll need the money for the burial, won't I?

277

Ida wanted to tell her about the help, that there'd been so much help from people round about, but the woman wasn't listening. And even with the help, the two days off work for Bill, more for herself, it was hard. They all needed to keep working. Ida had people to help out in the market, lucky for it, but if you'd a proper job like this lady, with a boss and all the rest, you couldn't afford to risk it, far too many others ready and willing to take the work out of your hands. What was the woman holding in her hands?

I go over the bridge along with all the others like me, up at four thirty and into the City to clean the offices before they all come to their desks. You'd be surprised the mess they make, some of them, no matter that they have ever such important work to do. What I find in the dustbins, beggars belief sometimes. Found things of value too, I have, on occasion, dropped in with the rubbish and not even noticed they're lost. Not that I've kept them, not often. Wish I had now, wish I'd kept all sorts, could have given half the things to my lad, a right magpie that one, we always said we had to be careful he didn't turn out a thieving little bugger, the way he liked his sparkly bits and pieces, watch chains and buttons and the like. We always said it . . .

The woman stopped, looked across at Ida, her frown deeper, You have a husband?

I do.

Well, there you are. We used to say 'we' all the time. Hark at me, I still do, but mine buggered off a couple of years back, took up with some tart down Camberwell, and she no better than she should be. Deserve each other they do. The bastard left me with these four. Three. She corrected herself, I have three.

The woman clasped the thing she was holding still harder, hitting it into her chest.

I cross this old river in the morning and I cross it again when I'm done. I have to walk against the tide by then, against the push of the men in their dark suits, force my way through sometimes, especially on a foul day when the rain's chucking it down and they can't see half a foot in front of them for the umbrellas. It's been a god-awful summer, hasn't it? Day after day like it.

She smiled, suddenly, it was there and then gone, Sometimes I think I could be sheltered all the way like that, hopping from one City gent to the other, each one of them with a big black umbrella. And now, since the boys went off on that ship, since we heard, since I've been waiting, when I go there and back, no matter how quiet at five, or how crowded coming up for eight, there's not a day that I don't look down into the river and spit. I spit into the Thames, telling it to carry my curse out to the sea that is keeping my boy. I curse the sea and I curse my old man for not being here, and I curse the day my lad left and I curse my own damn stupidity in letting him go.

She shook her head now, her voice almost a whisper, tears not far off, Ida thought, her own and this other mother's.

Because for all the spitting, all the cursing, he's not coming back. I know that. I've known since before he was born that I wouldn't keep him long. From the moment I fell with him, I knew I'd lose him. I just didn't know how, or when, my beautiful boy, my beautiful lost boy. And even when I'm not working, when I'm here, at home – not home now, doesn't feel like home any more – does yours?

The woman didn't wait for Ida's answer, not that Ida

could have given it, her own tears dropping down her face, soaking the hands in her lap, hands that wanted to be clawing, scratching, pushing their way out of that room, hands that lay still in her lap.

Even when I'm not working, the woman went on, that foul water calls me, wants me near it. Once I've given my babes their dinner, I go back, down to the docks and all along, to where they've built up the embankment, to the mud flats where the children, other mothers' children, not our children, are mudlarking and laughing and their laughs rip at me like barbs. I go down there every night too. My big girl is home at night, she looks after the others, takes care of them, she's a good girl.

Her voice changed to a whisper then, spittle on her lip, rubbing at her mouth with her free hand, Ida couldn't quite make out the words, but then the woman saw the frown on her face and repeated, clearly, too clearly,

The water will be splitting his skin. And I don't want to go there, to the dirty, stinking Thames, so damn full of people and boats and all that life, all of their hungry lives, but I don't want to stay indoors either, it's too dark indoors, even with the people who keep coming and bringing cake. Dear God, I don't want more damn cake, do you, do you want cake? Even with all of them, this place is too empty. It's why I can't stay indoors, why I'm always off out to that bitch of a river. When I have to, when I have to lie down because I can't stand another minute, I come and lie here, on his bed, because it's by the window, see? I mean, it is his bed, and I do want to be on his bed, the smell of him, the shape of his head in the pillow, but I want to see the sky, in case he can, in case my boy can see the sky. And between not wanting to be indoors and not wanting to be by the river, it's the river that wins. Always bloody well wins. I go to the river so I can curse it. Even though they tell me to hope and to pray.

She shook her head, whispering again, into her fists, as if she didn't want to speak ill of those trying to do their best for her.

So foolish of them to talk as if he might come back now.

She looked up at Ida, smacking the thing she was holding, a chunk of wood perhaps, or bone maybe, Ida still couldn't tell, smacking it now against her temple, against a bruise that Ida saw was already there, against a dark stain beneath her skin. Ida understood the gesture, the connection with skin and bone, she too wanted to break herself, cut, bruise, smack. She longed to feel any pain that might take her mind off the pain in her gut, in her belly, in the pit of her.

The woman was hitting her head with the thing she held and telling Ida,

I know it has him, and I am riddled with knowing it, wise to his death in my bones. And no bones of him to mourn.

Finally, the woman was quiet. She slumped back on the bed, curling up. Her temple was dark red where she had been striking herself. Ida reached out her arms and there was a moment when the woman might have allowed herself to be held, but as Ida leaned in the woman sat up, pushing her away.

You carry yours and I'll carry mine. You go up to that grave at Nunhead and you give thanks there's a grave to go to.

Then she reached out her hand and opened it, and sitting in her palm was the thing she had been hitting herself with. The woman was holding the bone angel.

I suppose it's this you've come for?

I came for you ... I had no idea ... why do you have it ... what?

The woman shook her head then, and Ida saw the touch of a smile at her lips, if not her eyes.

Ah. You'd have said no, I expect. Well, that's boys for you.

I don't understand.

The woman was calmer now, as she explained,

I've no doubt your Tom thought he'd got the best of the deal, but my lad had an eye for nice things. Not that we ever had any, but he'd always notice them, the finest bits and pieces in a shop. Magpie, like I said. He'd spend hours just looking at a painting in a schoolbook. When your Tom said they could do a swap, my lad, he was over the moon. I knew it wasn't right, the angel for my boy's old penknife. The blade's long had it, I knew who had the better half of the deal. But because I knew the knife was a piece of tat, God forgive me, I wouldn't let my lad take your angel on the ship with him. Said there'd be hell to pay if it were lost, and then he'd get your lad into trouble as well as himself. I made him leave it behind. Told him I'd take care of it while he was gone and I was sure your Tom would give him another few days with it, at the end of the trip. Told him he was doing the right thing, being sensible.

She looked at Ida then and held out the angel.

So now we've got the angel, you and I, and it's our boys

282

we've lost. Take it home. Please. What good has it done me?

Ida left, holding the angel. Crossing the Walworth Road she realised that even in the horror of the last few days, there'd been times she'd told herself that Tom had been holding the angel in the water with him, at least he'd had the angel watching over him. The angel had done no such thing.

Thirty-Three

Eventually he came close to shore, that last boy. They found him off Margate and brought him home. Five days after the huge spectacle of the other lads' funeral, a full eleven days since he'd been lost, twelve since his mother had last kissed him, the last boy was laid to rest alongside his fellows. The family had hoped for a quiet time of it, but even then the church was inundated with visitors.

Standing in a back pew, with the girls alongside her, to do right by the last boy's mother, Ida shook her head and whispered to May,

I've never set eyes on half these people, I doubt she has, poor cow. I don't know what they're doing here.

May shook her head, I think they want to be near it. Near her, near you.

Why would anyone want to be near this?

May thought, but didn't say, because perhaps it made them feel better even as it made them feel bad, life was hard enough for many, they had little reason to be glad of their own lives. Being this close to death was how they remembered.

Then the prayers began and the congregation bowed their heads, and a little boy's sobs were heard and afterwards a collective intake of breath and Ida caught the sidelong glances at herself and wondered if she might not have been better out of the way of their looks, both for her own peace of mind and for the lad who should have been getting all the attention now, another coffin, another draped flag.

Outside, as Ida joined the other mothers who were following on, a hawker came across, and after a cursory bow, he started on his patter,

Terrible loss ladies, terrible loss. I've some lovely cards here, ever so pretty, each of the lads' names on it, and the date of the tragedy, a little picture of the boat as she went over, a keepsake if you will. Would you like one? Just a penny for the remembrance, a penny each.

Ida couldn't stop herself, wouldn't have wanted to stop herself even if she could. She felt it rushing up from her belly, hot and furious, and her arms reached out, one to grab him, a hank of his greasy hair in her hand, the other to slap him hard, once, twice, three times. And then she was on him and fierce, spitting, screaming, nails in his skin, nails bent back, ripped from their nailbeds with the vehemence of her attack.

Eventually Ida was held, other women's hands digging into her own grey skin, holding her tight as the hawker, on all fours now grabbing for his spilled cards, rushing to get away, distance himself from the mad woman, the mad women, from his mistake.

Then Ida was calmer now, quieter, and no less furious for her soft voice,

My boy is gone, her boy is gone, and hers, and hers. All of our boys are lost. That's why we're here, why we stand. While you sell their memory for a penny a card. You're a dirty little thief, stealing my sorrow.

They walked away and there were still remembrance cards on the ground behind them, already dirty, another bloody grey, bloody damp day. They forgot the man, and held each other as the carriage moved on to Nunhead. At the cemetery they watched another woman in the place of honour, twisting her grief in her hands.

As she lay down that night, preparing again not to sleep, rejecting both laudanum and valerian because the dreams were worse than not sleeping, Ida was surprised to find her anger gone and, in its place, a scrap of sympathy for the man.

We've all got to make a living, and I know as well as any other about working a pass of people, but dear God, what a rotten bloody job.

Bill held Ida and they lay together, each of them alone in their grief. May had told Ida – and Ida believed her, May had lost her brother in the South African war, after all – that the best they could do just now was lie side by side, stay on with it. Even though Bill made her think of Tom, even though Bill couldn't look at Ida without seeing the baby Tom at her breast. They had to stay side by side because if they didn't they might never get over the break. And there were the girls to think of, so many days and nights and years ahead. Ida didn't want to think of anything but two weeks ago, before, and still she lay, holding Bill holding her.

Thirty-Four

When Rose married Charlie, Ida already had her own friends, had known Rose from round about, but she didn't need her cousin's wife to be her pal, and Rose didn't need her husband's cousin for that either. They'd pass the time of day and would always share a table at a family do, but that was as far as it went until the boys were a little older and then, when the lads had become great mates, Ida and Rose had more in common. It was the friendship between their boys that had brought them together. Now, with Tom gone and Jimmy missing his mate, and with the guilt Rose felt for having a living son, there was much less reason for the two women to be close, less still when Rose began to show properly.

When she'd thought she might lose the baby, early on, in those first days after the accident, when Emily had died and all around her was loss, Rose had also let herself think, just the once, that it would probably be fair. She had Jimmy and Ida had lost Tom, so in a way it might be fair, this baby for

that boy. And then she was horrified at herself, prayed forgiveness for her wicked thoughts, that she might keep this
baby. Rose thought of all those people who never seemed
to know how lucky they were to have even one child, who
hadn't lost baby after baby as she had. She thought how
hard she'd worked nursing Emily to her death, and that she
was a good daughter and she should damn well be allowed
to have as much as everyone else, and plenty of people had
two or three or four babies or more, plenty of them. And
so Rose reasoned herself past the shock of the clots and the
sharp sudden cramps and the fright and into a pregnancy
that she took pleasure in and was proud of. But not when
Ida was around. When Ida was around, Rose sucked in her
belly. When Ida was around, Rose Hatch was small.

Ida herself came and went in waves of grief that sometimes
had her clawing at Bill, screaming at him to make it better,
and other times subsided so far that she was able, for hours
at a time, to get on. It was better getting back to the barrow,
she remembered how she used to think it would be nice to
have someone pull the barrow for her, but the truth was,
she couldn't stand all their help. Every act of kindness only
reminded her why people were being so nice. It was better
when she was back at work, plying her own trade. But she
only went up the market with one of the girls beside her,
taking them out of school on alternate afternoons so she
was never alone, she couldn't yet risk hearing a mother tell
off her own raggle-taggle boy, those chance remarks that
would have her drenched in loss and unable to pack up the
goods, incapable of anything but numb tears.

She talked to May about it, her friend listening, nodding, knowing better than to offer solutions, knowing from watching her own mother broken with the loss of her brother in South Africa that there were no solutions. They were drinking tea and May added a tot of whiskey to the drink. It loosened Ida's tongue.

I go out walking every morning now, every morning, to Waterloo and back, where I said goodbye to him, where I let him go. It's getting darker and I'm not sure how much longer I'll do it, but I do it for now.

May nodded, it wasn't a long way to the river, but far enough to go there and back before a day had even begun. It made sense, looking at her, Ida had always been a little bit rounded, plump sometimes, comfortable in her skin, but now she was bone thin, and sharp with it, elbows and collarbones and cheekbones jutting.

Dear God, May, it kills me to say every, as if it's been a while, and it has. I've been doing it four weeks, since the funeral, four weeks tomorrow. I can't bear that it'll be a month soon enough. I can't bear the time passing.

May nodded again. Yes, she had felt this too. No, she wasn't going to say so. May knew enough about grief to understand that no amount of 'me too' made a blind bit of difference.

When I get back indoors I go to my bed or if I have my strength, if I get a second wind, I go along to the lane. Charlie's been taking care of the stall, but he doesn't do things the way I like, and it's not as if a young girl's going to come and ask him for a measure of pennyroyal, is it? Though I'm dead grateful to him for trying. Oh May, dead, how we use that word. I am grateful. But the lane feels all wrong, it's so quiet, now, isn't it?

May nodded again, following the thread of Ida's frayed conversation, the words spinning out, half a sentence here, another there. Even though the words sounded confused on first listen, they made a deal of sense if you put them together. Ida's attention was like a bird's now, May reasoned, a little sparrow, hopping here and then flying off startled by a blackbird, menaced by a starling, back again with a crumb or a worm half-dragged from the earth, pecked and pecked and released. It was hard work being Ida's friend just now, she needed proper listening. And even so, Ida was right. The lane was quiet. At first, it had been much busier than usual, people coming over the river to the funeral service, to get a look of the mourners, to feel themselves part of it. May knew enough traders to know it had been good business, awful business, but good business. They were paying for it now though, people were going up Borough High Street to shop, not wanting to be where the lads had been, scared to bump into grief.

Ida was talking again, quietly.

I walk first thing, before people are up, because it's harder later, much harder. I go down the street and people begin to smile because they recognise me and then they realise who I am, the woman that no one must smile at, in case I break. But I daren't stop indoors either, I'd go mad in the house all the time. The girls want me to, and Bill does, I know. He won't say it, but I think he's angry that I'm not making it normal for the girls, making it home for the girls. This is normal now, and it is not home. My dad, Aunty Sarah, they've both been kind, but I can't speak of our Tom, because it upsets everyone, and I can't speak of anything else, so there are no words left. Bill lies awake of a night, and I'm wide awake alongside him, and we hear the church clocks ring out the hours, and every damn note tells me they'll not bring my boy home again, he's up there for good. And so I can't even lie quiet with Bill because he's the man who gave me Tom in the first place, who gave me a lad to love, and if I'd never loved my boy I'd never have hurt like this. Bill's not to blame, and I can't stop blaming him.

Thirty days after the accident, Itzhak went back to the cemetery for the first time since the funeral, walking the same route up through Peckham. He took it slowly, his leg hurting him with every step, Shimon alongside, the old man trying not to lean on the lad, but also to lean just enough, to give Itzhak something to do, take his mind off his pain, something else to think about as they climbed another hill.

It was a quiet day, just the pair of them marking the contrast with the heaving, prying crowd that had accompanied Tom and the others. The crisp sunshine threw solid shadows across their path, new autumn showing in the high blue sky, London haze swept away in the high winds of the night.

The path took them past angels with wings wide spread and hands close in prayer, around a family mausoleum in stone and deep red marble, ornate gold leaf.

Shimon, who knew he'd never accustom himself to the excesses of a Christian cemetery, nor feel comfortable in one, shook his head at the ostentation,

Who is this for, all this show? Better to leave the wealth to the poor than to spend it on the dead. The dead do not enjoy the gold.

But if they wanted to, if it was their money?

And their children and grandchildren could not use the money themselves, the living might not have more need of it?

Giving the money to their children isn't giving it to the poor.

No, Shimon laughed, giving to one's own is not the same as giving to the poor. Yet the best of us do it, don't we, put our own family first?

Maybe the children chose the gold, maybe they just wanted a beautiful house to keep their mothers and fathers.

Itzhak didn't say to keep their grandfathers. He considered it, but didn't say it. The old man and the young man walked on.

At the grave, the earth still raised, fresh flowers laid along-side the old ones rotting, prayer cards sinking into London clods of London clay, Itzhak and Shimon stopped. The old man said Kaddish for the dead child. When the prayer was finished, when Itzhak turned into him, Shimon was ready, to hold his grandson, embrace the heaving shoulders.

I should have stayed.

Stayed?

In the water, I swam away, I let them go. I let Tom go. I was too scared when I should have been brave.

Child, we have a duty to our friends, yes, and when there is no more we can do, we have a duty to stay alive.

Itzhak saw again the dirty brown water, the yellowed foam, the faces of his friends, Tom calm and cold and whis-tling. Whistling to Itzhak because he had no more breath to call. Then the awful relief of those waves in the way, giving

Itzhak permission to swim. Shimon saw again the terror of those in his village, those fleeing, and those unable to run. The old, the infirm, his heavily pregnant sister, the many he'd had to leave behind to stay alive.

Shimon reached a shaking hand into his pocket and took out two small stones, giving one to Itzhak. The boy and the man leaned down to leave a stone for Tom, for the other boys, for Itzhak's loss of childhood, for Shimon's lost past. The stones held down the dead, laying memories in the earth.

Itzhak changed schools after the break. He went to a new school where the other children did not know that he was a swimmer. They did not know, or chose not to mention, that he had been in that awful tragedy at Leysdown, that he had been with those lads, that those were his friends up there at Nunhead. He didn't visit the cemetery again and he didn't go swimming and he worked hard on his portion of the Torah for his bar mitzvah.

Jimmy went back to school and, unlike Itzhak, he did answer the questions. He answered them honestly and plainly and, because the answers were ugly, because the newly growing patch of bright red hair on his head and the broken bone now hidden beneath the raised red scar along his arm did not look heroic, just painful, the questions quietly stopped. For the first time in twenty-three years of teaching Miss Mackay did not ask her children to write about what they had done in their holidays.

By Christmas Jimmy had stopped waking screaming every night. The colder weather gave him the first intimations of the aches he would suffer, worse in damp weather, worse in winter, for the rest of his life. The dreams still came, insides ripping out, bone tearing skin, Tom's face split open at the bottom of the sea, maggots crawling through his mates in their coffins, and water, always so much dark, dirty water. Jimmy would wake, gasping for air, but after a while the dreams came less often. Come spring, when Rose's baby was almost due, when his balls dropped, when his voice broke, Jimmy found the dreams began to let him be. Perhaps it helped that he eventually took out the map he had drawn for their trip, the map he had worked on in such painstaking detail and, having noted where they were when the squall hit, where the ship had gone down, marked the exact points that he could remember, he took the map into the yard, and fetching an ember from the scullery hearth, he set fire to it, burning the path they had taken.

Falling in love, or lust, he was only a lad after all, also helped Jimmy to feel differently. He hadn't been looking for it, didn't know it was possible, two months shy of his thirteenth birthday, to feel so all-consumed, so fiercely excited by the prospect of seeing the other, searching each other out in the playground, making the five-minute walk to school stretch into twenty, thirty minutes, a dawdle full of small talk and silence and hope. This time last year, Jimmy had been one of three, Jimmy and Itzhak and Tom, always Tom leading, Tom driving them on. Now Jimmy was just one and on his way to becoming a man, growth spurt and new hairs on his face, besotted with Arnold Grey from the year above.

Jimmy had no idea how to act on his infatuation, but luckily Arnie did. With not much prompting and no apparent fear,

Arnie kissed him after a long run up to Dulwich Wood. Both of them sweaty and panting and the snowdrops still on the ground, white flowers dotted about the green undergrowth. And then they were a two. Not so's anyone at school would notice, they weren't daft, and certainly not so anyone indoors could tell, Jimmy didn't need to think hard to guess what Charlie would say to a nancy boy for a son, but anyway, Jimmy Hatch fell in love.

He did miss Tom and he did feel rotten that Tom was gone and that he himself was all caught up with desire and a fearful excitement, but he couldn't deny that he felt it, and that it felt good.

Thirty-Five

It began quietly, a slow awareness, growing, that something should be done.

There ought to be a plaque, at least.

Poor little mites, there should be something.

What about their dear mothers?

Why isn't there ... ?

There should be ...

Someone ought to. Someone ought. Someone.

And so someone did. A penny fund was started, a notice placed in the *Daily Express*. Children sent in their pennies because they felt sorry for the boys who didn't have a statue to remember them by, and parents gave a few coppers, because they had their own children still and they felt bad about that as well as lucky, and some of the toffs who thought it a terrible show that nothing had been done, dreadful business, sent in their contributions too. And the fund grew and people's names were added to the subscription list and whole families sent in the coins they'd have spent on going for a picnic or a night in the pub. The subscription list was printed in the paper and that made even more people want to give, Scout troops from all over the country raised money by doing jobs and holding games and races and then, after a time, there were a hundred thousand pennies, from all across Britain, a hundred thousand pennies for the poor lads who'd lost their lives on the scouting trip.

Shimon looked down. His hands holding the hat were small, plump, they were the hands of a boy, ragged nails, fingers sticky with sap from a day working in the forest with his father. He looked down again and they were old man's hands now, nails yellow with time, knuckles swollen, dotted with liver spots, shaking. He was an old man holding his childhood in his childhood hands in his old man hands. He sighed and reached for the tissue paper, carefully winding it around the hat once more.

He left the house quietly, the old overcoat heavy on his back, but glad of it once he was in the street. The leaves might have the green of summer, but Shimon, the son of the woodcutter, woodcarver, knew that deep inside the trunk, in the branches themselves, the tree understood that autumn was coming. Each tree was readying itself to turn to red, yellow, gold, he could feel it in a breeze on the back of his neck, a smell of sap risen and now falling back. As a boy Shimon had run barefoot until his mother had to force him into boots right before the snow, he had always been happiest in shirtsleeves, now the slightest chill sliced his skin and his chilblains began to itch in September.

For five days now Shimon had placed himself just at the entrance to the market, sitting carefully on a stool borrowed from the pub, the tissue-wrapped hat on his lap. The collector would come eventually, Shimon was an old man and used to waiting, another day would not be too long.

The costermongers were beginning to pack up. Apples, also tissue-wrapped, laid in boxes, fish heads and tails rolled up for those who came shopping at the end of the day, a parcel of offcuts to turn into a stew. It was the same on the meat stall, Shimon watched Charlie make a young woman's day when she turned up as he stacked his boxes, asking for a few bones for the dog for the few pennies she had in her purse.

No bones love, got rid of them already, but here, look lively—

And the woman who had already started to back away, her dejected shoulders now up and hopeful again, turned to see Charlie pointing at a tray of pigs' ears, a snout in one hand and a trotter in the other.

Take this home to your old man, you cook up the ears and snout into a broth, serve him the trotter on top, he'll think all his Sundays have come at once.

He took her money, and then he took a penny more than she'd been hoping to spend, but the trotter was meaty and it was a gift. Both Charlie and the young woman had known there was no dog to feed.

Charlie looked across at Shimon, holding up a second pig's trotter, the skin fleshy pink where it divided into the cloven hoof,

I've got another here if you want it, break the habit of a lifetime?

They laughed. Charlie was always offering him a bit of bacon or a ham hock, gratis, just in case. Shimon had been tempted, once or twice, to take him up on the offer, just to see what he'd say, he wouldn't have to eat the treyf, there were plenty between here and the house who'd welcome it, but then he'd have to handle the meat, and Shimon couldn't quite bring himself to do that, not even to wipe away Charlie Hatch's smirk.

Charlie looked along the lane, the line of barrows being tidied up, ready to cart away and when he saw the hat, the briefcase, the well-made coat, he called back to Shimon,

Here you go mate, here's your man, make sure you drive a hard bargain.

Charlie didn't say aloud that he assumed the Jew would do exactly that. He didn't need to, Shimon heard it anyway.

It is an old hat, very special.

I can see that, may I ... ?

Lovett held out his hand and Shimon passed the hat over, his fingers itching to hold on to it, to say he'd changed his mind.

The collector turned the hat this way and that, held it up to the light.

Are you sure you want to sell?

Shimon sighed, I am an old man. If I say it is for sale, then it is for sale.

A deal was struck, money changed hands, the hat was given over.

Later that evening, Lovett caught himself thinking what a strange picture the old Jew had made, sitting on the stool and waiting to sell, clearly times were hard, no one would part with such an astonishing keepsake otherwise.

Occasionally he found himself feeling sorry for the sellers, sorry, but pragmatic. If not him, then another collector, one who might not be at such pains to note, to attribute, to record. At least now the piece would be kept safe and sound, on the shelf in a room built specially for the purpose, at least it would be recorded.

He sat a little longer in his study, soon he would go downstairs to join his sons and listen to their stories of the day. Young Edward was well, challenged in his occupation, and all to the good. Francis, less so, beginning to speak of moving on, rumours of repercussions from the problems in the Balkans. Lovett did not want the stories from abroad to tempt his son to a commission, the rumours might not develop into anything more, but it was a concern, nonetheless. He turned his attention back to his desk and the meticulous task of filling his pen with good ink.

Shimon took the money home. He felt as if he had just sold his father, his mother, his village, sold them all.

In the house, after the meal, after the blessing, the eating, washing his hands, another blessing, he took Itzhak aside.

This is for you, for your friends, for the memorial. Or, it is for your bar mitzvah. It is a good amount, you could buy yourself a new shirt, several, your brothers have used theirs too well, it is time you had your own to cover your back. It is your choice.

It was no choice. Itzhak knew it, and so did Mimi, and so did Shimon, but he had wanted to help the boy understand. He would be a man whether he read his portion of the Torah well or not. He would be a man whether he stood in front of the whole congregation or not. He had buried his best friend, he was a man now, already, no faithful rules or words handed down by the rabbis could create that for him. Itzhak had looked at his own death, and he had swum away from it, the bar mitzvah to come was merely a formality.

Itzhak gave the money to the memorial fund.

Late that night, the lodgers and her sons asleep, her husband just gone to bed, Mimi sat sewing, close to the light, while her father-in-law worked on a long, narrow piece of wood.

What is it?

I don't know yet, Shimon shook his head, I am waiting for the wood to tell me.

Mimi nodded, she felt the same with fabric. The making and shaping of things, this was where she and Shimon understood each other.

Shimon put aside the piece of wood, carefully wiped and then folded his knife into itself, he stood, his kneebones cracking, his back aching, five days sitting on a stool at the top of the lane had dealt with the sap of his bones as well.

I wish you good rest, Mimi.

Shimon, father, wait,

Mimi put down her own work, rubbed her red eyes redder, I would like, I should like.

She stopped, shook her head. After a time, she spoke again, the words she'd been waiting to speak for several days, waiting for quiet and privacy,

A shaynam dank.

For what?

For being a good grandfather to Itzhak, for showing him how to be a man.

It is my only work now, he smiled, we know I did not manage anywhere near such a friendship with either Nathan or David.

They are modern boys.

Yes.

The hat was a thread though, to your own parents, to your village, to yourself as a boy. It was good of you to give it up.

Shimon smiled, And they were Itzhak's friends, the families of the dead boys are our neighbours. It is important to be neighbourly, no? *Mir hobben à hime du.*

Shimon went up to the little room that was his own, just off the half-landing, and Mimi went on with her sewing.

Two long years after the accident, the monument was finally unveiled. Designed by Sir Giles Gilbert Scott and sculpted by Miss Lillie Read, who was also working with Sir Giles on the grand new Liverpool Cathedral. The statue was a life-sized Scout in bronze. He stood holding a stave, his head bowed as all heads had bowed, as the cranes of the Thames had bowed, for the boys brought home on the destroyer Fervent.

It was too long a wait for Ida. Although she went up to the cemetery with the other mothers and fathers, although she was grateful for the fund, for all the penny donations given, one by one, she agreed with the whispered voices that dared to suggest it was too little, too late. It should not have taken two years to erect a memorial to their boys. Perhaps they were, to those on the other side of the river, just Walworth boys after all.

Thirty-Six

Nathan died at Passchendaele in the autumn of 1917, David and Itzhak survived, they came home shocked and quiet, but alive. Itzhak had not thought it possible to see such loss so close again, and to still live, to stay sane. Yet he had, and he lived. Itzhak married a nice girl and eventually, when the time came, when Mimi could no longer care for herself, he and his wife welcomed her into their home in Hendon. They named their first son Shimon, giving him the second name of Thomas, unusual among their friends.

May was kind to Ida and took care of her in those first years after the accident, after the memorial. The two women held each other through the Great War when count after count of dead boys came in and their own losses were forgotten in the roll call of constant death.

In 1925, Edward Lovett published *Magic in Modern London*, the book detailing his collection. He ascribed no more than superstition to any of the charms he collected, certainly not a magic that he personally believed in, but it was noted that he made a personal amulet for his son to wear when that young man went away to war in 1916.

Tilly and Samson waited out the war and then sold up, everything they had, their little businesses, their bits and pieces, and they emigrated to Australia. The last Ida heard of them was a postcard from Adelaide, a scribbled note on the back,

Too darn hot and lovely with it. This country Ida, such a land. I should have come here a young woman, but we'll make a decent fist of it regardless. What I wouldn't give for a pint of winkles though. Your friend, Tilly.

Sir Giles Gilbert Scott enjoyed a good service during the Great War in the Royal Marines. He later designed the red telephone box.

Ida and Bill stayed together, lived in the same home, slept in the same bed, went to weddings and wakes together, but Tom stood between them. They rarely spoke of him and the girls grew up in the shadow of their parents' silence. Ida tried to be a good mother to her daughters, and both would have said she was kind and considerate, but Ida knew herself to be broken. She was a fine china cup, marred by a hairline crack, and tea poured too hot would shatter her. Bill was always careful to handle her gently. Ida had not been a careful girl or a careful woman, and the muted life with Bill after Tom's death was a second loss. She sold the angel to Edward Lovett just before the war. It was not special and it had not saved anyone.

Jimmy went to war, one of so many his age, his type. He went to war to fight for King and Country, to fight the Kaiser, to get away from Tom's ghost. Away at war, he found the young men like him, who preferred the company of other young men. He was lucky not to die with them, though it took a few years before he believed himself lucky. Eventually there was love, and a happiness of sorts, hidden and quiet.

Rose and Charlie loved each other, fought with each other, made love again. When the old house was finally cited for demolition, the council insisting the bomb damage was too bad to allow tenants to stay on any longer, they took the LCC's handshake and moved into the flats along from The Cut. From there, on a warm night, the windows open, they could hear the boats going up and down the river late into the night. Charlie died two days shy of his seventy-fifth birthday, still walking every day down to the market. His funeral was a glow of pearly buttons and Rose was happy for Charlie, happy he'd had a proper send-off. Three weeks later Rose Hatch, fit and well in spite of her grief, sat dead in her armchair. Her hair in curlers, her shopping list beside her. A broken heart the doctor said, though he wrote other words on the death certificate.

In 1969 the statue of the weeping Scout disappeared from Nunhead Cemetery. Had that amount of bronze been melted down for resale, it would have fetched perhaps forty pounds at the time. Had that amount of bronze been melted down it would have made any number of keys and doorknockers, belt buckles and shoe eyes, trinkets, amulets and charms.

Thirty-Seven

And now—

A boy who dreamed of crossing the seven seas, of sailing and running and journeying the world, a boy who imagined himself a captain of ships and died in a dirty little squall off Leysdown, who died two years before the First World War, two years too early to suffer an inglorious death in the mud and dirt of no man's land, finally steps away from the pedestal that has held him still for so long.

It is a cool evening, London is swinging down the hill, over the river, the cemetery is quiet, a field mouse runs across his feet, again, and finally it is enough, he has stood here for his fellows long enough. There is a life to be lived. The weeping Scout steps off his podium and away.

He is light and hot, molten, he is liquid, running fire. He has been boy and never man and now he is remade. The boy who only made it as far as the mouth of the Thames in life, is bronze and he is everywhere.

He is the key jingling in your pocket, he is the lock on a door five hundred miles away, he is the belt on a buckle that journeys with you, all the way to America and beyond, he is the eyelet on a handmade designer dress strutting catwalks in Milan, New York, Paris, he holds the masthead on a brand new yacht, sailing from Plymouth to the world. He is on the Tube wall and the Overground signs, he is in the London Eye and the Olympic Park, he sits deep at the bottom of a muddy, tidal river, and he is revealed when the old river sucks its own banks dry. He is in the City and the country, he sails and now, astonishingly, who would have thought, who would have believed it possible, he flies.

Tom is bronze, he is golden, he is everywhere, he is all of London, he is all of the river, he is all of us, and – finally – he is home.

The plaque on the original memorial at Nunhead Cemetery read:

IN MEMORY OF

PATROL LEADER   WILLIAM BECKHAM   *aged 12*

PATROL LEADER   HARRY GWYNN   *aged 13*

SCOUTS

ALBERT EDWARD DACK *aged 12*   NOEL FAULKNER FILMER *aged 14*

THOMPSON JAMES FILMER *aged 12*   PERCY BADEN POWELL HUXFORD *aged 12*

JAMES SKIPSEY *aged 12*   EDWARD SMITH *aged 11*

Of the 2nd Walworth (Dulwich Mission) Troop of Baden Powell's Boy Scouts
and FRANK MASTERS *aged 14 of the Training Ship "Arethusa"*
who were drowned off Leysdown on the 4th of August 1912